Carnival of the Mind

E.M. Peterson

The Wasteland

First I am nowhere, then I am here.

I'm sprawled on top of sand. In fact, I'm not so much on it, as slightly in it. As I pull my arms free, grains stream off me, forming into miniature ridges, topographies that swirl of their own accord. I come to a sitting position and look out over a barren expanse. Rolling dunes spread before me, broken only occasionally by clusters of spiky succulents. It must be day because the sun is beating on my neck, yet the murky quality of the light makes the landscape feel twilit. The sky is close with muddy clouds. Nothing stirs below.

I grasp for any recollection, but the space on the other end of consciousness, the space where memory should be, is a yawning nothingness that resists my efforts to fill it.

The dry pain in my throat is what ultimately brings me to my feet. I put aside the larger, more difficult questions, and focus instead on my need for water.

A dull yet persistent rumble—the only sound I can hear—pulls me forward. Maybe at the other end of that noise is a gorge containing a rushing river. I walk toward it, sand sifting between my toes. Why the hell am I barefoot?

As I crest each dune, I stop to catch my breath, looking out for a glimpse of water or civilization. But nothing has changed. The dunes continue in their rolling patterns, and there's nothing but randomness to the growth of the cactuses.

The sound grows closer though. Eventually it becomes so loud that I think the body of water making it might be the ocean rather than a river.

As I stumble into the deepest valley yet, the noise of water becomes a solid wall. I look up and see a roiling wave pass over the top of the dune above me. I turn to run. As I do, my attention catches on a beeping plastic object around my wrist. I just have time to see that the tiny LED screen counts upward with every chaotic step before the water is upon me.

My arms churn wildly against the force of the wave as I'm carried up the ridge. Soon the water is so deep that the desert's previous shape is lost completely beneath the waves. The water has a hold of me, and anything I do makes little difference. Huge waves bounce me up and down like a human cork. My only focus is keeping my mouth high enough to choke down breaths.

At the top of one wave, I can see for miles, and the effect is no less startling than the emptiness of the previous landscape. The former desert is now a single green ocean, with the high waves of a stormy sea moving over it.

No cactuses, though.

I realize with morbid satisfaction that the water streaming into my nose and mouth isn't saltwater. At least I won't be thirsty while I drown. I gulp greedily, choking a few times when water gets shoved down the wrong pipe. The water may not be salty, but it's not entirely fresh, either. It tastes almost sweet, like sap freshly drawn from a sugar maple.

My legs are already tired. My arms burn from the effort of keeping my head above water. There's no sign of a break in the waves. Even if I were in control of my direction, as far as I can tell there's nothing to swim *to*. My only choice is to keep afloat. The current is taking me the direction I decide to think of as east, opposite the sun, which hasn't moved since I awoke.

My conception of time is surely skewed, but it can't be more than a few minutes of treading water before I spot a break. Not a surface exactly. My eyes lose it as I'm swept down the leeward side of a wave, but it's still there when I crest again. Something—a skin of algae, possibly a school of fish—appears to be growing on the surface. I swim toward it frantically, hoping it can hold my weight and allow me to rest for a few minutes. Every time I look up, the patch has grown, until it covers close to three-hundred square feet of ocean. As I thrash toward it, I'm suddenly aware of the water resisting. Soon my arms can't even break the surface. I pull myself up onto the soft, porous surface, and lie on my back, exhausted.

Water splashes through the buoyant substance that is supporting me, but it holds me a couple inches in the air. There's nothing particularly organic about the brown mass under me, and yet it's replicated so rapidly that I can no longer see a single unoccupied patch of ocean.

I think vaguely that I should be worried about this being some hostile life form that will consume me as it continues to clone itself. I reach down, trying to get a better grasp of what exactly it's made of. It's coarse, and comes away between my fingers, resolving into dark clumps of...

Is that sand?

The sea has slowed its rocking as the sandy substrate on top of it counteracts its natural motion. Then the world stops moving completely and I'm thrown off balance.

I'm once again on a bed of sand, dunes rambling far into the distance. A few cactuses have begun to grow again from the top of the dunes. Something is deeply wrong with this place.

With my thirst quenched and my limbs exhausted, it seems pointless to move just yet. Sand cakes my entire body. The device on my wrist displays the number *973*. I tug at its elastic band, grating sand into my arm. I pull harder, trying to find any seam. But there is no discernible way to remove the device. I give up, wishing the water had destroyed it.

I rub the sand from my hands and wipe my face. My fingers expect to find the faint divot of acne scars—lower on the right side so that if you're close enough to notice them, I begin to look a touch lopsided—but there's nothing but smoothness there. My chin feels weird too, in that there is just slightly too much of it. The long, thin limbs splayed out in skinny jeans and a plain gray T-shirt are definitely my own, but are missing several of my less prominent freckles. On the upside, the hair on my toes is missing, giving the clusters of drying sand less to grab onto.

As much of a leap as it is, I begin to consider my location no longer merely a question of geography, but possibly one of astronomy. Maybe I'm an interstellar traveler who frequents planets millions of light years apart, and my amnesia is merely a symptom of a particularly rough jump between different points in space-time?

I think if I was something that cool I would remember it. Besides, where's my damn spaceship?

Over the next few hours, the landscape's cycle repeats three more times. A roaring wave rises over the dunes, engulfing the desert with seawater. Then the landscape settles, the waves' crests becoming the crests of dunes.

I notice a few things I couldn't before, when I was distracted by the whole "trying not to drown" thing. First, the water changes each time, both in color and in flavor. The following wave is too salty to drink, while the next is yellow in color but—thankfully—tastes of pure spring water. Second, the water always flows in the same direction, away from the sun, which I can now confirm has not seen fit to rise or set a single degree since I've been here. And third, the dry part of the cycle is about five times as long as the aquatic one.

My thoughts turn toward food. I try extracting the meat from one of the cactuses. As I place my hand between the spikes, the cactus squirms. I nearly cut myself pulling away. But looking closer, the movement was not in response to my touch. The entire trunk is moving upwards in a swirl of morphing flesh. The cactus is growing before my eyes.

"I really wouldn't touch that if I were you," comes a voice from behind me. I jump so violently that I almost cut myself again on the cactus. A young woman sits at the top of the next dune, watching me. She stubs out a cigarette on the sand. One side of her head is buzzed, and the rest of her chin-length hair falls in a manicured arc over the buzzed area. Though I can't see any tattoos on her arms, she gives the impression of having at least three or four.

"You have a name?" the young woman says, seeing that I'm too surprised for an intelligible response.

"Matthew." Got that at least. My voice feels like it's rattling through a rusty tube. "And you are?"

"June. Good to meet you, Matt."

"Matthew's fine."

"Whatever you say, Matty."

June gets up. She's about my height and probably a year or two older than me, likely in the first couple years of college. The thought of college fills me with a combination of excitement and dread.

"Do you know where we are?" I try.

"Yes," June says. "That's why I'm going to take you somewhere much better." She looks at the dull sky and kicks the sand disdainfully.

She turns and walks directly toward the sun, and I realize I have nothing to do but follow. She takes strides that are considerably longer than her legs should allow, forcing me to maintain the awkward middle ground between a walk and a trot to keep up.

"So you know the way out of here?" I say.

"Out of here and all the way to the Carnival," she replies without turning around. "But of course, you don't know anything about the Carnival." She gives me a shrewd look. "In fact, you don't seem to know much about anything, do you?"

Though technically true, I'm not about to agree. "What is the Carnival?"

"The Carnival's where we're going. It's my home, and not at all like the Wasteland. Trust me, there's nothing to worry about there. The Carnival's about as close to non-stop excitement as you can get without actually forming your own cult."

"You don't make it sound like a real place."

"It's all real," June responds. "Though *place* is probably not the right word."

A couple minutes later, a wave crashes over the top of the next dune. Once again I am swimming, doing my best not to fall too far behind with the water's flow. I look up between strands of hair that have fallen in my eyes, and see June sitting gently on the surface.

"You're a pretty good swimmer," she says.

"Not any better than you, apparently." My words are interrupted by the occasional splash of lemon-flavored water in my mouth.

"I've never really been into swimming while wearing shoes, they always take forever to dry out." She indicates her black combat boots, which are folded under her crossed legs and, though touching the top of the water, are completely dry.

While we wait for the water to re-solidify into sand, I ask June if there's a trick to not having to swim. She replies that of course there is. When the waves disappear, we're walking again, the sand grating beneath my wet feet. June offers me shoes, but I turn them down, knowing I might need to do more swimming.

I wonder where she would even be keeping shoes, as she doesn't have a bag with her.

Hours pass, but night never falls in the Wasteland. We continue toward the sun, halted periodically by the rhythmic return of water. There is no change in the land itself, but the sun grows larger with each passing hour until it takes up a good third of the sky.

"It's not really the sun," June says in response to my confusion. "Think of it more like a heat bulb. It gives off light and enough heat to keep the Wasteland a reasonable temperature. Now that I think about it, that's basically what the sun does. That's a head-scratcher for sure."

"So we're going to, what, pass the sun on our way?"

"Pretty much. Although you've also gotta pass through the Substratum to get to the Carnival." June sighs. "More boringness to get through, sadly."

"Sorry me being unwillingly deposited in a barren desert/ocean is so uninteresting to you."

"It's okay, it's not like I was busy negotiating a peace treaty between the Armageddeons and the Apocalyptians or anything."

"The Armaged—"

"Those guys will simply not stop fighting."

June springs over a small cactus, her boots grazing the uppermost needles. I skirt around it. I don't want to hear about the Armageddeons. I just want to know what's going on. And then leave.

The device on my wrist buzzes as June picks up her pace, as if goading me on.

"That's all fine, but where the hell are we?"

"The Wasteland." June puts up a hand, anticipating my response. "I know that's not what you're really asking. But you have to understand this place before you can define it. Anything else would be unsafe."

"Unsafe?"

"You're not a stable entity, at least not yet. You could do a lot of damage both to yourself and to the people around you." She gives me a pointed look.

As we rise over the next dune, I see the first change in the landscape. Beneath the bottom curve of the massive sun runs a range of mountains. They rise in square, uniform peaks. From this distance they look like they've been carved out of bedrock by an obsessive god. Our pace quickens with our destination in sight, and we only have to deal with one more flood before we reach the base. This time I note that the floodwater comes from the top of the mountains, pouring down in an orange cascade.

We reach the mountains just as I'm starting to dry. I look doubtfully up, half expecting another wave to crash down from overhead. June leads us quickly up the rectangular steps carved into the solid rock. As we climb, it becomes apparent that the squareness of the mountains themselves informs the composition of everything within them. All squares and rectangles, perfect edges form steps, columns, and cliff-faces.

June turns to me as we begin our ascent. "Welcome to the Substratum."

The Substratum

There are no railings in the Substratum. It's hard to notice much else as I narrowly avoid falling hundreds of feet off the staircase into the chiseled ravine below. June keeps a quick pace, taking two steps at a time. I take June up on her offer of shoes, and she produces a pair of neon green running shoes from a beat-up tote bag, saying, "They have incredible arch support." They fit. I try to focus on how strange it is that June knew my shoe size and that she suddenly has a tote bag, rather than on the drop next to me.

While the Wasteland was silent except for the cyclical roar of water, the quiet in the Substratum beats on me. Sound echoes off the rock, but in a cold, dead voice, as if the sound itself has been stripped of its life. Even June—who navigates effortlessly around bends, between forking pathways, and up stairs that become so tall that we have to scramble up them—seems uncomfortable here.

As we climb further, all of the questions I want to ask June bubble toward the surface. I start to ask how she knew where to find me, but she shushes me. Even that sound echoes off the gray rock, before being swallowed by the chasm.

She steps close and whispers, "Your voice is vulnerable here. Speak too loud, and it might become a permanent part of the Substratum."

I imagine the voice being ripped from my throat, condensing down to the size of a stone and melting into the surrounding rock. I keep my mouth shut.

At the top of a steep rise, we come to the entrance of a cave. The trail winds its way through the cavern, but June pulls me up short. Our voices remain at a whisper.

"I should warn you, this place is disturbing," she says. I study her face, but nothing in her expression indicates anything besides sincerity. "It's really the only way through, though. If you want you can close your eyes and I can lead you, but to me that sounds scarier."

"I'll keep my eyes open," I say, partially because I do think it would be scarier, and partially because I'm internally screaming at the thought of being led by the hand like a child. "What makes it so disturbing?"

"The rest of the Substratum is constructed, it's built from the ground up. It's all intentional, which at least means it's controlled. The things we're about to see in that cave are not constructed. They're much older than the rest of this place. Even older than the Wasteland or the Carnival. It's a wilder, more primal place."

After the rigid order of the mountain, the jagged walls inside throw me off. We follow a worn but uneven trail inward. Though no source is visible, there's plenty of light to see by, even after we've passed out of sight of the entrance. June leads more slowly.

The first indication of anything wrong is a low growling that makes the hairs on the back of my neck stand on end. It grows louder and more bloodthirsty as we continue, until it consumes the whole cave. I want to run, I want to leave this place and get away from whatever is making the sound. We press on. As quickly as it had come, the growling stops. Silence. Save for our echoing footsteps.

A shape catches my eye to one side. I flinch before I see that the shape is not in front of the rock. It's part of it. Buried in the rock wall but still eerily visible is the outline of a wolf, its mouth locked in a distorted snarl.

The wall on the other side holds the stretched image of a baby, its limbs horribly bent, its mouth open in a cry. The horror is overwhelming.

"Keep moving," June says.

Images become more frequent along the walls. Trees, other green things, a naked woman and man, with their arms stretched downward so we have to walk below them. More sounds arise, deep sounds, ones I can recognize without naming. The wail of an injured child, the rumble of a storm moving up a valley, the sprinkle of rain in trees. With it comes the unmistakable scent of ozone, that questioning smell that precedes a coming shower.

It's not all frightening, but a lot of it is. Most of the images, sounds, and smells raise instinctive fear. At one point smoke rises before us, and we have to put our shirts over our mouths to keep from choking. My heart pounds in my ears, and I can feel myself sucking involuntarily at the smoke-clogged air through my shirt. My eyes water horribly as my visibility is cut to just a few feet. June shows no sign of panic as she leads me forward.

Everything in me says I should turn around and head back the way we came. Even the imposing silence of the Substratum would be a reprieve from this. In the part of my mind that can still think rationally, I understand that the fear is not coming from the images, the sounds, or even the smoke. It is emanating directly from this place into me, through me, around me.

The smoke resolves, but the fear remains. It is only growing.

When I am close to my breaking point, we reach a blank space where the trail should be. A chasm yawns below us, with no discernible path on the other side. And no discernible bottom. As I wait for June to offer an explanation, the cave walls behind us move, closing rapidly until there is no opening at all. My heart lurches with the claustrophobia of it, only to lurch again when I realize the solid wall behind us is now moving in our direction. Toward the edge.

My world feels as if it's collapsing, and the only way out is a mind-shattering drop. I'm powerless before the forces of nature and gravity.

"Don't freak out, Matt," June says. "We're almost at the end. We're almost out. This won't be very fun, but trust me, it works."

"What isn't very fun?" I ask, scrabbling against the wall. But June is already leaning backward over the edge of the cliff. I shout as she falls into the blackness below.

The wall continues toward me. The space below my feet only looks emptier and emptier. I want to close my eyes so I can imagine this isn't happening. The path I'm standing on is now only a foot wide. I shove against the wall. It's futile. All I have to do is follow June. Making up your mind doesn't make it any easier to jump, though.

I try not to scream as I leap from the edge. I don't succeed.

I'm falling, where a moment before all was forward motion. Lights flash across my mind's eye. The world wrenches violently, twisting into pure centripetal pain.

Metal crashes around me.

A voice says *give him a bit more*, and I sense relief coming. I fall back into numbness.

Pain courses through my legs. My back feels as though it was whacked with a dozen tiny hammers, and my head pounds against itself. June stares down at me.

"I F-ing hate this place and everything about it," I say.

"That was a very manly scream, I have to say. Very masculine and dominant. As a woman, my screams tend to be much higher pitched and more helpless."

"Shut up."

She offers me a hand and yanks me to my feet. The device on my wrist makes a cheerful dinging noise, and begins counting up again as we walk. June looks at it with amusement.

"You did a good job, all in all. No broken bones even. The fall tends to shatter a couple things if you get pushed."

We're standing on a flat stone surface in the middle of an open area surrounded on all four sides by even walls. Above, I can't see any sign of a ledge. One of the walls has a square door.

"We're out of the cave?" My voice sounds almost pleading. I don't think I could take much more of that.

"We're out of the cave. Not too much farther."

Though this area is as cold and uninviting as the rest of the Substratum, leaving the cave has lifted a weight. It no longer feels like we shouldn't talk. About halfway across, the floor turns into uniform rows of square holes two feet wide and two feet deep. June runs through them, lifting her knees high like she's doing an agility exercise. I plod behind her, still massaging my back.

"It's fun to not be lazy!" June calls back to me.

Another couple of narrow corridors, followed by a descent of several hundred steep steps, and we come to the first green we've seen since entering the Substratum. Scrub grass clings to the rock around us. As we near the bottom, the steps become less uniform, and then fade out altogether into a dirt trail with the occasional root. Before long we're in a forest. The terrain remains rocky, but the gentle slope makes it relatively easy going. A pleasant breeze stirs the trees, and for a moment the landscape feels almost natural. A tired, coming-home-legs feeling comes over me, like the last stretch of a hike. Maybe once we reach the Carnival we can rest. Though it doesn't sound like a super restful place, going by the name.

"So what's so great about the Carnival?" I ask.

"The stories, mainly. Any story you want, as long as you're willing to put in the effort. The thing about the Carnival is that what you imagine tends to come true there."

"What if you imagine something really horrible?"

"Well yeah, don't screw around with that responsibility."

A quarter mile later a high wooden fence blocks our way. The trail snakes to the left, winding its way around the last large stones and to the towering structure of a wooden gate. To one side is a crystal-clear lake, flanking what I can now see is a walled city.

I hear them before I see them. Low croaking sounds, surrounded by human voices. A surge of fear springs through my chest.

Four large figures make their way down the branching path leading away from the gate and the lake. June calls out to them, and they turn in formation toward us. The shapes are much too large to be human. Only once they get closer do I realize that they are in fact four humans, riding on the backs of large animals.

And those sure as hell aren't horses.

Eight clawed feet pound the dirt track as the beasts, ranging in color from white to black with stops at gray and brown, squawk toward us. Their riders sit in the crook formed by undersized wings, and behind each trails a plume of rainbow feathers. There's no two ways about it, the riders are mounted on giant, six-foot birds. They pull up in an uncomfortably close semicircle around us. If I had to guess, I'd place the age of each of the riders, who are all men, at about fifty. I would have to pass on a guess at the age of the birds, whose bobbing heads look more like the heads of chickens with each passing moment.

"Hoy, travelers!" one of the men says. They make no move to dismount, and the way their legs conform to the shape of the birds, I'm not convinced they're physically capable of doing so.

"There are no travelers in the Substratum," another says.

"But here are two," says another, "including June."

"Whatcha call two lone wandering souls, if not travelers?"

"Seems your theory's been disproved," says the first, critically.

"Exception proves the rule, sometimes."

"Sometimes not, though."

"Hello," I manage. The heads of men and birds snap to me in unison.

"Oh yes, hello. Who are you, and are you a traveler?"

"He's asking for a friend."

"That's me. Got a hunch a friend is wrong about something."

I take a deep breath. Speaking with these men feels like being dumped violently and repeatedly in a tub of nonsensical water. June rolls her eyes.

"I found him wandering out in the Wasteland," June says. She turns and greets each of the men, although how she tells them apart is anyone's guess. "Larry. Rob. Bob. Steve."

"Lost, by the sound of it."

"Disoriented."

"Mixed-up."

"Confuddled, even."

"Pleased to meet you," I say, before they can come up with more synonyms. "Thankfully June got me un-lost. At least we're out of the Wasteland."

"Not the nicest place, the Wasteland," says I think probably Larry.

"Difficult to navigate."

"You can try a compass, but it won't point to anything."

"It's sort of a blank slate type of place."

"Really all it's got going for it."

I can feel the heat rising underneath the collar of my T-shirt. I recognize the same rage I used to feel at the time-wasting idiots in my Model UN club. Model UN. Huh, more a snack than a full meal memory-wise, but I'll take it.

"Boys, I've got this handled," June says. "You can consider yourselves dismissed."

"But Bailly will want us to bring the traveler to him."

"Not necessary," June says. "He'll see Bailly soon enough, but if he hangs out with the chickenmen for any longer he's going to end up irrevocably lost."

"Rude."

"An aspersion—"

"—and an unfair one—"

"—on both our intentions and intelligence."

"No one's insulting your intelligence," June says through good-natured exasperation, "you're perfectly capable of doing that just by opening your mouths."

"Thank you."

"Anyway," she continues, "Bailly sent me himself. End of discussion."

I don't know who Bailly is, but the thought of June acting on someone's orders feels like a bad sign. It's hard to imagine anyone ordering her around.

"Bailly?" I ask.

"A question for later," June says, shish-kebabing me with her brown eyes. She turns back to the chickenmen. "Always entertaining to run into you, chickenboys. See you back in the Carnival."

The four men turn their mounts and amble off back the way they came. June watches them go before directing her attention back to me.

"They mean well, you know," June says. "I've heard they didn't always used to be like this, that it's just being here so long that's mushed up their brains."

We walk toward the gate, which grows larger and larger above us with every step. A brass handle in the middle of the gate appears much too large for human use, and giant rusty hinges hold the gate in place. In faded gold letters, someone has written:

Welcome to The Carnival(e)
Please remove shoes before entering

"You don't have to take off your shoes," June says as she hoists the latch. "Someone's idea of a joke. Or one of the old laws of the Carnival. I'm not actually sure, the two tend to resemble each other pretty closely."

The door swings open and a blast of light and music greets us. I walk forward warily, but June is off into the mayhem beyond, and I am forced to follow.

The Carnival - Valdrada

The people of the Carnival stretch all definitions of humanity. We encounter a cascade of faces, most with between zero and seventeen eyes, and with complexions representing all colors, though mainly the primary ones. They tend to have a modular appearance, as if they've been stuck together from a box full of assorted arms, legs, and torsos. A man with the skinniest legs has a massive upper body, and four arms ending in saw blades. A woman with two necks and only one head steps past us. Try as I might, my eyes can't move fast enough to process the strange array of people.

We enter in a central square, with market stalls along its sides, and a row of occupied tables in the center. People buzz back and forth between shouting vendors, as above them fireworks flash, flying between the two sides of the square as if they're at war with each other.

"The city is called Valdrada," June says over the din. "You can think of it as the capital of the Carnival if that helps, and if you're okay with ignoring thousands of years of complex history."

Everywhere tiny brightly-plumed birds scurry between feet or roost on the tops of stalls. The residents ignore them, or else shoo them away from their food.

"Microgriffs," June says. "Nobody can figure out how to get rid of them, and nobody wants to see them harmed because they're so damned pretty."

They are pretty. Their feathers are a rippling gradient from white at the tail to a striking teal at their beaks.

"A real pest," June says, but is interrupted as we nearly get trampled by a horned creature resembling a humanoid rhinoceros. June smiles. The smell of frying dough envelops us. They took some aspects of the Carnival name seriously, at least. We swing past a food vendor on one side and June hollers to the man at the stall.

"Jayson, what's in the dumplings today?"

"June, where ya been?" Jayson says. With cooking grease that covers him from head to toe, he looks as if he only recently crawled out of a fryer. "You know I can't answer that. Chef's special, same as always."

"Can I get a preview?"

Before I know it, we're walking away from the stand, June juggling two steaming dumplings. She passes me one and I shove it in my mouth, mainly to keep it from burning my hands.

There's no precedent for the experience. Beyond the salty broth inside is a delicate blend of meat and vegetables, with a slow-roasted sweetness I can't put a name to. June slurps hers down and eyes me, waiting for a reaction.

"This is incredible," I allow. I forgot how hungry I'd been.

"Damn right. Hope you brought your appetite because we're celebrating tonight. We'll have a real feast. It's not every day someone wanders out of the Wasteland. But more importantly, we celebrate because it's today, and we exist, and we're in the Carnival."

Not all of Valdrada is as loud as the main square, but all of it is as strange. We pass streets made entirely of vines, people composed only of shadows, and a giant pair of eyes peering out from the end of an alleyway. Every so often the eyes sneeze noselessly. On a soapbox in one of the more public streets, a preacher extolls the need for faith. The absence of any indication of what exact type of faith they mean is far less disturbing than the fact that the preacher doesn't possess a head, and their voice projects directly from a gaping hole in their neck.

Past a long walkway, above which hangs a reflecting pool of water, we come to a sign for "Night and Dragon," which features a sleeping dragon with tiny armor-clad legs poking out of its mouth.

"This is the best bar around, Matthias. I also happen to have some business to take care of here. Grab a drink. It shouldn't take too long, then we'll eat."

Brightly woven cloths provide privacy for each booth inside, but every seat I can see is filled, both in the jumble of seats on our level and in the balcony that hangs haphazardly above. The loud conversation of revelers in various stages of inebriation surrounds us. There seems to be no restriction on bringing animals into the bar, as three men ride miniature ponies through the crowd, their presence unremarked upon. One gesticulates grandly as if in the midst of a ribald story, but a moment later falls from his horse. His somewhat less intoxicated friend picks up exactly where he left off, and the riders leave their friend behind.

We come to the main bar, which features bottles of dozens of types of alcohol I don't recognize. June points for me to sit at an empty seat at the bar.

"I'll be right back. Tell them to put it on my tab." June disappears into the crowd. I fidget with my hands on the bar. To my knowledge I've never been to a bar before. In fact, I feel an instinctual repulsion to the idea of ordering a drink. I strain my neck watching the other customers talk over drinks and food. In the back, a person dances on a stage at balcony level. They move slowly, in time to low music that blends a dozen different musical styles, with the primary influence apparently being some form of chanting. As the dancer sways, their form shimmers and becomes soft at the edges. Then there are two identical dancers, moving in the same languid motions. As I wonder if two will suddenly become four, a voice at the bar breaks my trance.

"What are we having, love?" The woman before me is far more human than most of the guests. She wears a kind, easy smile.

"Um, I'm with June."

"Lovely girl, Juniper. She'll be meeting with Pavel, I expect. Those Apocalyptians won't come up with a peace treaty on their own."

"She said something about that."

"Can I get you something to drink?"

"I don't believe I drink alcohol," I say, feeling more than a little idiotic. But the sentiment burns as a fixed point guiding my actions, even if I don't know why.

She cracks a wide smile. "Tea then?"

"Sure. Thanks."

"Not a problem. I'm D'Angeline."

When the tea comes it's another revelation. Smoky, a little bitter, but with a rich aftertaste I want to go on forever. D'Angeline laughs at my expression.

"Good, right? I grow it myself. Not the most usual, I know, owning a bar and growing tea."

"You own this place?"

"Always have. Best bar around. Has been for as long as anybody can remember." I'm beginning to get the sense that most things in the Carnival always have been whatever they are. As strange as it is, it's a place made up of consistent reference points.

"It's a great place."

We watch the dancers. There are indeed four of them now. Their rhythm picks up as large translucent boxes begin rising from the stage to envelop them. The music surges. The boxes stop when the dancers are fully enclosed. The boxes' surfaces snap into complete opacity. A crowd of people by the stage moves toward the boxes, pointing wildly and yelling. After a chaotic few seconds, the boxes fall back into the stage, and a single dancer stands where the box on the far left had been. Some of the onlookers groan, others cheer. The entire area gives off a playful, back-patting vibe that makes me chuckle to look at, and more than one wad of bills exchanges hands.

"Not the most refined trick," D'Angeline says, "but a crowd favorite."

"That dancer, they're amazing."

"Shimmer's about the best at what he does. I tried to get him to stop the box trick, at least for a week, but he's immune to anything I say when there's cheering involved."

"Is it common to be able to do that? That replicating trick, I mean."

"Not remotely. He's honed that type of creative influence for years. That's why I'm always wary of giving him a talking to." She mixes a drink and delivers it to the woman next to me, though I can't recall her having ordered. "June's taking a while. I'll bet you're hungry. Let me grab a snack for you."

A moment later she's back, carrying a plate of purple cheeses. "Here you are, love."

She sets it down in front of me. My eyes set on the slight folds of skin on her finger as she does, and something about the voice draws me in. I feel warm, safe, taken care of. Like all my worries can be solved by a kind word and a snack.

I remember something, spurred by that voice. Weeks spent not at school when I should've been. Busy hands, hands that kept making snacks for me even long after I was full. Hands that kept massaging the empty space on her ring finger, and occasionally rising up to wipe moist eyes.

Here you are, love.

The bar pulls me back, its noise overwhelming any further dive into my mind. But despite the happy uproar around me, I'm deeply sad. Something is missing, and I feel inexplicably angry.

"Sorry, Pavel likes to gab," June says, materializing next to me. "Ready to grab a table, Mattchu Picchu?"

June orders at least six courses—and several carafes of wine for herself—and by the time the dishes have stopped coming out, we're both holding our bellies. She's chatty and clearly buzzed, and seems in a much better mood than earlier. I feel better as well. I haven't touched the wine. Now that her tongue is loose and I'm not feeling quite as overwhelmed, it seems like as good a time as any to ask some questions of my host.

"June, can you tell me what this is?" I ask, holding up my arm to show the device on my wrist. As I raise it, a gif appears on it. With the screen's low resolution, it takes a second before I register that the image is of a golden retriever giving me a withering side-eye. June snorts.

"It always amazes me that anyone thinks a smartwatch is a flattering fashion accessory."

"It's not a smartwatch," I say, tugging at the band as the device's display flashes back and forth between exclamation points and no-entry symbols. Tug "It's an unremovable..." Tug. "...piece..." Tug. "...of semi-sentient..." Tug. "...garbage!" I give up, my wrist chafing under the effort.

June examines it closely. "I've never seen anything quite like it, but it sort of looks like the biotracking devices people in the steel city wear. And I do mean only sort of."

"Can we go there, then?"

"You want to go all the way north to the steel city just to ask them if this vaguely similar tech is something they maybe might, possibly, know the slightest bit about?"

I sigh. "Maybe it doesn't matter. I have bigger questions." I lower my arm to the table, and the device clacks against the wooden surface. "None of which you've done a great job answering."

"How about you try asking me about something I actually know about? That would be the best way to get an answer."

"Fine. Tell me about the Apocalyptians. Seems like you love those guys."

Despite the copious consumption of wine, which I roughly estimate at two full bottles, June annunciates her words clearly. "The weird things about the Apocalyptians is that they might hate peace, but they don't really like war either."

"Those seem like sorta opposite positions."

"You might think. You might think." She leans forward, clasping her hands on the table in front of her as if she's a speaker on an academic panel, getting ready to begin her portion of the lecture. "But they're more or less human, and that means one overriding thing. That means they're lazy. Do you know how much effort it is to fight a war? Even if you've got perfectly good reasons, i.e. being hell-bent on ending the world and everyone in it due to your cult-like religion's ingrained beliefs and traditions, it takes a lot of energy to get that ball in motion. I mean, have you ever seen the parts requisition order for a single tank?"

"Is it long or something?"

"You bet your sweet ass it's long. I spend so much energy acting as the go-between for those two horrible groups of people, drawing up resolutions, writing charters, negotiating land deals. But sometimes I think I'd be better served just tallying up the vast level of human effort required in blowing each other up and presenting it to them via PowerPoint."

"Going by their names, I'd think they'd be good at it."

June bobs her head somewhere between a nod and a shake. "Yeah, they're good at it if they ever get around to it. It's putting the wheels in motion that's hard. I'm a piece of gunk in the machinery of war, keeping the cogs from turning."

"You're relatively human-looking, as gunk goes."

"And that," June says, "is the nicest compliment anyone has ever paid me. Thank you, Matteus."

"So what now? The chickenmen were talking about someone named Bailly."

"We'll see Bailly soon."

"Some sort of bigwig around here?"

"The biggest of wigs. He's a kind of leader, though as far as I know no one's elected him to shit. He just feels like he should be in charge. Around here, that's good enough to mean he actually is in charge. More importantly, he knows much more than any of us about the way this place is structured. He might know why you were wandering around in the desert acting like a horse kicked your memories out of your head."

"And you don't?"

June eyes me, but lets me finish my thought before responding.

"You knew where I was, and where to find me," I say. "You seemed to know right away that I'd lost my memories. But you're not like these other people ..." I haven't been able to fully form this thought, but when I compare June to the carousers at the bar, to the people out in the square, or even to D'Angeline, I know it's true. June is different at a deeper level. She feels more powerful. And more dangerous.

"You don't trust me."

"Why should I?"

June takes a generous swig of wine and swishes it around like mouthwash. "This is fair. It must be strange to feel like someone knows more about you than you do. But the fact is that I only know what Bailly told me."

"You work for him?"

"Not officially," June says. "Sometimes he asks me for favors, and most of the time it's to your advantage to oblige him, especially if you want information outside the scope of the Carnival."

"Maybe I don't need his information. Maybe I just leave."

"Do it." June shrugs. "I'd genuinely like to see you try."

The Carnival is bizarre enough that I feel like there should be a trick to it. Maybe I can close my eyes, lose a sense of gravity, and sink beneath the fabric of it. Or maybe it's as simple as finding a door.

June snaps her fingers just inches from my nose.

"Come on, man," she says. "Wake the hell up. The only way you're going to figure out how to get out of here—or even what here is—is if you go to Bailly and find out everything you can.

In the meantime, I'm going to show you why you'd be an idiot to want to leave in the first place."

An earnest gleam shines in her eyes. As I stare back, I feel my resolve crystalize. I'll go to Bailly, I'll go wherever June asks me to. But I am also going to do everything I can to find the way out on my own.

I sleep that night at a little inn off one of the quieter side streets, not far from the Night and Dragon. The sign out front is in the same style as the bar's, and features a sleeveless coat, with an unoccupied round hole at the top, but sleeve holes and a wide bottom where arms and legs stick out.

Deep in the night, I suddenly become conscious. My limbs don't respond, like my mind is awake but the rest of me isn't. I am aware of a dark pea coat hanging on the back of my room's door, reaching nearly to the floor. Maybe a previous guest left it? A breeze from the open window ruffles the thick fabric, which begins to sway. The breeze stops. The coat keeps swaying. It's fluttering now, undulating from side to side, trying to dislodge itself from the hook.

It waves violently and comes free. I still can't move. Fear grips me. The arms and lapels of the coat stretch themselves to their full length.

And a *face* peers at me from its folds. It's too dark to see detail, but I have the impression of a long nose, wrinkles, and incisive eyes.

With three quick flaps the coat and the figure rocket toward the window. It streaks out into the night. Only when it's gone does control of my limbs return.

I rise shortly before sunrise. Thankfully, the sun behaves in a normal cycle here, although it does have a tendency to change colors when it doesn't think you're looking. I walk out onto cobblestone side streets. There are only a few people out and about. Doing my best to keep track of the turns I've taken, I make my way toward what I think is the opposite end of town from where I came in, moving away from the main square and into the unknown maze of Valdrada.

I try to be as methodical as possible. Valdrada seems like the most likely place for a door that leads out of the Carnival, given that it's supposed to be its center. I don't even know if what I'm looking for is a literal door—I keep my eyes peeled for anything resembling a portal, a threshold, a crossing point to another dimension.

My efforts at an efficient search quickly go south, as the town turns out to be a warren of unplanned streets, many of them stopping in dead ends where moments before they appeared to offer three-way intersections. I realize that I've been on this same road before, and that no matter which way I turn, I end up back at the previous intersection. In the calm that only early morning can provide, I retain my composure. Rather than seeing if a road takes me in the direction I want to go, I start out thinking that the road I'm already on ends in my desired destination. Then, when I take that road, it's already going the direction I need to go. Simple.

Following this strategy, I manage to escape the narrowest roads. I come out in an area populated almost entirely by short, elfin creatures. The slate roofs of their homes are built at aggressive angles, and all of the creatures are scowling. They pay me no notice. As I walk among them, I see that many hold oblong boxes of wood with a metal crank at one end. They turn the handles determinedly as they walk. I have half a mind to ask about this when I notice one of the contraptions lying on the ground. I pick it up, surprised to find it extremely heavy. The unbearable urge to turn the crank comes over me. Before I can do otherwise, I'm turning the machine's handle, hearing the satisfying whir and click of gears inside the box. This feels right, like my strong, claw-like hands were made to do this, like my short arms were designed to hold the box under one arm, and turn the crank with the other.

I almost scream as I look down. The rest of my body has also morphed into the shape of one of the elves. My hands trembling, I stop turning the crank. *I mustn't stop cranking. I can't. This is my box, I must crank.* I throw the box down on the cobblestones so hard that it smashes into pieces. I straighten up, feeling my limbs lengthen, my face return to its normal shape. My knees feel incapable of supporting my weight.

An innocent pile of pieces sits in the street. The wooden box, its contents now visible, is entirely empty.

I run from this neighborhood, feeling that what I've just experienced is far worse than anything that happened to me in the Wasteland.

I soldier on. The world that yesterday felt so rich with chaotic possibility now feels larger and scarier than I could've imagined. I fear walking down the wrong side street could result in me losing myself, and never returning to human civilization. As I worry about this, I notice several people around me rubbing their mouths. I pause in front of a middle-aged man, who has stopped sweeping the sidewalk in front of his house to massage his jaw. As I watch, he reaches into his mouth and pulls out three of his teeth. He studies them impassively. They're not bleeding, nor do they appear to be causing any pain. He raises an eyebrow, then drops them onto the sidewalk and sweeps them up along with the dust and bits of newspaper.

All around me, others are undergoing the same process. It's so pervasive that soon I have to pick my way carefully around discarded molars, canines, and incisors.

Everyone appears more or less unconcerned with this loss. I feel my own teeth, but luckily they're all firmly in their correct places.

Off the street a few dozen yards is a shady orchard. A man bends down under one of the trees. Even at this distance I register the slight hesitancy of his motions, the way he holds out his hands to feel the space in front of him, and realize he's blind. Assuming he's also lost his teeth and is searching for them in vain, I start toward him to help. But I come up short as a woman steps out from behind another tree. Her pregnant belly juts out in front of her. She says something to the blind man and, with only a slight pause, steps up onto his flattened back. The purchase allows her to reach up into the branches, from which she plucks a perfect green pear. No one around us has offered to help, content to allow the man to be used as a human stepstool. Meanwhile a ladder leans against a tree on the far end of the orchard.

As time goes on, the town moves into rush hour. The strange variety of the Carnival's citizens slouch to whatever serves as a job here, and an increasing tide of carriages carries the wealthier residents along.

A few merchants attempt to take advantage of the passing crowds, arraying odds and ends on tables or on canvas at the curb.

"Fake relics here, fake relics!" one man declares. "I sell only the finest fake relics—both religious and spiritual."

I make the mistake of catching his eye, and he follows me into the flow of pedestrians.

"Sir, you look like you could use a quick salvation," he says, tugging at my arm. "I've been swindling folks like yourself for nearly twenty years. If you buy my relics, I promise that you will gain no benefit either to your present or future life! What do you say?"

"I don't have any money," I say. "Sorry, really they do look like great relics." The shabby oddments on the table are almost indistinguishable from the kind of junk that pops up at most yard sales. "Really, very nice."

There's a flash of something in the man's eyes, which I identify as a cousin of both joy and sadness.

"That's very kind, sir. Bless you and yours, and remember that if you ever need a purely heretical and inefficacious route to heaven, I'm your man."

He falls back, and I continue into the growing rush. The number on my wrist device passes *10,000*, then rewinds itself back down to *0*. Occasionally when a passerby jostles me, the numbers will be replaced by question marks, before re-shuffling to a value similar to, but usually not the same as, what was displayed before.

Most cities give an immediate impression. Even if it's partial, walking through the streets of New York, or Glasgow, or Beijing gives some indication of what it might be like to live there, who its inhabitants are and what sort of lives they might lead. But Valdrada is remarkable mainly for its lack of this consistency. Though the microgriffs are everywhere, and at each intersection you might see two or three carriages with more or less the same design, for the most part this city is slippery. Its architecture changes without preamble, flashing from Greek revival, to Spanish portico, to any number of Victorian styles. Once I emerge from the close walls of a Hutong to find myself looking at houses and lawns that are unmistakably suburban American. Here it feels like it's perpetually a summer afternoon, a lawnmower running in the distance, a sprinkler casting a faint rainbow over a sidewalk. The houses are benignly neglected, so sterile and generically sturdy that their occupants could take a thousand year vacation and return to find the same mowed lawns, the same drawn shades, and the same comforting blandness of a summer afternoon.

I retreat into the chaotic warmth of the Hutong.

"Hey, boy," a voice calls from the eves of a ramshackle house built into a bend in the road.

I spin around, hoping the voice is talking to someone else. As if.

"You're the one they brought in from the Wasteland last night," says a man sitting in a rocking chair in the shaded corner where the buildings meet. He has graying curly hair and sparkling green eyes.

"I suppose so. Matthew."

He doesn't get up, but scoots the rocking chair around so he's facing me. Rain bounces off the underside of the chair. "Carl. Good to meet you."

"What do you do around here, Carl?"

Carl smiles broadly. "Some days I sit in my chair and watch the world go by. Others I decide which way the world will go. Depends on my mood."

A few people passing by wave at Carl.

"How do you decide which way the world will go?"

"Not as hard as it looks. All you need's a little realism, and a healthy dose of decision-making. To be honest, the latter's a bit easier to come by around here."

"You're telling me."

"I am, aren't I? Don't mind me, I tend to put my paws in places they have no business being." He nods down at his paws, which I'd taken to be human hands. They're covered in a somewhat ragged coat of gray fur.

"No, no, I need all the help I can get," I say, and Carl practically beams at me. "Is there anything you can tell me about this place? I don't even know who I am past my name."

Carl stops the chair's rocking with a leg and leans forward. "You don't ask these questions as if you expect me to know the answers."

"Maybe I don't. No one here's big on answers so far."

"The Carnival does that to people. There's this whole unspoken 'don't act like it's weird no matter what' rule that makes us all dishonest. Sometimes I wish it would just rain from the sky and we could have one day where coffee tasted like bitter bean juice instead of a floral bouquet with vanilla undertones."

Three microgriffs that had been pecking in the gutter make their inquiring way over to Carl's leg. He strokes one of their heads. In return, the creature belches a tiny ball of flame, which singes the hair on Carl's paw.

"Little bastards." He watches them bob away before continuing, "I want to help, but everything has a price here. I have some jobs need doing, which you seem to be uniquely suited for. You come work for me, I'll give you so much information your head'll explode."

"What sort of work?"

"The illegal kind, obviously. Immoral, for the most part. Some of it downright dastardly."

"How do I know you've got the information I need?"

Carl taps his nose knowingly. "Good man, keeping me honest. A sampler, then, to whet your appetite? Here it is. The Carnival is not the destination. It has an exit, and that exit leads to another plane, much in the same way the Substratum leads here. There may even be another plane beyond that."

An exit. A way out. It's something, at least. At the thought of it, a tremor runs through the ground, as if the Carnival itself is objecting to the topic. Carl raises an eyebrow.

"Think it over."

"Matt?" a familiar voice comes down the street. June jogs toward us. "There you are. Dangerous place to pick for a stroll. Hi Carl. We should be going." Her words come out coated in ice.

I follow her reluctantly back toward the inn, giving Carl a nod that I hope says *I'll think it over,* and not *yes absolutely I'll do whatever you want.*

"You can't trust a word that guy says," she says.

"Why? He seemed friendly enough."

June easily maneuvers through the throng, and I run into a couple of people as I try to keep up. "Yeah sure he's got the kindly uncle thing going on, but he uses that to lure people in. More mayhem has been caused by Carl than pretty much anyone else."

"What does he do, stick out his foot as people are walking by?"

"Don't be dense, Mattinee. Carl's head of the mob."

"I'm not sure we're talking about the same person."

"We are. Stay the hell away from him. He's bad news."

"So far everyone I've met here has been bad news. If he can help me, I'm gonna do it. Same as Bailly. But I'm not gonna give special preference to one just because you said so."

"Your cynicism is admirable," June says. "I'm glad I finally taught you something." She claps her hands together, and her voice takes on the tone of a cruise director walking passengers through the day's activities. "Your decision to align yourself with the Carnival's most insidious elements aside, I have a plan for us today. We're going on a little adventure. It'll be fun. And in return for having fun, which I know isn't really your thing, we can go up to the steel city."

June points to the device on my wrist. Strangely, at a couple points today it has counted down rather than up. It seems to happen in certain areas in the center of the city, though I haven't been able to pinpoint exactly where.

"As much as I may have roasted the idea," June says, "whether or not it comes from there, the technologists in the steel city know their stuff. They might be able to tell you what that thing is. It's a nice contrast to Valdrada too—you should see that there are options here."

Part of me wants to keep looking around the city, but in the few hours I've spent exploring, I've found nothing of immediate use, and have almost gotten myself killed or lost at least three times. This is something concrete, at least.

"Fine. We can have fun, but only on the condition that we do the less fun thing directly after it."

June rubs her hands together. "That's what I like to hear."

The Carnival - The Steel City

Outside Valdrada's gate, we walk through tilled fields and past farmhouses. At one point we pass a single glittering skyscraper sticking out of otherwise undeveloped land. June hurries us past without a word. We begin to climb a mountain path of brick red dirt. The going here is easy, and I soon lose myself in the sights. Shallow caves bore directly into the hillside. People mill around the entrances, or bask in the sun. Every few minutes a group of children trails behind us, giggling and shouting. A few times adults step into the path, offering us cold tea or slices of warm bread with butter and honeycomb.

The Mountain Folk mainly occupy the foothills, so as we climb further the caves become less frequent. The foliage grows thicker, the trees crisscrossing until we can't see more than a few feet beyond the path on either side.

"Spooky, huh?" June says. It's not. Despite the strangeness of it, nothing feels threatening here. A dozen buds spontaneously bloom in a riot of blue and purple in the canopy above us. Though the branches and leaves obscure the sun, the path itself glows with red light. As we walk a little farther, the trees curl back from the path, exposing us all at once to light both from the sun above and from the ground below.

"We've got a choice," June says. "If we continue on the path, it'll take a couple hours to get to the peak. There's plenty to see along the way, but it's not the quickest route."

"What's the quickest route?"

"The quickest route is, I get a little creative."

I picture us bushwhacking our way through the trees as we march straight up the mountain. But my curiosity gets the better of me.

"Creative sounds good."

"Sick. Please hold." She closes her eyes. I wonder if I'm supposed to do something, so I opt for staring stupidly around, taking in the way the thick trees bend almost horizontally in the wind. "Okay."

A gap opens in the foliage. The trees have not so much bent back as been cut away in a rough circle, forming a tunnel running perpendicular to the path. We walk down the tunnel, briefly leaving light behind, and then emerge on a sunlit plateau. My stomach drops. We stand high up on the side of the mountain, not quite at its peak, but no more than two hundred feet vertically from it. A river valley spreads below us. Valdrada gleams at its far end.

An even taller peak stretches upward to our right, capped with pristine snow, which periodically cascades down in wispy tendrils. Past Valdrada on one side I can make out the blocky shape of the Substratum, wreathed in gloom compared to the brightness of the valley. On the other side a calm sea laps against a sandy shoreline.

Something about the view, its vastness, its gentleness, sweeps upward like a rushing wind. I breathe deeply, and no air has ever been fresher.

June pulls a metal water bottle out of an unseen pocket. She takes a swig from it, giving a satisfied sigh before offering it to me.

"It's probably wine or something," she says in response to my questioning look. "No pressure. It's cool if that's not your thing."

A hand reaches out, holding an old seltzer bottle, though I know by the tint of the liquid inside it's something else.

The mountainside fades, replaced by the warmth of a fire it had taken us hours to get going. My friend Lewis' face falls as he realizes his mistake.

"Sorry dude."

I tell him it's okay, even as bitterness wells inside me.

But the hand holding this bottle is not Lewis'. Rings cover enough of June's fingers to be reasonably considered armor. Crisp mountain air pulls me insistently into the present, away from whatever half-remembered past caused me to blanch at Lewis' offer. The smell from the bottle is sweet, not sharp like the scent of Lewis' breath. And the aversion that springs up automatically feels disembodied. It's a reflex, nothing more.

I take the bottle. One more look down the mountain. An anticipatory twist in my gut. This time I do mean it when I say: "It's okay."

I take a sip. I want to say I'm transported, but if I am, the destination is right here, on this mountain, with this strange young woman.

June laughs. "Slow down, you'll need your wits about you."

"For what?"

"It's not that hard. The air is thicker up here, so you don't even have to be that aerodynamic. Just don't try flapping your arms, that's an idiotic look to have as you're falling out of the sky."

"You mean..."

"Don't worry, I have a lot of influence up here. In order to hurt yourself you'd have to do something even out of your league stupidity-wise, M-dash."

The wine moves through me, activating every pleasurable corner of my brain. It doesn't sound so crazy to step forward and let the wind take me away. And no sooner do I think it's not so crazy than I'm over the edge.

The moment of panic is short. Not because I'm any less afraid of what appears to be miles of space below me, but because almost immediately the wind buoys me. I extend my arms behind me, leaning forward. I accelerate as I do, careening down almost at a diagonal. I laugh as I pull up. I slow and lift higher on the force of my momentum. I'm flying. A roar fills my ears, but not enough to block out June's voice behind me.

"YEEEE-HAWWW!"

I cackle madly and slow to let June catch up. She dive-bombs me, pulling off at the last second and spiraling away. I dart after her. She's more experienced at this, but I feel like a natural. I chase her around the edge of the mountain, then settle into formation beside her. June points ahead toward one of the snow-capped peaks. We zigzag our way toward it, above a river a mile wide. Rainbow mist rises from the water. Towns dot the river, some with watermills, others with long piers. Near the river's head I make out a huge concrete dam running all the way from one side of the valley to the other.

There is no comparison for this pure rush of elation. I catch June watching me, satisfied.

Wide open farmland sweeps in rows, which are interrupted periodically by bales of hay wrapped in white plastic. I can't hear any sound from this height, but my eyes catch on a stream of movement between the marshmallow bales. Close to thirty animals of all kinds run in a loose flock: chickens, pigs, and cows tripping over each other in haste. I look for something chasing them—what else would cause this odd display—but see that they're the ones chasing. A red fox barely outpaces them, its tail high as it sprints away. It carries something in its mouth, but we break off before I can tell what it is.

We make a huge bank turn around the back of the mountain. Huge shapes unfurl themselves along the craggy, frosted cliffs. What had at first appeared to be giant ice floes reveal themselves to be massive creatures, white and snakelike, with bodies composed of a large head and a single long tail run through with webby skin. As we watch, one launches itself into the air. My mouth hangs open as it undulates its body, floating as easily as we do on the mountain air. It bellows, and the sound cuts so deeply into me that I think it will tear me apart. An avalanche falls over the mountain like a wintry waterfall.

The creature floats lazily. My stomach does a dance as I see June banking toward it. She has a *trust me?* smile on her face that I don't like, but she hasn't steered me wrong yet. We glide toward the beast from behind. The creature is covered in white scales, each at least three or four feet long. Though they look hard, when it waves its body there's no noise other than the rush of displaced air.

June keeps a respectful, if not comfortable distance, falling into line beside the creature. I do the same as I keep my eyes on the jaws that support hundreds of teeth, each the size of my leg. When I catch its giant multicolored eye, I'm struck by something elemental. In some ways it reminds me of what we saw in the caves of the Substratum. Yet unlike in those caves, I know I have nothing to fear. I know I cannot understand rationally, but I also know that I don't need to understand. June shouts something over the wind. Its body forms a wake of air that buffets us up and down. It grins at its unexpected travelling companions.

I thought the air up here felt warm. A voice like heat lightning blazons itself across my mind.

It's a beautiful day for a flight, another voice says, this one clearly June's, although deeper and more resonant than her voice out loud.

All days are.

We fly in silence. June takes a sip from her wine bottle, before flying over to offer me some. I have to focus to avoid spilling it all over myself. When the creature turns, it does so slowly, giving us plenty of warning. We make a long arc around several more peaks, before pointing back to the creature's home.

Eventually we break off from our companion. A deep sadness fills me at his departure, as if I've lost a part of myself that can never be returned.

We spend the rest of the day flying. As the sun lowers itself gingerly over the Substratum, we streak toward the steel city, flying up the river, past the dam, and through a narrower valley where the river is little more than a creek. Train tracks divide the rocky landscape, disappearing into the sides of the mountains.

The doors of the steel city are embedded directly in the mountainside. The entrance is a landing pad covered in all manner of flying machines. Helicopters, ships that look designed for space travel, and even a hot air balloon made entirely of metal. Mechanics bustle around them performing repairs. No one notices us as we land in one of the few empty areas. My legs feel wobbly after so much time spent off the ground, but it's nice to have my feet on something solid again.

June leads us toward the doors, which are locked open wide enough to allow several hundred people to enter at once. The place feels nothing like Valdrada. The people cover as wide a range of shapes, sizes, and colors, but they all wear the same gray and white uniforms, with allowances for extra limbs and other unusual physiognomy. There's a quiet order to this city. People queue to be scanned at the entrance. Every wall is smooth metal.

We join the short line waiting to enter. When we get up to the window, a robot with a creepily friendly face asks us what our business is in the steel city.

"We've got an appointment with the IT Guy," June replies.

"And do you intend to stay longer than three hundred and eighty-seven days?" the robot asks.

"No, probably less than one."

"Permanent visa not required. Please see an immigration agent if you intend to extend your stay."

"Thanks, will do."

The robot's eyes light up. "Please extend your wrists." We put our bare wrists—me selecting the one without the device on it—out in front of the robot. Its eyes flash, and there's a prick of pain on my arm as a faint barcode appears on my skin. "Entry authorization confirmed. Enjoy your visit."

We leave the booth behind, me still rubbing my wrist, and make our way through another long hallway into the heart of the steel city.

"IT guy?" I ask. "Is that his official title?"

"*Her* official title," June corrects. "And no, she's got a long, acronym-intensive title that I can't remember. But everyone who needs something from her just calls her the IT Guy."

"How does she feel about that?"

"She'll install a virus on your device if you call her anything else."

The city feels like a beehive. Above us are metal residence cubes, with a miniature train running between them and lifts rising directly from ground level. Dozens of shops and restaurants line the floor level, all with a gray color scheme, promising hearty meals or utilitarian goods in muted lights. Robots walk among the pedestrians. A moving walkway rockets people along at insane speeds down the center of the road. The road itself stretches endlessly forward, with the same housing structures continuing in an unbroken grid as far as we can see. The houses look as if they were designed to the exact minimum requirement for sheltering a human. Nothing here takes up more space than it needs to.

We pass sensors at even intervals. Occasionally one of the people around us will break off suddenly after we pass them.

"Constant diagnostics," June says. "If anyone's running below full capacity, the sensors alert them so they can eat a supplement or see a doctor."

"I would find that inconvenient, I think."

"Most procedures here take under a minute. Not bad to keep you at peak condition." Something about this place gently suggests you should speak in a voice a little above a whisper, which June does.

"You did say it wasn't that homey."

"Homey and efficient are rarely interchangeable, MC squared. The life expectancy here is nearly three hundred, though."

"Is there a lot of disease in Valdrada?" I couldn't remember seeing anyone who looked sick.

"No. You see, here they've recognized the rationality of inevitable death. It makes all of this healthcare apparatus necessary when, strictly speaking, it might not otherwise be."

"You're saying people in Valdrada don't get sick because they don't recognize the inevitability of death?"

"I'm more saying they've got a good healthcare system here. Whether they really need it is a moot point. Come on, let's check out the manufacturing hub. We've got a bit of time before our appointment."

We take the moving walkway, which turns out to be a lot safer—though no less scary—than I thought it would be. It grips your shoes, and in order to exit you just tap the side rail, and the portion of walkway you're on slides off to the side and deposits you gently, if a little dizzily, back on solid ground. We ride for close to twenty minutes, every passing bank of homes and shops a reminder how vast this place is. The living pods form a visual wall of sameness. When we get off, it's near a door with a radial handle so massive that only a seventeen-foot tall robot could open it. We make for a smaller entryway to one side.

Another moving walkway takes us at a more reasonable speed along a balcony overlooking machines and thousands of people. Massive interstellar ships are under construction by a combination of automated machine arms and human laborers, while an assembly line churns out dozens of new robots a minute. One area houses a dog-sized dragon made entirely out of titanium. Around it, elf-like creatures frantically turn the cranks on their wooden boxes. The only difference between these and the ones in Valdrada are that these wear gray and white suits. We're still in the Carnival. There is one set of rules, or one set of a lack of rules.

It's all too much for my eyes to take in. Too much metal, too much noise. The wheels of industry turn at an impossible rate.

We continue deeper into the factory, into a smaller room with a single cylindrical container in the center. A machine consisting of three carriages worth of tubes and pipes injects liquids and spurts of air into the cylinder.

"One of the most complex processes," June says. "They're transmuting metals."

"Like alchemy or something?"

"Or something." June checks a clock on the wall. "It's time to see the IT Guy."

We don't leave the factory, instead climbing into a service elevator. A couple dozen workers from the factories travel with us, some carrying machine components, others chatting as they consume tubes of what I can only assume is nutritional gel intended to serve as lunch. We drop close to thirty floors. People get on and off, but as we descend deeper, the crowd thins out, until June and I are alone on the elevator. A few floors from the bottom, the elevator lights suddenly flick off, and the space is lit only by the blue glow of the emergency lights in the top corners.

"Don't worry," June says at my obvious concern. "They change the lighting to accommodate some of the workers who don't do as well with light. They're the ones who built the steel city originally, so they're given special consideration."

As if on cue, the elevator door opens, and a single person steps in. My eyes take a second to adjust and scan the round, androgynous features. The person's eyes are at least three times as large as a normal human's, and have no differentiation between iris, pupil, or sclera. Their eyes are basically black all the way through, and squint at the faint illumination coming off the emergency lights.

They nod to me and June, and get off at the second to deepest floor. We get out a minute later, at the last available stop.

We exit directly into a mess of wires and the noise of fans. Lights flash on racks of servers that form a loose grid through a massive room, which runs so far in each direction that it's not clear where it ends, or if it even has an end.

June sniffs. "I love that smell."

"I don't smell anything," I say.

She leads me around a bend in the servers, and past tower after tower of panels and routers. "It's the smell of technology. Of information. Of connection. It's the guts of all of it."

"It just smells like ... I don't know, hot plastic and metal."

"But what hot plastic and metal it is!" says a voice from the stacks next to us. We turn to see a woman sitting at a desk tucked in between the shelves. Her desk and chair are completely covered with wires, and my stomach jolts when I notice that the wires appear to be disappearing not into each other, but into her arms and torso.

"Matthew, meet the IT Guy," June says.

I shake the woman's hand. The wires move with her. She looks like she's somewhere in her mid-forties, incredibly pale, and with dark buzzed hair. She wears a shapeless, unzipped gray hoodie over a shirt sporting a comic strip written entirely in some coding language.

"Nice to meet you," I say, taking a seat beside June, who is moving a stack of laptops onto the floor to clear a space for us.

"I'm not what you were expecting," the IT Guy says. I thought I'd done an okay job hiding my surprise at her appearance, but apparently not good enough. "It's okay, the title throws everyone off. I've found that being an IT Guy is more a state of mind and being rather than anything related to gender."

"It also throws people off the scent so they don't realize she's not only a computer genius, but also a complete smoke show," June says.

The IT Guy glares at June, but there's humor beneath it. "June knows my position on flattery, and exploits it mercilessly."

"Just calling it like I see it," June replies.

The machines around us whir in a staccato that sounds like a laugh.

"I understand you're here about an unusual device," the IT Guy says, placing an outstretched hand across the pile of circuit boards on the desk. I let my arm drop into it, the device on my wrist facing her.

"June said you might know what this is."

She studies the device closely, turning my arm gently so she can take in the entire screen, the lack of any apparent buttons, the elastic band running in a circle.

"I'm guessing you haven't been able to take this off?" she says.

"No," I say. "Is there some technology keeping it there? And why would it have been attached to me in the first place?"

"We were wondering if it was steel city tech," June jumps in. "That shit tends to be annoyingly persistent."

"I appreciate that description of my designs," the IT Guy says. She stares for a long, long moment. "But no, this isn't ours."

Shit. Another dead end.

"I've never seen anything quite like it, to be honest," the IT Guy continues. "However, I do have some thoughts about its origin."

I sit up straighter in the chair. A nudge in the right direction isn't much, but I'll take it right now.

"Its origin?"

"This is not really technology, at least as we conceive of it here," the IT Guy says. "No one anywhere in the Carnival made this. This is a self-emanation. That's why you can't get it off—it's a part of you."

"Couldn't you, like, cut it off?" I ask.

"I wouldn't advise you cut off a part of yourself just because you don't like it," she says, her voice sharp.

I look down at the device again. Every so often, it counts upward. Earlier today, I noticed that when it reached 10,000, it dinged and a huge checkmark appeared on the screen, along with a smiley-face emoji. It then reset to zero.

"Is there anything more you can tell me?" I feel the desperation in my voice. "What does it mean that it came from me? Can anyone else tell me about it?"

There is a crashing noise, and the IT Guy's eyes flash to the source of the sound, where a server tower has gone up in a plume of flames. She sighs.

"Come on, Matthew," June says, forcibly pulling me to my feet. "She's busy. She told you everything she knows."

"Please," I say. "Is there anything else?"

The IT Guy stares deep into my eyes as she stands, trailing wires behind her. "I would recommend looking into yourself to understand why you—why who you are—would emanate such a device. Only you have that answer."

We have dinner in one of the steel city's restaurants. The food is good, but not as satisfying as the meal back in Valdrada. It's perfectly seasoned and proportioned, but...

June notices me looking down at my steak.

"I know what you're thinking," she says.

"You always seem to."

"It's perfect, right?" She twirls spaghetti on her fork. "Nothing out of place, crafted to perfection. Almost makes you sick, doesn't it?"

"It does feel off somehow."

"Exactly. Are you starting to see some of the problems of the Carnival?"

I think about this for a second.

"I guess the problem is that it's not really one thing. It's a kind of jumble of different elements stuck together. Like someone took a box of toys and shook it up before opening it."

"Also those freakin' microgriffs are everywhere." June breaks off another piece of bread—leaving the last piece for me—and butters it generously. "Ugh unsalted. See, we've got the Substratum on one side, holding us in place. Like an anchor. Some things come from there, but those tend to be the basic, fundamental things. Organizational structures, government, that kind of boring crap."

"And on the other side?"

June blinks at me. "The Carnival goes theoretically forever on every side except the Substratum. It's as boundless as the Substratum is bounded. But there is of course something beyond. I can't tell you if it's a true boundary, but at some point you come to the Superstratum."

Superstratum. This must be one of the layers Carl was talking about.

"How would you get there?" I ask.

"You can't. And you wouldn't want to. As I understand it, the Superstratum isn't much more than a sort of filter."

"Why wouldn't you want to go to the Superstratum?"

"Lots of reasons," June says. "The main one being that every time someone tries to leave the Carnival, they end up upsetting things. There's a balance here. A lot of people could get hurt if that's upset."

June looks at me meaningfully. A robot waiter comes up, scans us to confirm that we don't require any more sustenance, and slides away.

I can feel the usefulness of this conversation slipping away, so I head down a different route. "Sorry I'm not much fun to talk to. Losing all your memories really cuts down your conversational options. Do you have any memories from before?"

"A lot more than you ended up with, for whatever reason. I remember getting through a year of college. Computer science. Don't think I made it to sophomore year, but I remember that first year pretty well. I had as many friends as you could ask for, and it turns out I'm pretty damn good at writing code. My mom wanted me to be pre-med, or pre-law. Something stable. She says all computer science majors end up working for failed start-ups. I don't think she grasps that most of them make six-figures right out of school."

She catches the look on my face and smiles. "Come on, you know I'm not that shallow. Six-figures isn't nice just to have it. I want to be the kind of person that does something with money, that contributes to causes and supports public radio and shit."

"I also seem to remember liking NPR only semi-ironically."

"See? I'm helping already, unlocking your most trivial memories. Anyhow, college also taught me that capitalism is evil, and that education is just a means of creating more workers for the oligarchs' machine. Nice when a school gives you a meta-narrative as it's churning you out."

"It's only fair."

"But those days are behind me, of course. College is all fine and good when you're on a path from childhood straight to stable adulthood, but that was never what I really wanted. I wanted a life that meant something beyond myself."

"Is that why you're out there creating peace treaties between warring nations?"

"You haven't met the Apocalyptians. They don't do war for any cause. They do war because they love it. They've built their religion around slaughtering their enemies, and sometimes their friends. It's in their version of the Bible and everything. How cool is it to keep a country like that out of conflict? How many nineteen-year-olds do you know who get to do that?"

"What about the Armageddeons? Some kind of cult too?"

"Nah, they're just assholes who like hitting other people over the head with things."

June's leaning forward in her seat. The intensity in her eyes makes me want to go out and be part of a cause too. But that sense is immediately tempered by the weight of everything she still hasn't told me.

"We all want a narrative," June says. "It took some time for me to figure out what it was, but I've found mine here."

What's my narrative? Surely I had some idea about that before... And I do find I have some idea. I'm wearing a suit, raising an indignant hand, giving a speech to a fired-up crowd. But what does that crowd want? What do I want?

"Do you know how you ended up here?" I say. "It must've been a different process if it didn't steal your memories."

June frowns. "It was a straight shot to the Carnival. That's the most obvious difference. And Bailly met me right away. It could've been disorienting, but with Bailly right there, it wasn't. We'll go see him tomorrow. I think he could help you too, James Mattison."

I'm about to respond when I see a flash of black among the gray forms outside the restaurant window. Am I imagining that it's a tall figure wrapped in a long black coat? It disappears. It's hard to find anything supernatural or scary here, though. I must just be paranoid.

"Do you think Bailly can tell me about this thing?" I ask, holding up my wrist, and the device on it.

June waggles her lips noncommittally. "The IT Guy said it was coming from you, which means that you're really the only one who can answer that."

"But I don't know anything about myself!"

"That is sort of an issue, I suppose."

"Stop enjoying this," I say.

June wipes the grin off her face, but the light stays in her eyes. "One thing I'm almost positive Bailly can help you with is giving insight into who you are. Maybe even what lies in your past. That sounds like a decent recipe for self-understanding, no? And by extension, understanding what the hell your self is doing when it makes a weird pedometer thing show up on your wrist."

I sigh, then nod and start to get up. If Bailly has answers about my past, then that's the next step. My mind returns to Carl, and his promise of a way out. None of this would matter if I could just leave. But what reality would I be returning to? What if this is all that's real now?

We sleep that night in one of the guest pods in the rafters of the steel city. The room has two twin beds, and I listen to June's soft breathing, my thoughts buzzing too loudly for sleep. My mind, trying to wrap itself around the vastness of the Carnival, feels as if it's expanded tenfold in the past day.

And then there's June. As annoyed as I started out at her, that annoyance has morphed into something else. I consider the possibility that I might have a crush on her, but that doesn't characterize it. What I feel is more a sense of being continually impressed with her as a person. Not once since I've met her has June doubted herself. She's never paused or vacillated. Every decision is a confident direction already taken. I don't have the memories to back it up, but I'm sure this respect comes from a certain amount of envy, that confident decision-making is something I both struggle with and desperately want. I can learn a lot from June.

A nascent thought first sparked by the order of the city grows in the quiet. Something about routine. My eyes fall on the hard lines of the sleeping pod. My ears take in the low hum of a white noise machine that fills the space with fake nature sounds. School's an obvious part of the routine. Sports. Model UN. But it's not so much about the things I did. It's more about a way of being in the world. Studying during my free period before soccer practice. Friday night spent catching up on administrative duties for at least three clubs. Homework all day Saturday and Sunday except for volunteering at a food pantry. Steady. There was a plan, and a lot of spreadsheets to track it all. Boxes checked, colors coded. I wonder if it's projecting to think that June would rip this sort of plan to shreds and light it on fire.

I look over. She's on her side facing away from me, her long legs bent, mismatched socks poking out of the covers.

I turn over, no closer to sleep than I was an hour ago.

The Plan. In my head I capitalize it. It must have had a goal to mark its final endpoint, but in my mind the Plan itself is the dominant force.

I only realize I've been dozing off when the entire pod shakes, yanking me awake.

I hear shouting, and klaxons blare. The pod shakes again. I look out the window and see that the whole city is vibrating. People run back and forth in confusion on the catwalks.

"Shit, shit, shit," June says, pulling on her boots. I grab my sweatshirt from over the back of the chair and stuff it on over my T-shirt.

"What's going on?"

"Some sort of instability. Big one too."

We run out onto the catwalk as it rocks again. A metallic snapping sound comes from the walkway in front of us.

"We've gotta get to one of the lifts, head to the exit."

Sprinting side-by-side, we move toward the nearest lift. But when we get there, the shaft has crumpled halfway down. One of the pods lies smashed on the floor below.

"Jesus Christos," June says.

"What about that one?" I point to an intact lift a hundred yards to our left.

"Good thinking, MC Hammer." We're off. A piece of metal shakes loose from the roof and smashes onto the catwalk in front of us with a scream of tearing steel. June sizes up the hole created by the falling debris, then, without hesitating, runs forward and leaps to the other side. I follow, starting my run before she's even landed.

"Not bad, not bad," June mutters to herself as we dash to the lift. I slam the door behind us. Thankfully the controls are still working, and we rocket to ground level. We're about to run straight across the floor toward the entrance when an entire catwalk collapses. It smashes to the ground in a shower of sparks and shrapnel.

I hear the shriek of the falling catwalk as if through tinny speakers, and for a second I watch a figure I know to be another version of me, one with less luck or more foot speed, fall beneath the onslaught of metal. Yet I'm outside this course of events. It gives me no fear.

With a jolt, I reel back from the falling debris and yell over the din. "Too dangerous that way. I have an idea though."

I run into one of the restaurants, June behind me. It's closed, but its glass door has been smashed. We sprint across the empty restaurant, straight into the kitchen, and through.

"Are we looting?" June asks. "Please tell me we're looting."

"Delivery system."

I don't know how I knew it was back here, but when I saw the restaurant and remembered how clean it was, I matched my cold rationality to that of this city. There must be a rear entrance, where all the food comes in and refuse goes out. Now that'll be our way out too.

A cart half-loaded with food scraps waits in the corridor. It's technically a two-way street, but it's a tight fit for two carts to run in opposite directions. There's no key, but the cart starts right away. Guess no one wants to steal a literal pile of trash. June and I exchange a *who should drive, you or me?* look.

"This is your escape," she says. "Take us out."

I drive the cart altogether too fast down the corridor, weaving around pieces of fallen metal and cement, on one occasion having to swerve past two overturned carts. The device on my wrist jumps fifteen or twenty numbers each time we drift, now not just capturing the change on an LED screen, but actually projecting in the air in front of me.

Fragments fly through the walls behind us. I chance a look as the entire corridor shakes. I think I see a piece of catwalk slam through the place we'd been a moment before, and half of a cylinder resembling the one we saw in the transmuting section of the factory yesterday bounces almost lazily past. I gun the motor.

Two more turns, and we're out in moonlight. The loading dock has a strong roof overhead, and there doesn't seem to be much that could fall on us. I pull up. Tremors still shake the ground, but they're less frequent than before.

"I think that's the worst of it," June says. "Not the most splendid of times to be stuck underground."

"Where the hell did that come from?" Down in the valley, the river has grown past its banks. Some trapped cache of water deep in the mountains had dislodged itself and come roaring down like a charging army.

"Not here, nothing in the Carnival could create that big of a disturbance." June frowns. "We'll just have to hope it was a one-time thing."

"Oh good. Hoping for the best is always my go-to plan for natural disasters."

"Nothing natural about that." She looks me over, confirming I wasn't skewered by any sharp metal objects. "Good call with the delivery system. That was quite the innovation."

"Not sure how I remembered it was there."

June laughs.

"You remembered it, did you? Amazing. How come when I was sitting in the restaurant I saw a delivery robot drop a pod of supplies through a chute out front and collect a pod of trash the same way?"

I blink. I did indeed see a robot outside, but I assumed it was doing something unimportant and pod-related. Oh.

"You're ridiculous." June is now roaring with laughter. "You misunderstand one thing and you end up redesigning the steel city's entire delivery and waste management system!"

"Sorry, I really didn't mean to."

This just cracks her up more, and it's several minutes before we can return to normal conversation.

We make our way down to the train station, several levels below the main door to the city. It is pristine, with clear glass walls all the way around. In the five minutes before the next train, as we sit on padded white chair, I ask June the obvious question about our recent escape.

"So, you know how I apparently redesigned a bunch of stuff just now?"

June giggles. "Classic Matthematics right there."

"Why was I able to do that? Every time I got lost in Valdrada, the streets stayed the same way they'd been, and I stayed lost. I wasn't able to just point them in whatever direction I wanted. Come to think of it, I didn't see you fly in Valdrada either."

"That's because I can't," June says. "I told you in the mountains that I have a lot of influence there. That's true, but it's also true that the mountains are a place where *flying is appropriate*. One might argue they're designed for it. The whole point of creative influence is that your power matches the place. So I couldn't fly in Valdrada, but either of us probably could have rearranged the systems underpinning the steel city. That's because the steel city is a place whose identity is about the systems within it. It's a place of rules and logistics, so the creativity you can express is within those very rules and systems."

My mind doesn't feel like it's fully caught up to any of this, but I'm following close enough to ask, "So what type of place is Valdrada? What powers could operate there?"

June smiles, as if I've asked the exact question she was hoping I would. She looks toward the platform, where our train is speeding into view. It whizzes past—it will let everyone off at a separate platform, and then come back to collect us after a rapid cleaning.

"Valdrada is one part maze and one part multitude," June says. "So anything that brings you further into the maze is something you could very well manipulate. But more importantly, Valdrada is a place of places. There are different rules on one street, and different rules on the next. Different rules in the factories, and different rules in homes."

"So Valdrada is a lack of specificity. That makes things hard."

"It's not a lack of specificity, it's an overflow of specificity," June corrects me. "That distinction is important."

We get up as the train floats back onto our platform, and the wide doors slide open.

"Remember that," June says. "You will have power in whatever you identify to be a place's essence. Valdrada just happens to be many, many places."

I wish I had slept more, maybe then I could process this information better. But it's enough, along with the information about the wrist device, for me to mull over. I follow June into our private train car.

The Carnival - Valdrada

The train runs on magnetic tracks that create a smooth, if mind-bogglingly fast ride. Perfect for catching a substantial nap by the time we pull up outside Valdrada. The train's only stop in the area creates the illusion of a sleepy country station. One platform sits in the middle of a field, which abuts the lake on one side. Across the field, it's a short five-minute walk to one of the main entrances.

The sun is beginning to make its presence known when we reach a wooden gate off a side street. I rub my eyes.

"Thissit?" is my bleary approximation of human speech.

"Yep. Bailly wants to talk to you alone. I could afford to do something productive, i.e. shower, as well."

June holds the gate open, smiles as I go inside, and slams it shut behind me. June always cast Bailly as some near-supernatural being. Someone slightly outside of the Carnival, at least based on his extensive knowledge of it. I feel a twinge of fear at who I'm about to meet, mixed with excitement at what he might tell me.

The narrow breezeway inside is open to the sky above, with high walls on both sides. A hammer lies across a wooden board on top of a workbench, and nearby a wheel is propped up against a wheel-less wheelbarrow. At the far end I approach another wooden door.

Mrow. A shape drops down from the windowsill next to the door, and I nearly jump backward into the wheelbarrow before realizing that it's nothing more than a gray cat, almost small enough to be a kitten. The cat has bright orange eyes and raises his long tail as he weaves between my legs. He feels like a living piece of silk that happens to be vibrating gently. I scratch him behind the ear.

My uses exhausted, the cat leaps onto the wheelbarrow, then to the top of the wall, and struts away, balancing along its edge. I take a breath and knock on the door.

A deep voice calls me in. The cat watches intently as I ease the door open and step inside.

The interior is not what I would have expected, given Bailly's reputation. A comfortable living room, with a low fire in a screened-in fireplace. Bookshelves line the walls, but I don't recognize any of the titles. Most appear to be travel journals to places I've never heard of, some conspicuously handwritten.

"Welcome, Matthew," Bailly says from the doorway to the kitchen. He fills the space with his height and a square-shouldered frame. He's movie star handsome, a light brush of stubble over his cheeks, and eyes so green I have flashbacks to water rising over the dunes of the Wasteland. His hairline is one even I'm envious of, and the black strands are flecked with gray in a proportion that brings the word "distinguished" to mind.

"Hi."

"We have a lot to discuss, and I think perhaps my study would be better suited to this conversation. I've just made coffee, would you like some?"

"Yes, please."

"Excellent, have a seat. I've recently re-discovered café con leche, and I must say, I'm somewhat addicted. The key is to scald the milk." His conspiratorial smile is dazzling.

"Oh, yeah, sounds good." I feel my face flush as I step into the study and take a seat in the less worn of two chairs. These walls have bookshelves, but they are filled with file folders instead of books. Here and there a stray paper pokes out, but I can't get a good look. Bailly comes in with two cups on saucers, setting one beside me on the desk, and resting the other in his lap as he sits opposite me.

"Thank you, I was just admiring your study," I say, mainly to have something semi-polysyllabic be heard coming out of my mouth.

"It isn't much, but it serves my needs. It's where I keep my records." He points to the shelves.

"Records on what?"

"All the citizens of the Carnival. Everyone has a file, at least one page. A dreadful amount of work from an organizational perspective, but someone's got to do it."

"Is that, like, your job?"

"I'm a sort of record keeper. The last arbiter of account, as it were. Not that that will matter to you. You're here for more practical reasons, I trust?"

"Practical?"

"You're missing some memories."

I start, surprised by his directness. "Yes, actually."

"Good, standard stuff. Nothing to worry about."

"So you can tell me what this place is? How I can leave?"

Bailly frowns. His frown makes me want to apologize profusely. It's like I've personally disappointed him because he cares so much about my potential. I seem to remember a similar look from a baseball coach who I'd told I was quitting the team to focus on academics.

He gets up and reaches for a box high on his shelf. It's wooden. When he pulls it down, I can make out an inlay of gold around an illustration of a naval battle.

"Leave? I suppose that's only the natural response to being thrust into so disorienting a circumstance. But you have to understand that the Carnival is not so much a place one leaves from or arrives at. You simply are here."

"There's no way out?" I say.

"I didn't say that. What I am saying is that leaving would be very bad for you—I would venture disastrous—and disastrous for this place as well. To leave would be to turn your back on unlimited possibilities."

"You sound like June."

"I take that as a compliment. June is a remarkable young lady. Though come to think of it, I don't know how much she'd like being called 'young lady.' In any case, I'm talking about more than possibility. You have a role to play here, and turning your back on that role would be a tragedy."

He sits back down, swapping the coffee for the box in his lap. I take a sip of my own coffee, and damn but that's good. His milk-scalding technique almost seems a more important point of inquiry than the nature of the Carnival.

"This box is where I keep only my most important records." He opens the box. I lean forward, but he gives me a *keep your grubby little eyes off the secret records* look, before pulling out a single sheet. "Ah, here it is. Your record."

"Mine?" I'm sure he's made a mistake. My record can't possibly be one of his most important. But Bailly doesn't seem the sort of man who makes mistakes.

"Yes, yours. You're an important part of everything that's happening here. A bit dramatic, I know. Sorry about that."

"Am I a Horcrux or something? Or the only one who can resist the power of the One Ring?"

Bailly laughs.

"Not exactly. You asked what this place is. This place is simply a story. Some of it is a story that's already been told." He waves a hand at the records on the wall. "But more importantly, a story *waiting* to be told. Every corner of the Carnival possesses the potentiality for narrative. You're asking questions as if the key to understanding is understanding what it is in a literal sense—the earth, the wind, the water. You have to look beyond the form and see the potential. That, in the realest sense, is the definition of the Carnival."

"I'm not sure I understand," I reply, "but I'm guessing that's okay."

"It's more than okay. The question now is what narrative you will embrace, what story you will tell."

"What story have you told?"

Bailly smiles. "That's not my role." He holds out the piece of paper. My record. My breath quickens as I reach for it. I expect to see a history of me, if not in detail then at least a basic sketch of who I am, where I'm from, why I'm important enough to have my record kept in the special box.

What I see instead is a blank page.

"You've got to fill it up, Matthew. Fill it up with your story, and the keys to the Carnival will be yours."

Two things exist in parallel in my mind. First, that Bailly's offer sounds enticing. Second, that I have no idea why it sounds enticing. I don't know why I'm here, or who I am. Why should I care about the proverbial keys to the Carnival?

"I feel like there are more productive ways I could be spending my time," I say. I'm tempted to fold the paper, but instead I keep it between my fingers, my head bent over it. "Since I've been here, all I could think about was how to leave. June has shown me some amazing things, but I still can't bring myself to want to stay fully, to explore those stories. Does that make sense?"

Bailly smiles beneficently. "It does. How about this, in exchange for you building your story, I can give you a glimpse of what came before. At least until you realize that writing your story on that—" he points to the paper "—is so much more important."

I nod my agreement, and instantly I am somewhere else.

I get out of the driver's seat of my beat-up Honda Civic. The car was somewhere between a birthday gift and a reluctant acknowledgement that it was easier for me to drive myself to high school once I had my license.

The door creaks shut behind me as I circle toward the back of the house. My excited footsteps spray grit onto the recently planted flower beds by the driveway.

I've guessed right, and my stepfather is in the backyard rather than inside the house. He likes to read out there once the weather inches to 49 degrees or above, and today the early spring sun is shining.

Russ sees the expression on my face, notices the way my clothes are disheveled—tie loosened, shirt untucked under my blazer—and puts his book down.

"Good news?" he says.

"Great fricken news," I say. I'm holding a piece of paper with a running tally on it. "We more than doubled the contribution goal. We're well over eleven-thousand and counting."

Russ' reactions never push much past calm, but I believe him when he says, "I'm so proud of you. You built this from nothing, and now look where it is."

I almost say, "No, *we* built this," but I don't get the chance as he stands and hugs me so tightly I can't say another word.

As suddenly as the memory came, it is gone.

I am back in Bailly's study. He watches me with eyes just as approving as Russ'.

"I am only able to give you a glimpse at a time," Bailly says. "But show me what you've done, and I'll keep showing you what I can of your past."

I spend the bulk of the afternoon and evening exploring the streets—at least those that end up not looping back on themselves or stopping in dead ends. I clutch a second piece of paper in my hand. Like the blank one, this one is also the size of an index card, but has a scrawled name and address across it in perfect cursive writing.

After what Bailly showed me today, I have more questions than answers. I admit, too, I have a lingering desire to light the paper on fire and toss it over the side of the city's outer wall, where I'm now standing. As if in reaction to my thoughts, the paper bursts into flames. I drop it with a cry of pain, and frantically bend to put it out. The card dissolves to ash as it falls, the fire winking out. Panicking, I pick up the one corner that hasn't burned completely. The entire address is gone. I've burned it up through sheer thought. I imagine Bailly's look of disapproval, before noticing a slight poking sensation in my pocket. I reach in to find the same card, with the same address scrawled across it. I look around. Guards patrol along the top of the wall, but they don't seem to have noticed my accidental magic show. Outside the wall, a breeze stirs the lake. Bright stars shine above, but create no reflection on the water.

Bailly said I have a role to play here. Something about how he said it, the surety and the knowledge behind it, makes me believe him instinctively. It's even easier to believe him when I have more than a hint of a past unfurling itself behind me.

Whatever Bailly is, he's more than a record keeper. He's some sort of guide. Hell, he may be the hub of this misshapen wheel, and all of us are the spokes. I don't know. What I do know is that the past day has brought me to my knees. June showed me a world of wild possibility, a world it might even be worth telling a story in. I think about her peace talks between the warring nations and wonder whether I can top that story. I probably can't, but I don't need to top it. I just need to tell my own.

The paper in my hand flaps brightly in the breeze. I climb down off the wall and make for the address.

The Carriagemaker's Union office takes up an entire block in one of the farthest flung corners of Valdrada. I go inside after watching an assortment of sturdily built men and women pass through the open doors. Inside, a dozen or more workers sit around a table, some playing cards, others chatting over a beer. I ask a young man on his way out the door where I can find Jer's office. He points vaguely toward the back where a door with block lettering reads *Union Master*. It's open, but I knock. A gruff voice comes from inside.

"No wage increases since you last asked, Sanford."

Jer sits behind a heavy desk covered in papers. In fact, the desk itself seems to be made entirely out of paper—if there's any wood involved, it's not structurally significant.

"My mistake." He waves me in. "Have a seat. Bailly told me you were coming."

"He did. Good?" Bailly seems more sure of what I'll do than I am. If it wasn't for the possibility of him giving back my memories, this would probably worry me.

"Your assistance is required," says a squawk of a voice from the corner.

I snap my neck to see a white bird perched in an artificial tree.

"Don't mind me," the bird says. Though its feathers are white, its eyes have the distinct keenness of a crow. "I'm just a fly on the wall."

"Really, don't mind him," Jer says.

"Thanks for seeing me," I say, still distracted by the talking crow.

"Of course, Bailly said only good things."

"And if we're honest, Jer is entirely unequipped to handle the current crisis his union is undergoing," says the crow.

"Shut it, bird." He turns back to me. "We could use a little help though."

"That's why I'm here," I try.

But the bird interrupts again: "You know, the last help we had didn't go over so well, come to think of it." Jer stands ponderously, hiding a grimace. "You want to fill Matthew in on where you got the money to pay for that 'consultant' who ran off last month?"

"On second thought don't bother sitting," Jer says. "We'll talk at the factory."

"I'll give you a hint," the bird continues.

"He don't need a hint," Jer snaps.

I shake my head as Jer guides me forcibly toward the door.

"I guess we'll find out, won't we!" the crow says as the door slams shut behind us.

"Idiot animal." Jer pats me on the back. A pat from one of his strong arms is enough to send me stumbling back into the main hall. We take the back door, walking down a bustling alley. Jer wears a bowler hat that probably used to be a distinguishable color. He tips it to everyone we pass.

"Don't know how much you know about unioning," he says. "Only thing to it is that my people make carriages for the factories owned by Hendricks Carriagemakers. No finer carriages, I'll warrant, and the credit goes to my people. They're the wheels on the carriage, so to speak." He laughs grandly, with a timing that suggests this isn't the first time he's whipped out this gem of a metaphor. "You know the drill. Corporate's looking for any opportunity to stiff us, so our job's to protect the working fellows and felloweses. It's mostly a losing battle. But if we can manage to lose it slowly enough, then our union members can have good lives along the way. It's a decent living, you know. Good, honest work. Maybe too honest."

We continue on to the factory gates. The inside could not be more different from the manufacturing hub in the steel city. Machines whir overhead, but they're made primarily out of large pumping gears. Below on the assembly line, the workers hammer and saw away, some inches away from the teeth of the machines. Everything looks to be designed around the workers doing as much work as possible, as the machines only handle the heaviest lifting, bringing a steady stream of parts up from below.

"Ain't she a beaut," Jer says.

"How many carriages do they make a day?"

"Quota's twenty-one at the moment." We walk along the factory floor, having to dodge the occasional wood splinters flying off a saw blade. Jer puffs out his chest. "We're in charge of supplying the entire area with carriages. But Hendricks keeps upping the quota, and they refuse to hire more workers. So do they do the logical thing and increase pay? Give the current workers more hours? No sir."

"Sounds like the union needs to do something."

"They sure do, but here's the thing. I pressed too hard last time. The Hendricks got wise and shut down the factory for a week. A reverse strike. The workers are hungry for change, but they're scared. They don't want to piss anybody off upstairs, the need to put bread on the table and all still withstanding."

"I've seen a lot of things since I've gotten here, and granted I've only been here a short time," I start, "but it seems to me, there's a whole range of possibilities that aren't being explored, outside of more labor and more hours."

"Such as?"

"Well, and this may be a touchy subject, everyone appears to be acting very normal and working in a very conventional way. That is, everything is being done very manually, and with strict adherence to the laws of physics."

"Are you suggesting we embrace automation like those godless swine in the steel city?"

"No, no, not at all. I'm suggesting something simpler, but less conventional."

Jer finally catches my drift. He talks tough, but he makes me realize that one downside of having a head you could smash through the company's bargaining table is that it takes a lot to get information through from the outside.

"You're talking about using some of our more imaginative outlets?" Jer asks.

"Exactly."

Jer shakes his head. "No go. We've got strict bylaws in the union charter about using creative influence inside the factory. It dilutes the craftsmanship. And every word in the charter is enforced to the letter, with extreme force."

Bylaws, charters, it sounds in keeping with my vague understanding of my past self, including the glimpse Bailly showed me. I have to follow my instincts, the way I've seen June do, the way I did myself when we escaped the steel city. If I'm going to follow this path, doing so halfheartedly is not an option.

"Change the charter then. It's the only way you'll keep up with these quotas. Besides, think of how much extra free time your workers would have. Look at them."

I've positioned us over a convenient railing with a view of seven laborers hammering wooden pegs to make up a carriage's frame. Sweat drips off their foreheads.

"Creative influence *will* work here," I say. I remember how June described the ability to influence things being tied to a specific place. We were able to fly in the mountains because it was the place for it. We were able to reorganize the steel city because it was a place where form and function were inextricably linked, so changing the function would change the form. "I've walked that floor with you, I can feel the potential down there. It's still craftmanship, just faster and more imaginative. What do they work, ten, twelve hours a day? They should be spending that extra time with their families, or starting their own businesses on the side. Maybe one could start a carriage factory of their own."

"Not if the non-compete clause has anything to do with it."

"Something else, then. It doesn't matter. All I'm saying is, don't waste your people's potential."

We start back toward Jer's office. He's so lost in thought he barely acknowledges the workers who stop to wave to him.

"You're talking about amending the charter, that's no small thing."

"I know it's not. But the benefits will be well worth the effort. Bailly sent me here because he knew I could help. This is what I'm offering."

"Thanks for stopping by, kid," Jer says once we reach the main union hall. "You have my word I'll think it over."

He'll do more than that. The workers are actually in much worse shape than Jer let on. Bailly told me that they'd missed their quota seventeen out of the last eighteen days, and that there'd been two pay cuts in two months.

My ears buzz as I leave the union hall and factory, both from the noise of hammering and sawing, and from excitement. Having Bailly's recommendation is an automatic ticket to negotiating with the most important people. I'm beginning to understand why June enjoys her high-level talks with the Apocalyptians. For the first time I can recall, something real, something that matters, is riding on what I do.

So here I am, Bailly, creating a story about a kid advocating on behalf of oppressed laborers. Definitely a good start, one my suit-wearing former self would approve of.

While I wait for Jer's answer, I pull another thread. Bailly is who I should rationally follow, the powerful and benevolent guide who can show me my past. But Carl's offer of information on a way out is enough for me to look past his seedy reputation. The thought of escape still tugs at me. I'm now following two masters, each offering one part of the understanding I need.

That's how I end up on a stakeout in a single horse carriage just inside the city gate. My companion, Alyssa, is an unsmiling woman in her early thirties. She carries around a pair of improbably large binoculars. My wrist stings with an insistent buzz, as if the device there disapproves of my presence. Eventually it gives up, and returns to climbing upward past *8,000* at seemingly random intervals.

Carl had reacted almost with glee when I agreed to help him.

"How long you been working for Carl?" I ask, hoping to break the silence of the past twenty minutes.

"Long enough. How long you been asking nosy questions?"

I sigh. "Any sign of him?" Our mark is a man wearing a black suit, who is medium-sized and has an air of having too much money. Wearing something as normal as a suit is a sure way to stand out around here.

"Nothing yet."

We sit in silence for a while longer. I have to consciously avoid twiddling my thumbs. So far working for Carl hasn't been the exciting journey of discovery I expected. My eyes catch on movement at the gate. A carriage pulls through, and I spot a nondescript face through the window. Below it, a necktie.

Alyssa drops her binoculars and climbs up front. We inch forward slowly, falling into line a half block behind our target. Townspeople melt away in front of us, and we are soon pursuing the carriage down the main drag. I keep my eyes locked, and point out unnecessarily when the carriage turns. It heads down the quickest route to the street that houses most of Valdrada's restaurants and bars. The carriage pulls up, and Alyssa stops us as the man in the suit climbs out. He waves his driver on. He's wearing sunglasses, which don't seem particularly useful in the dusk.

"I have to park this thing," Alyssa says. "Don't lose him."

"Right." I hop out and follow the man's suit. I realize quickly that he's making for a landmark I recognize, the Night and Dragon. There's no one around the entrance, so I walk past as he steps inside, counting to ten before I backtrack and enter the noisy bar.

The crowd is thicker than the last time I was here. A twenty-five-piece band performs a jazz number. I have to push my way through bodies, and when I emerge into an open space at the top of the stairs leading down into the main bar area, I fear

I've lost the man. But my eyes catch a flash of black a second later, and I see him directly in front of the stage, being led by a waiter, who seats him in a booth with orange and gold drapes.

"Looking for a table?" Another waiter's voice startles me out of my sleuthing, or more accurately, my standing at the top of the stairs like an idiot.

"I'll just look for a place at the bar."

"Good luck finding a spot. When Jeremiah's Eardrum plays, all bets are off seat-wise."

"Thanks." I ignore the waiter's puzzled look and make toward the bar. I position myself near the end closest to the booth.

I order a tonic water with lime—on June's tab, of course—keeping my eyes on the closed curtain.

It's surprisingly difficult not to stand out by yourself in a crowded bar. Nearly everyone is obviously part of a group, some in large gatherings standing around one of the raised tables in the center of the bar, some in couples flirting on adjacent barstools. I sip my drink with a flourish that suggests it actually has alcohol in it, and direct my eyes and ears toward the band.

The band is indeed very good. I must have been in a jazz band, because the syncopated rhythms set my middle three fingers tapping out unconscious rhythms. Trumpet?

A bank of saxophones belts out the melody in perfect rhythm, and when the time comes for what would usually be solos, they take on the challenge two at a time, coordinating their on-the-spot creations in harmony, eyes closed, swaying. It's like watching a doubles tennis match with a perfectly coordinated pairing. Their timing is unplanned yet closely aligned, and every movement augments the other. With each note, a different colored wisp of smoke flies from the saxophonists' fingers, twirling up to join the pleasant haze above.

I reluctantly wrench myself away from the music. The drapes are still drawn on the suited man's booth. I return my eyes to the stage, having to remind myself not to get lost in the music again. My tonic water and lime tastes regrettably like tonic water, yet here even quinine is tolerable.

A hand touches my shoulder, which I take for a slightly too drunk person bumping into me on their way to the bathroom, but instead when I turn I meet four eyes on a single face, and they're unmistakably looking at me.

"'scuse me, you the kid wandering around the carriage factory the other day with Boss Jer?"

His teeth are the pointiest I've ever seen, and his thin lips make his mouth look like just a hole in his face. But as I stare at him and get used to his presence, his features resolve into a more or less human face.

"Yes I was," I say, too taken off guard to even consider lying. Maybe this man is from Hendricks Carriages, and is about to kick my ass across the bar.

"You've created a big ol' stir, that's for sure." I realize that what I took for a grimace was in fact a smile, slightly bleary and drunken, but a smile nonetheless. He shakes my left hand since it's the one not holding my fake adult beverage. "I'm Mini. There's talk of your offer around the hall. Nobody can get the idea of creative influence out of their head."

"Really? That's good to hear. Let's hope the talk trickles up Jer's way."

"Jer's a good boss and a better man. But new ideas aren't really his slice o' pie. It'll take something a lot more dramatic than conversing about the relative merits to get him on board with changin' up the charter."

"You make it sound like I don't stand a chance."

"I ain't about to root against ya, kid. Not if there's a shorter workday and no more pay cuts on the other side of it. I'm just sayin' it's gotta come from the people." He thumbs a nearly empty mug of beer. My eyes dart to the booth, but there's still no sign of movement.

"I appreciate your support, Mini. Don't you worry, I'll get the job done."

"'ppreciate it. I'll leave you to whatever it is you're doing. But if you want to stop by any time and say hi, the drinks are on us." He points at a dozen men and women standing around a table.

"'ppreciate it," I respond, realizing too late that I sound like a parrot.

Mini laughs and lumbers off toward the bar.

Alyssa pulls up beside me moments later.

"He moved at all?" she asks.

"He's still in the booth."

"Is he still in the booth, or has he not left the booth?"

I don't give Alyssa the satisfaction of asking a confused clarifying question, and instead follow her toward the back of the bar, between the stage—where the band has stopped playing and are now throwing instruments at each other in what appears to be a fight over creative differences—and the booth. We can't quite see inside, but I catch sight of D'Angeline waiting a table nearby. She gives me a kind smile before setting her tray down and coming over.

"Need something, dear?" D'Angeline's voice is like being set down in bathwater. When her eyes fall on Alyssa they fill with disapproval, but by the time they turn back to me, they're all warmth again.

"This may seem like an odd request," I say, "but could you please check if there's a guy in a business suit in that booth?"

"I really shouldn't. My customers expect a level of discretion." She looks at the drawn curtain, as if seeing through it. "But I think in this case it may not be an issue."

"Thank you."

"Of course, dear. I will expect, in return, that you come back and have lunch with me one of these days. And no spy stuff!"

"Sounds lovely."

D'Angeline flutters over, not even pausing before pulling the curtain back to reveal the interior. She waves us over. The booth has room for four people, but it's empty now. A couple full mugs of beer sit on the table.

Alyssa shoots me a look, as if I should've anticipated this.

"Lunch, remember?" D'Angeline laughs and leaves us to it.

I can see an opening once I step inside the booth, tucked behind the seat on the right side. A narrow staircase spirals downward. We start down it. The stair rotates at an impossible rate, and I find myself having to keep my hand along the smooth wall in order to keep my footing. With a lurch of vertigo I recognize that the stairs are becoming smaller and smaller, until soon only my heel fits on each step. Eventually I abandon my single step understanding of staircase travel, and let my footfalls cover three or four steps at once. The numbers on my wrist count down instead of up as we descend.

Then we are surrounded by trees. They are broad-leafed, tropical, and tiny orbs of light fill hollows in many of their trunks. The orbs cast flickering shadows through the twilight. We're no longer on a path, but the plant growth is thin enough that we can move without too much difficulty. The trees gives a strongly sylvan impression, as if at any moment a party of elves is going to do a forest dance and sing *tra-la-la-lally* at us.

"It's the Grove," Alyssa says.

We pick our way through soft ferns. Some end in tiny luminescent spheres and curl toward us as we walk by, bathing our entire presence in silver light. Not exactly the stealthiest way to travel.

But the Grove feels like a place where it's impossible to worry about things.

I put my arm out to stop my companion as a scrap of rigid black catches my eye. We approach more slowly, keeping to the thickest vegetation. Where we emerge is not a clearing, although it feels central in the way a clearing usually does. Our target stands motionless in front of one of the trees. The only difference between this tree and the ones around it is that veins of chalky blue run down it, creating a shifting, rippling pattern.

The man in the suit has his eyes closed, and sways as if pushed by an unseen breeze. Sweat has collected on his clean-shaven upper lip and strong brow.

"I meant no disrespect, of course," he says through gritted teeth. "Partnership is how humans think of it, but I know true partnership is impossible given your ... status."

A groan emanates from the tree, and the man laughs uneasily.

"I confess, I'm still not accustomed to your particular style of humor. But thank you. Your consideration is all I can ask for. The Armageddeons are grateful."

He bows and turns quickly. We take a rushed step back, but fortunately his exit takes him in another direction. We wait until he's gone before making our own exit.

"The good news is that our mission has succeeded. We've learned everything we need to," Alyssa says.

"Bad news?"

"I'll let Carl explain the bad news. He's good at that."

After the encounter with the tree, the wood doesn't feel quite as inviting. The trees still glow, and though calm remains, I get the sense it's a narcotic, coercive calm. Alyssa stops us at a tree a short distance from the stairway.

"That doesn't look good," I say. The entire base of the tree, from its roots to four feet up its trunk, is riddled with holes. I pull back as something moves through one of them. My stomach twists. A massive worm is methodically carving its way through the soft flesh inside. The assault has done so much damage I wonder how long it will be before the tree keels over entirely.

"This is different," Alyssa says. "Perhaps the Grove's cooperation with evil forces has corrupted it. Come on, it isn't safe."

When we've made our way back out of the Grove and up the staircase, D'Angeline is waiting for us in the booth, looking at the opening in vexation.

"I thought I'd fixed that," she says.

"What is it with the Armageddeons and wanting to cause the end of the world?" Carl says. He's joined us in our carriage. He prefers to conduct his business exclusively in moving carriages—Hendricks if possible—which never seem to be going to any destination in particular.

"It seems on-brand, at the very least," I say.

"This is more than a little disturbing," Carl continues. "You said the tree seemed amenable to some kind of offer?"

Alyssa nods.

"The spirits of the Grove are temperamental, but I wouldn't expect them to be this reckless. We don't have to speculate much to know what the Armageddeons could want out of the arrangement, but why the spirits would even agree to meet with them is a question I can't fathom."

"Could it be a changing of the seasons?" Alyssa says. "I'd think we're due for one. The Carnival has gotten a little ... crowded."

I look out the window. We've just passed a lane where a dozen elves turn cranks on their empty boxes. I've noticed more and more of them throughout the city. I'm almost accustomed to their disconcerting presence. Almost.

"These spirits of the Grove, what would they want from the Armageddeons?" I ask.

Carl's mouth gives an approving twitch. Something about the gesture—perhaps the control, combined with the slightly paternal gaze—reminds me of Bailly. But Carl puts me much more at ease.

"Spirits don't understand the world in terms of transactional exchange. Much of the Carnival is a nominally capitalist society, but the more powerful forces, the older presences that under-gird this existence, they don't look at the world through that lens. They destroy and remake in their own time. It may be that this is simply the time, and the Armageddeons are merely a convenient tool." He pauses to change the subject. "What I've just told you may be the most important truth about this place, but I know I promised you something else."

Alyssa rolls her eyes. "He should be content to be paid just like the rest of us."

"That's not for you to say," Carl snaps. He takes a breath, calming himself. "Here's what you need to know about the Carnival: The Carnival is a mirror. Everything here is a reflec-tion of something else. That's the fundamental truth of this existence—nothing that happens here is a fact in itself, it exists only in relationship to an *other*. Sounds hopeless, right?"

I catch a movement on Carl's face, but it's more than a simple twitch of emotion. His entire body is rippling along with the carriage seat he's in. He seems not to notice, and things slowly pull themselves back into place.

"Keep in mind that every mirror, no matter how deep the reflection, has a surface, a point where it physically touches the world it's reflecting. The Carnival is no different."

I can tell Carl has revealed about as much as he's going to. It's not nearly as much as I wanted, but I understand. Information is a commodity, and Carl won't give it all away at once.

"I don't have another job for you yet, but when I do, I promise I'll tell you where the surface of the mirror can be found." Carl turns to the window and opens it to speak to the driver. "Drop me off here, please."

We pull up, and Carl disembarks without saying goodbye, blending instantly into the crowd.

I wrack my brain, but I can't think of a single time I've seen my reflection since I've been here. No bathroom mirrors, no polished metal surfaces. Even during daylight, light passes through windows unreflected. When I notice this, there's something colder about Valdrada. It's as if every missing reflection is an attempt to erase my existence, to convince me that my presence doesn't project into the world.

But that's ridiculous. I've been talking to people since I got here. I've negotiated with a union boss and gone on dubious stakeouts with potential criminals. I most certainly exist.

But maybe that's not the point. Maybe the mirrors themselves are the point.

I can't help thinking what this means for my own existence. Is there a real me somewhere else? If I find him, will I just disappear?

The Carnival is a mirror. Everything here is a reflection of something else.

When I think about it, though, I do feel like some sort of shadow. I know so little beyond my own name and partial memories—both the brief flashes that seem to come unprompted, and the fuller scene Bailly gave me.

I'm so caught up in my thoughts that, "There are no mirrors here" is the first thing I say to June when I see her the next morning.

"Then how the heck do I look so flawless?" she responds through the tail end of what I can only assume is her third cigarette of the day.

"I assume it's because you're the most naturally perfect human in existence," I say.

"Oh yeah, you're right."

She's taken the news of the Armageddeons' deal with the spirits of the Grove surprisingly well. I assumed she would be off trying to salvage the situation, but while she's given me endless grief about working for Carl, she decides to tag along while I interview members of the Carriagemaker's Union. With no small amount of prodding from Mini, I have a full slate of appointments this morning. Jer allows me to work from a small records room off his own office. I go in with planned strategies to get them talking—I have a whole speech lined up about how powerful creative influence can be, but it turns out the carriagemakers are only too willing to share their experiences, and it's not long before they fall into a familiar pattern.

Low pay and ratcheting quotas is an obvious burden, but what stands out are the terms the workers put the struggle in. They're surrounded by a world where the implausible is happening constantly. Limits feel arbitrary in this environment, and they resent the union for the limits it imposes almost as much as Hendricks Carriages. Hendricks is supposed to be the bad guy. They'll cut hours, raise quotas, clamp down on wages. They do these things because it's how they're expected to behave, and the workers don't question it. But when they speak about the union, about how it limits their ability to meet those demands through their strictures on creative influence, the workers' eyes turn to fire. The union is the reason they see their families less and less, the reason their wages are lower than last year, despite them doing more work than ever. At one point I have to close my office door to prevent Jer from hearing the string of expletives coming from a particularly riled foreman.

June sits in the corner through all of this, only making snide comments after my interviewees have left the room. I can see why she's such an effective negotiator. She always feels in control, and matches her demeanor perfectly to the pitch of the room.

I don't know whether the fact that she doesn't bother when it's just me around should offend me or not.

By the end of the day I have a catalogue of notes, as well as sixteen signatures on my petition to expand the acceptable use of creative influence.

Mini stops by the cramped room a couple minutes after the last worker leaves.

"Told you they'd talk," he says. He looks down at the scrawled signatures approvingly.

"There's definitely demand," I say. "But only a three-fourths majority of signatures from union members is enough to amend the charter. There are, what, eight hundred total members? We have sixteen signatures."

Mini laughs. "Eight hundred and twenty-six, in fact. I wouldn't worry. I set you up with all of the most vocal and active members. By the time anyone else sees this piece of paper, they'll have gotten an earful."

"Three quarters should be easy then."

"Ain't nothing easy in a Hendricks union, kid. But whatever you gotta do to make it happen, I'll be right alongside you. It's high time the minds of the people were allowed to run free."

I envision a wild scene as hundreds of workers exercise their most creative impulses on such a mechanical process. Carriage parts fly in every direction. They shrink down and come together to form what appears to be a model carriage in mid-air, only to expand again into a fully finished product. No doubt what actually happens will be far more chaotic. But also much, much quicker than what they're currently doing.

Inviting union members into the office is one thing, but for the next several days we pursue a more aggressive strategy. We show up at their doors on their days off and during the evenings, presenting our proposition in full to every single one of them. We do our best to make sure their families are present. Having the beneficiaries of less time spent in the factory in the room drives our point home in a way I couldn't on my own. I present the pitch, while Mini puts the practical tilt on it. June takes on more of an advisory role. I suppose she's mainly curious to see whether or not I'll mess it all up. I don't, though. As I get into the rhythm of knocking on doors and making my case, I feel buoyed on the winds of momentum. This is *me*, and I'm in my element. The promise of another memory from Bailly almost feels irrelevant.

Nearly everyone we speak to either agrees to think about our proposal, or signs on the spot.

We close out our third day talking to Lorna, who leads a coalition made up mainly of younger workers.

"You know my people have been pushing this for years," Lorna says. We're sitting in a four-walled courtyard. She and fifteen others share the building that encloses it. Low shrubs have been trimmed to allow seating room, but the entire space feels as if at any second the plants might decide to reclaim it.

"It sounds like now is the time, then," I say.

"Maybe." Lorna leans back in her chair, which looks dangerously close to tipping over on its flimsy legs. "You know, most of my generation doesn't identify with the union the same way the older folks do. As long as it benefits us, I don't give one-sixteenth of a damn about preserving traditions."

"It needs to adapt," I say. "That's a theme I've been hearing with almost everyone I talk to. Preserving the union and its strength means changing, and maybe even abandoning, some of the old ways of thinking."

"Precisely." Lorna tends to point a single finger as she makes each point. "I'll tell you one thing: people like Durro, and even Jer, they don't really care about the union when it comes down to it. All they care about is doing things the same way so they don't feel like the dinosaurs they are. You talked to Durro yet?"

I glance at Mini. The names are starting to flow together.

"Not yet," Mini says. "We'll be getting to him later tonight."

Lorna rocks forward. The front legs of her chair crash back into place, sending a spray of gravel upward.

"Tell that bastard that he and his buddies need to stop standing in the way of progress."

"I'm sure he'll see reason," I say.

"Reason?" Lorna is getting more agitated by the second. "Reason abandoned that incompetent fogey seventy-four years ago, back when he should've retired."

June is clearly doing her best to suppress a laugh, but I'm more focused on the challenge this represents. The enmity between these two groups clearly runs deep. It's hard to imagine them agreeing on anything.

"If not reason then at least their own self-interest," I say, keeping a smile up. "They'll see that it benefits them. Even if we have to twist some arms to make them see it."

"Please do," Lorna says.

"I take it we can count on you to back our proposal, then? Your support, especially with the engagement of your constituency, would be incredibly helpful."

"We'll sign. It's high time we moved into this century."

After we've shaken hands and are shuffling out, I turn to June and ask, "Which century is it, exactly?"

"Eighteenth or twenty-seventh, depending on who you talk to," June says.

"Yeah, sounds about right."

Lorna's support speeds up our next set of conversations. Almost anyone who joined the union in the last five years follows her lead, and some even sign before we give them our pitch. I approach one door—a garden apartment beneath a twelve-story tiered tower—only to have it fly open in my face. A young man with a striking set of ornamental neck pincers grabs the paper out of my hand, signs, and slams the door before I can say another word.

The momentum carries us into the evening, but as the hours pass, our meeting with Durro looms closer. With a chime my wrist device begins counting down from *568* rather than ascending. *567.* Each number a step from Durro, I guess. Mini does his best to prepare me. Though the group Durro leads is older, they represent the largest single voting block in the union. *421, 420.* Without them, we'd have to convince virtually every other single member to sign. Though we've made good progress today, the odds of that are slim, not least of all because some union members do not possess either the hands or the frontal cortices necessary to sign or even understand the amendments.

15, 14, 13.

"He's next," Mini says, pulling us up in front of Durro's door. *2, 1, 0.*

"What are the odds that he hears Lorna is supporting this, and murders me outright?" I say.

"Not zero," Mini says. "But keep to the pitch. It's worked so far."

I pat Mini on the back. I should feel nervous, but all I can identify in myself is pure resolve. I knock on the door.

Durro's orange skin is the texture of an old baseball mitt that no one has bothered to oil. He leads us into a dusty living room. On one wall hangs a set of porcelain plates, each with the picture of a different orange child. He offers us bourbon, which Mini and June accept.

When I turn it down he says, "What's the matter, you don't drink, kid?"

"I've got ten more people to see tonight, gotta keep a clear head," I reply.

"Nothing clears your head like a glass of whiskey," Durro says, taking a swig that would be generous even if he were drinking beer. "I appreciate you taking the time to come out here. Charter amendments are serious business."

"My goal is for as close to unanimity as possible," I say. Mini nervously sips his drink, more quickly than is perhaps wise.

"That should always the goal. Unrealistic as it may be." Durro smiles at me.

I dive into my pitch, which I'm all but certain Durro has heard before. He's exceedingly polite throughout. He doesn't interrupt me at any point, and nods along in understanding. When I finish, he leans back in his chair. I'm leaning forward with one elbow on each knee, and immediately feel thrown off balance.

He finishes his drink, sets his tumbler down on the table, and pours himself half of another.

"You've got a couple problems here, as far as me and my people are concerned," he begins. "First, you're essentially telling the old-timers that their hard work is for nothing. We made those carriages with our hands. Now, we're going to let them be made with this influence? No craftsman with pride would allow that to happen. Second, I see that upstart Lorna has already signed. I'd bet the nickel I don't have that she sees this as an opportunity to screw my people over."

"I understand there's some distrust between you," I say, but get cut off.

"Distrust? That's quite the turn of phrase. No, distrust is reserved for fellow humans. Lorna and the rest do not even come close to meriting that classification."

I scratch my cheek, but that's as much nervousness as I'm willing to show.

"We presented Lorna with the benefits as they related to her own interests, and the interests of her people," I say. "I know this type of change is difficult, but I wouldn't be here if I didn't believe it was in the best interests of all, not just one faction."

"They're not distributed evenly, though. Lorna knows that."

"That's why we're prepared to offer you some protections."

Mini gives me a *we are?* look, while June sips her drink, betraying nothing. Durro crosses his arms.

"You've been asking for tenure rules in the charter," I say. "How about we piggyback that amendment on this one?"

Mini watches in horror as I offer way more than I'm authorized to, including guaranteed hours and pay increases based on tenure, calculated in terms of the total number of units produced, since time is often difficult for people to agree on. I watch as Durro's eyes light up.

As we leave Durro's house, we step over a swarm of microgriffs. June taunts one until it shoots a fireball at her, which she dodges with practiced grace.

"That was a wonderfully effective trainwreck," June says.

I don't think Mini's yet decided whether or not he's mad at me.

"You know there's no way Lorna is going to let you keep her signature if she hears about this," June continues.

"Have some faith," I say.

"Yeah, I definitely don't," she says. "But I'm beyond happy I came along to watch this."

When we return to Lorna's house, thirty or forty people fill the courtyard. Smoke of all kinds rises from a variety of cigarettes and pipes, filling the air with odors ranging from oppressively pungent to light and pleasant like the smoke coming off a campfire. We ask around, but no one seems to know where Lorna is.

We stand awkwardly in a corner, near a short statue of a pudgy, grinning man holding a flowerpot. We're debating whether we should come back when we hear a "psssst" from behind us. Lorna is crouched in the bushes behind the statue.

"Hey guys, through here," she says. She moves the branches of an overgrown bush aside to let us through onto a porch that, were it not so overgrown, would overlook the courtyard.

"We were looking for you," I say, too taken aback by her strange entrance to say anything more intelligent.

"I thought you might be," she says. "Glad you stopped by. We're having a surprise party."

Something tells me it's a bad idea to ask if that's why she was hiding in the bushes.

Lorna leads us into a living room off the porch.

"So, did you meet with the ball of wrinkles?"

"We did," I say. "He's agreed to sign."

Lorna walks over to a writing desk. She opens the drawer and pulls out a long, thin purple object it takes me a second to realize is a cigarette. She twirls it between her fingers.

"Under what conditions?" she asks.

"Well, we had to offer him a sweetener, since he had concerns that creative influence would negatively impact the standing of the old-timers."

"And I doubt you suggested that they all retire and get out of everyone's way?"

"Real missed opportunity, Titus Andromattus," June says. I'll have to ask her later if she would've been at this party anyway—she and Lorna give the impression of having a friendly history.

"I did not," I reply. "I didn't think suggesting he was too old to take part in his beloved profession would be the most tactful approach."

"Fair," Lorna says. "So what's the sweetener?"

"I offered him something that in practice is effectively useless, more a gesture than anything else. I offered him a tenure clause."

Lorna's face goes cold. Her hands stop twirling the cigarette. "Tenure?"

"It's meaningless. With creative influence taking over the factory, production is going to go through the roof. Tenure is determined based on overall units contributed to. What will happen is that everyone in the factory will have tenure in a few weeks. It's a raise for everyone."

I raise an eyebrow as Lorna paces the room. The sound of laughter rings outside in the courtyard. I imagine how fun it would be to spend an evening getting to know new people, staying out until dawn washes over the balconies.

"I don't like the idea of even having it in the charter," Lorna says, "but we move forward." She extends a hand. Her firm handshake contains the entire weight of the deal. "I can't wait to see the look on Durro's face when my people receive their tenure and he realizes his obstructionism is for nothing."

That night June and I stroll around the main square, which is alive with the perpetual party that's raged since we first arrived. We stayed for a few minutes at Lorna's, but there were so many union people there I got tired of talking about charter amendments. Mini took the petition to the last several houses on his own. If he does well tonight, we could hit our three-fourths majority. A familiar anxiety plays over my entire night. I'm proud of the work I've put in, but having the outcome out of my hands is driving me insane. I feel a relentless need to push forward, to continue working, to see it through.

This feels like the kind of story I'm supposed to be wrapped up in.

At the outer edge of the square, a staircase leads up to the top of the city wall. We clamber up it, and look out over the mayhem below. The fireworks have not slowed despite the fact that they started a little after noon, and the food merchants still cook at top speed. We lean over the parapet, the distance between us and the chaos just far enough not to be overwhelming. June's sloping chin and the slight upturn of her nose reflect the flashing lights below. Dramatic shadows follow each explosion of light, making it look like her face is contorting in a staggering array of emotions. Yet during the brief interludes—when the unseen pyrotechnical folks restock their explosives, I assume—it's clear her expression never changed. She's a calm pool upon which the world projects.

"This Armageddeon shit is pissing me off," she says.

"Is it possible your first mistake was trying to prevent a war between two factions whose sole purpose is the annihilation of each other and the entire world?"

"As much as I very much approve of your sass, and believe me I do, I'm a little too annoyed for banter right now."

"Did you expect them to behave differently?"

"Well, not in theory. I've been working mostly with Pavel on the Apocalyptian side. The Apocalyptians just agreed to put a pause on hostilities for their midwinter festival. Usually the midwinter festival is a chance for them to pillage more than usual in order to honor their gods of destruction. A hold on carnage for this period could set the tone for the next year. But I can't in good conscience leave out the fact that the Armageddeons are apparently planning on invoking the spirits of the Grove."

"What exactly would happen if they did?" I ask.

"The Grove forms a natural basis for the Carnival. Every time you see a tree or flower, every animal, every unnaturally large chicken, the Grove had a hand in its existence."

"It's like a creative force or something?"

"I didn't say it had a hand in their creation, I said it had a hand in its existence."

Amid the festivities, a brawl has broken out between two sets of tall, bendy creatures. They're resolving their dispute by flinging various human projectiles at each other. All parties involved appear to be enjoying themselves immensely.

"The fear is," June continues, as if this is a completely normal sight, "if the Grove will decide to rebel entirely, to stop supporting the existence of the Carnival."

"Would it do that?"

"I can't pretend I understand spirits. But I don't think the answer is necessarily a firm no, and that scares me."

June who, on multiple occasions since I've met her, has thrown herself off impossibly steep cliffs and is completely unperturbed by the strangest presences, is scared by what the Grove might do. I trust that if June is scared, I should be too.

"Do you think peace is still possible?" I ask.

"It's always possible. Just looking less and less likely. We have to hope that the Grove will reject the Armageddeons' offer. The spirits have been known to change their minds before. In the meantime, I'm on damage control. I still don't know if it would be wise to confront the Armageddeons with this information. I don't want to spook them, and this is the exact kind of thing that could throw them into war."

We fall into silence. Below, Rob, Bob, Larry, and Steve have arrived on their chickens, and are weaving among the crowd. They look for all the world like they're charging the battle lines of an enemy, though short observation makes it clear that they have absolutely no goal in mind, and are running in random patterns. Townspeople dive out of the way or are sent flying by the feathery chicken breasts. Yet none of them direct any particular anger toward the chickenmen.

"Are you asking all this because you care about it, or because you're worried your work with the union might be for nothing?" June asks.

It's a harder question to answer than I would've thought. Wrapping myself up in the activity of the last few days has given me less time to think about the strangeness of this world.

"Oh, neither. I'm just concerned about my investments in oil futures."

"I'm sure your thirty-seven dollars will yield quite a fortune, if invested properly." She pauses. "That was some wild shit today,

Mattress. Durro and Lorna have been at each other's throats for years. Having them agree to the same amendment might be some kind of record."

Was that a compliment?

"Let me ask you, though," she continues, "which one did you lie to? Because you definitely lied to at least one of them. Like directly onto their face."

"The objections they had to creative influence and tenure weren't substantive. It wasn't about the benefits or disadvantages. It was about their own pride and making sure their rival didn't get what they wanted. I probably lied to both of them—in reality I would guess creative influence will make acquiring tenure no slower or faster, but I can tell you that its overall benefits will outweigh all of that."

"I guess it should be obvious by now that I was just teeing up an opportunity to call you a prag-Matt-ist," June says.

"Seek help, please," I say with a laugh.

"I can't be helped, baby." We watch the crowd for a couple more minutes before June points. "There's your guy."

Mini emerges from between the booths at the edge of the square. He's holding a fat envelope. He stops at the base of the wall, looking up to where we lean over the edge.

"I have something for you," Mini says.

The envelope flutters upwards, as if caught on an updraft, and deposits itself in my outstretched hands. I open it carefully. The petition inside is worn with the oil of many hands, and in the signature portion, which is much larger than I remember it being, I see hundreds of signatures. If a quick count is right...

"There were a few holdouts," Mini shouts, "but we got over eighty percent of the union to sign. Creative influence in the Hendricks factory starts tomorrow."

I've succeeded. I wonder if Bailly knew this role I'm filling, this story I'm telling, would appeal so naturally to me. The act of using my voice to create consensus is intoxicating. Even if there was a bit of somewhat backhanded wheeling and dealing required to make it happen.

But as great as I feel about the victory itself, the real prize is the memory Bailly promised me.

The device on my wrist stops counting up as I make my way toward Bailly's house, and the numbers start descending. I feel far more nervous than I did when negotiating with the powerful leaders of the union. I'm about to see another glimpse of my past.

Bailly is waiting for me in the breezeway between his inner and outer door. He sits at a picnic table, deftly shelling peas by hand. As I sit across from him, I can tell he already knows about my success with the union.

"I'd offer you something, but uncooked peas don't make the most tantalizing snack," Bailly says. They're an almost fluorescent green. They were obviously picked just minutes ago.

"I'm not here for food," I say.

Bailly smiles. "A man in search of a memory. You've more than earned it."

A peapod *snaps* between his fingers.

"I do have to ask, though," he says, "are you sure you want it?"

Another *snap*.

"What do you mean?" I ask. Of course I want it. That was the whole point of me helping with the union. I told this story so I could learn my own.

"You took so naturally to your role. It's like it was made for you. You will have plenty more opportunities to explore similar roles, if you wish. The Carnival is limitless in that way. But be warned, the further you go down the road of exploring your past, the more resistant the Carnival will become to supplying you opportunities. It will soon become more shaped by your past than it is shaped by you, by the reality of what you need."

"So knowing too much about my past could ruin the Carnival?"

"Or at the very least undermine your ability to make the most of it." Bailly dumps a pile of shells into a compost bucket sitting at the end of the table. "I will supply the memory if you want it, but I couldn't pass it along without this warning."

I nod, trying to mirror his grave expression. His warning makes me pause, but whatever I've been able to make out of my time here so far, the yawning chasm that is my past still pulls me toward it. I need to know, if not to escape, then at the very least to understand why staying is the right choice.

"I want the memory."

Bailly doesn't admonish me further. He just puts down the last pea pod, and extends his hands, palm up.

Then I am in a memory, and I am in pain.

My hip feels like it's filled with pins, and the way I'm sitting—both legs up, pillows propping me in place, in what can only be described as a hospital bed—makes it obvious that I'm recovering from an intense injury. A half-empty bottle of painkillers is on the table beside me.

I'm alone in a room painted neutral, inoffensive colors, reeking of antiseptic and commercial-grade cleaners. I try to shift to take some of the pressure off my back, but the small motion sends a blast of fire into my hip. I grit my teeth.

Next to the painkillers, I find my VR headset and a controller. As I lower the set over my head, darkness enfolds me. Then it is quickly displaced by light as I turn the headset on. It boots right up to the pause screen of the game I had been playing.

When I restart the game, the pain fades into the background. I am in the eyes of a warrior in a fantasy realm. My job is hunting monsters, and I am paid handsomely to do it. I rub shoulders with royalty, and am enemy number one for the disciples who worship the monsters as gods. I have been at this particular iteration of the game a while, and my level 41 character is a match for most enemies that are thrown my way.

But the progression through levels isn't why I play. The reason I play is that every quest is an opportunity to do something good for someone, or have an unexpected event take me in a completely different direction. I slay a monster threatening a mountain village, only to find out it was the only thing keeping an even worse beast from plundering the village. I help an old woman reclaim a lost heirloom, and she turns around and uses it as collateral in a pyramid scheme.

All of the stories, when I'm immersed in this headset, feel completely real to me. The graphics may stutter at points, or I may feel the occasional twinge from my hip, but these feel minor when this reality is so much more engaging than the stale sight of my hospital room.

In here, I have become powerful.

In here, a health potion is all that's needed to heal a grievous wound.

In here, life is structured and important, not arbitrary and painful.

I leave the memory just as I reach the end of the quest, and my character levels up to level 42.

I must have put my head down between my hands when the memory started, because I have to look up to meet Bailly's eyes.

"That's it?" I ask. "My whole memory is just me playing a video game?"

Bailly laughs. "That's it. The shorter the memory, the more powerfully its implications extend into your past. I have a sense this one matters."

My first feeling is anger that this is all he showed me. What implications extend into my past?

I can't piece together the actual events leading up to the memory itself, but I do feel their presence. And what I feel within them is pain. Not the same pain of an acute injury, but the more nebulous one. Not the need for a painkiller, but the impulse to put on the headset and be transported somewhere entirely different from my present reality. To escape.

Wrapped around this particular moment in the hospital, almost choking it, there is a large swath of time where I obviously wanted to be somewhere else. To be someone else.

Shit.

Bailly is still looking at me, and I can't handle the understanding and compassion in that look. I get up to leave.

"Thank you, Bailly," I say. I'm not able to meet his eyes again.

Mini insists that I come to his home to celebrate. Other than Bailly's cozy residence, this is the first home I've been to in Valdrada. He ushers me inside, off a side street near the end of town closest to the river. His house is a single story tall, but the interior's subterranean feel gives the impression that it goes down several levels. Tapestries line the walls, many of them depicting people working on carriages or more primitive carts. In one, a man who looks almost exactly like Mini fashions a wheel out of stone.

"My family have been craftspeople for generations," Mini says when he notices me eyeing the tapestries. "Weavers too."

I have to duck to clear the low ceilings. The scent of spices permeates everything, and though a dish involving cumin and possibly cinnamon is cooking, the smell is omnipresent, baked into the fabric of the house like the seasoning on a well-used pan.

We squeeze into chairs in the kitchen. The table is designed for four place settings at the most, though there are eight chairs around it. Mini's wife, Tilla, offers us tea or spiced milk.

"This is a dry household," she says with a pointed look at Mini. He grins at me.

I accept a spiced milk and we sit and chat while Tilla finishes making dinner. Mini drains his with a bitter determination that marks his drink as an inferior substitute for something stronger.

"Going on twenty-six years now," Mini says when I ask how long he's worked at Hendricks. "When I first got out of school I thought I might go off to the steel city, maybe work on the maglev train or some of their flying machines."

"I like those metal balloons," I offer, "though honestly I have no idea how they keep those things in the air. You know, physics-wise."

"And physics was never Min's strong suit," Tilla says.

"She's right there," Mini says. "But you don't need to know physics to work in the steel city. An assembly line is the same anywhere. You make your piece, the next guy in line makes his piece, and you keep on going until there's exactly one unit of whizbang at the end of it."

"But you ended up here."

"I tell you, no matter what when you're young, leaving home seems a grand old adventure. You get to go make your way in the world, leave your little town behind." He fixes me in his gaze. "But I tell you what, when it comes down to it, nothing beats the flavor of home."

Tilla gives me a smile that suggests there's more to it than that, but doesn't say anything.

"I think I, out of anyone, can relate," I say.

The light in the simple wrought-iron chandelier above the table begins to flicker, casting the space into intermittent bursts of shadow and light.

"Damn thing," Mini says, getting up to adjust it. As he stretches, his belly protrudes over the table.

It doesn't feel like he's going to respond to my last statement. Tilla begins to ladle the soup out into bowls. I get up and, despite her protests, begin ferrying the bowls to the table. The soup has four different kinds of root vegetables, and is a searing orange.

"Call the kids up, Min," Tilla says.

Mini walks over to the wall, and opens what at first I had taken to be a cupboard. Inside is a long tube snaking down into the cellar.

"You know, when he says 'flavor of home,' he really means my cooking," Tilla says. "He couldn't possibly have left me behind."

"He'd miss you too much?"

"That, and he's incapable of doing anything I tell him not to do."

"Best kind of husband to have," I reply.

"Kids, time to eat!" Mini bellows into the tube. A chorus of indistinct higher-pitched voices calls back, and soon the ground shakes. Mini motions for me to follow, and we slip around the corner into a narrow hallway. Past the opening segment of carpeted floor are six circular holes, all in a row. Almost simultaneously, six children, all resembling their parents, scurry up from spiral staircases.

"Say hi to Matthew," Mini says.

There's a long train of greetings from each of the children, but none so much as pause as they rush around me and Mini—impressive given that Mini takes up well more than half the doorway—and into the kitchen.

"I guess they're hungry," Mini says. With eight chairs for nine of us, one of the younger children sits on one of the older children's lap. They settle into this arrangement without a word from their parents, as if it's a common occurrence to be so casually displaced by guests.

The soup is delicious. The root vegetables are tender with a smoky aftertaste, and I slurp the tangy, sweet broth down by itself once the vegetables are gone.

The children chatter about their days and sibling squabbles. Nothing in the conversation is particularly dramatic, and I have the rueful thought that it's the first at least semi-normal meal I've had in a long time. I could almost be sitting at the table with one of my friends from a big family, going through the mundane details I never appreciated until now. More than once I notice that when Mini speaks, every single one of his children turns toward him with an expectant face. They give the impression that it's special to have him around. How much more pleasant would the lives of these children be if their father didn't have to spend all his time at the factory to support them?

Not even the fact that every few minutes a rumbling beneath our feet shakes the entire room can keep me from appreciating this improvised normalcy.

After the meal I help Mini round up the children who, as soon as the corn flour cakes we have for dessert are gone, begin running around the entire ground floor. We chase each of them down, scoop them up, and deposit them in their assigned staircase. When we do, the staircase becomes a slide, and the child shoots down into their room, cackling in delight.

We find the last child hiding under a set of sawhorses in Mini's small workshop, repeating "you can't see me if I can see you." When we finally manage to catch him—a task involving an orchestrated flanking maneuver—we discover that he's stolen a frying pan, which he brandishes as a weapon despite the fact that it's larger than half his body. Extricating the pan from his grasp proving too dangerous a task, we launch the child, pan and all, down the shoot to his room below.

We return to the workshop, breathing heavily and chuckling. It's a tight fit with two of us—the sawhorses block the entrance and one wall is composed of a large workbench covered in a messy pile of tools. Mini pulls away a thick cloth covering the opposite table.

"Really more a hobby than anything else," he says. I study the geometrical wooden shapes—triangles, squares, trapezoids, all stuck together to form fist-sized objects. "Here."

He hands me a flat piece. The frame is t-shaped, but around it runs a rectangular piece of flat wood. I realize the flat part is actually embedded in the frame itself, so tightly joined that it doesn't even rattle when I move it. Seeing my confusion, Mini smiles his thin-lipped smile, and takes it back from me. He puts it behind his back and wiggles his elbows dramatically. When he brings his hands back around, the object is in two pieces, one in each hand. A puzzle.

"I like making things," he says, "I like the way things are put together. But I think it's only really fun if you can take them apart too."

There's a loud clacking as he smacks the two pieces back together. Before I can see how, they're back to being a single object.

He puts the puzzle back on the table and carefully covers it with the cloth. He puts a strong arm around my shoulder.

"You're doing a good thing here, kid. You're making things better for my family and hundreds of families like ours."

"I'm happy to think I could help."

"You have. And that's no small thing, kid."

With the expression on Mini's face, any doubt about my course of action fades. Bailly said I should have a role, and this is as good as I could've hoped for.

The Carnival – The Carriage Factory

The next morning I walk over to Hendricks a little late. I can never quite figure out time here. No matter how hard I try, I either wake up in a cold sweat hours before I need to, or in panic realizing that I actually am late. I go in through the main factory entrance. There would usually be twenty or more workers on break milling around the entrance, smoking cigarettes and joking around, sitting on the carts that bring carriage parts inside. But the carts are abandoned. I reason that it's probably still too early for anyone to be taking a break, and even if it isn't, the introduction of creative influence is likely exciting enough for those not working to want to watch.

When I enter the factory, silence envelops me. The normal chug of machines and clatter of hammers is an echo. I walk out to the railing and look over the factory floor. The space is empty, clean—pristine, even—and in the outgoing loading dock are scores of brand new Hendricks carriages. There's not a worker in sight. The clock on the wall reads $\Omega{\approx}\Omega{\approx}$, which means it's been under thirty minutes since work started.

"Boy!" comes a yell from the direction of the union office entrance. Jer tears toward me. Based on the expression on his face, he should probably be holding a hammer or some other blunt and bashy object.

"This is a disaster," he says, "an unmitigated cluster-F."

"Did they use the new rules we voted on?" I ask.

"They sure did. They used them for all of the ten minutes it took to fill the entire quota for the day." He points to the carriages with disgust.

"Sounds like it was more efficient."

"It was so efficient that Hendricks has decided it would be more cost-effective if they fired all but three of us."

"Why though? Don't they want more carriages?"

"The quota is the demand for their product, you economically challenged buffoon. They don't need four thousand carriages a day. That means they don't need my people anymore."

His ears have gone the red of burning coals, and with each sentence he jabs his finger into my chest.

"This is what you can expect when an outsider comes in and tries to *fix* everything. You don't understand our world. You think we're too stupid to come up with the right solutions ourselves, and that you're the only one who can save us." He bruises my chest one more time.

"I—I'm sorry."

"You should be." He turns away, and for a second I think we're through the worst of it. Then Jer turns and kicks clear through the railing I had been leaning on a moment before, shattering the wood into dozens of pieces that clatter onto the factory floor.

"Picket lines form at six o'clock tomorrow morning."

By the time the echoes from the falling railing have subsided, Jer's slumped form is halfway back to his office.

My thoughts turn to Mini. What will he do, with Tilla and six children depending on him? Their hope that they would see more of their father and life would be better after this change has turned to ashes. Maybe this situation was like one of Mini's puzzles, requiring a delicate touch and knowing exactly where to apply pressure. Instead I've gone and smashed it into pieces with a hammer.

I wonder if Bailly will think I've let him down. All that talk of creating my own story, and it's looking more like a tragicomedy than anything else. I may be a long way from seeing my next memory.

In any case, I am not late for the picket lines the next day. June joins me for "moral support," which so far has consisted entirely of making jokes like, "I hope the workers won't be too busy to show up—oh wait, none of them have jobs anymore, we should be fine."

The workers did indeed show up, forming a wall at least ten deep around the factory entrance. Between the workers and the main door are a half dozen men and women in old-fashioned police uniforms with skinny ties. Most also wear bowler hats, and carry aggressively long rifles.

"Pinkertons," June says as we fall into line. "Security for hire, though mostly they specialize in shooting peacefully assembled people at inopportune moments in order to start riots."

The workers are already rowdy. A sense of desperation fills the gray morning air. Insults fly at the Pinkertons. Despite their relative calm, the Pinkertons hold their rifles in both hands, ready to use them at a moment's notice. A large proportion of the workers have brought tools from home that, though not specifically designed for crushing a human skull, could do the job given enough patience and persistence.

I catch Mini's face through the crowd. He projects the same determination as the rest of the strikers, but I don't miss the deep tired pouch under each of his eyes.

The factory door opens partway, prompting a jeer from the picketers. Chants of "Let us in! Let us in!" start up, and a few dozen cabbages volley harmlessly off the Pinkertons. A man in a suit and bowtie steps out. His salt and pepper hair is slicked back over severe temples. He's at least a head taller than the Pinkertons on either side of him, who sport billy clubs and self-important smirks. The man's gangly appearance is made ganglier by the fact that his suit pants don't quite make it to his ankles, revealing the fabric of thick orange socks underneath. His gait has a canted, uneven bearing. In fact, his entire body is slightly slanted, even his thick chin, which juts out to one side and is covered by uncomfortably translucent skin. But for all that, he's strangely handsome, and holds himself with poise. The sight of the man sends the picketers into a frenzy, and soon the air is filled with rotting vegetables. None seem to make it to their target. His guards dump out the contents of a large crate, and set it upside down. They make a show of inspecting the crate's integrity, fussing over a slat that wiggles slightly before the man in the suit waves them off and steps onto it. The workers fall instantly silent, as if the lights have just gone down in some sort of perverse, participatory theater.

"For those of you who don't know me," begins the man in a measured voice that's still loud enough for all of us to hear, "which I would be surprised if is any of you, I am Roland Hendricks." The boos are deafening. June joins in wholeheartedly. Roland waits for the noise to die down before continuing. "When my great-great-grandfather, Roland Hendricks, first bought this little plot of land, he had nothing more than a dream and a simple design for a carriage more elegant than any yet in existence. He also had the help of his assistant, Theo. Now, Theo wasn't a smart man. He was well known to be able to keep exactly one thing in his head at any given time. But one thing Theo could do is carry out my great-great-grandfather's designs to perfection. They had an innate understanding, the two of them. It was like Roland was the mind and Theo was the hands.

"This is not so different from how we are. You are the skillful hands that put the brain's—my, if you will—ideas into being. Without that relationship, there would be no factory, there would be no carriages, there would be—" his chin veers even further to one side as he shudders dramatically "—no Hendricks. You have been a vital part of this partnership, and I want to thank each and every one of you for your contributions. You have my eternal thanks and appreciation."

"How many times have they been on strike this year?" I ask June.

"I haven't really been tracking it, but I'd say at least eight to ten. That's strikes though, there have definitely been a few lock-outs, lock-ins, slow-downs, shutdowns, sit-ins, and other less formal actions. I doubt even Jer can keep track of them all. Don't worry, though, this is definitely by far the worst situation they've been in." She smiles and gives me a ringy thumbs-up.

My attention returns to Roland as he says, "I have always been a student of history, particularly my family's rich history. I seek to learn not only from their successes, but also their victories, because I believe they all present learning opportunities. When Roland and Theo started the factory, they made only one carriage every two weeks. They sold out an entire year's run within a month.

"So he hired a half dozen kids from the local orphanage, who had no parents to grub over their wages. You see, even then, while still a young man, Roland had a head for maximizing profit and value. Soon Hendricks was the largest carriage manufacturer in the entire Carnival, and also the largest employer of parentless children.

"As his success continued, Roland came to realize a couple things: first, while he appreciated Theo's contributions to the company in executing the superior Hendricks designs, the paradigm had changed. It didn't make sense to have one relatively highly paid employee, when he could hire fifteen more employees for the same amount. Production relied more on many motivated hands, and less on two highly skilled ones. Second, Theo was not served by this change. He was a living fossil on the assembly line, and keeping him there was a disservice.

"When Roland let Theo go, it was the hardest decision he ever made. But it was the right one. I told you I'm a student of history, and as a student of history I have a perspective many of you likely lack. I understand that this moment represents as large of a paradigm shift as Theo's obsolescence. It is clear that we now no longer need so many hands. Hendricks will continue its unparalleled production, but now with only the few workers with the best creative influence, who can accomplish the same work without requiring extraneous expense. Your work yesterday clearly demonstrated this, and I will always be grateful to you for helping me understand this lesson. I am truly humbled, and know that future generations of Hendricks workers—though much smaller generations, obviously—will admire what you've accomplished.

"But the time for lofty words is over. Reopen the factory!"

Down the sloped gravel path leading to the main door comes a tight cluster of people. In front are two Pinkertons with long wooden rods, flanked by a half dozen more security guards. Three people in factory garb are wedged between them. They look no different than any picketer, save that these three still have livelihoods. The line turns from Roland, who has stepped down with a bow and returned inside the factory, timing his exit so the attention and howls of rage are directed at the scabs rather than him.

For the first time tempers truly boil over. If most picketers brandished heads of lettuce or overripe potatoes during the speech, now the improvised weapons are ready. Violence seems inevitable. The Pinkertons force themselves through the tide of people. The crowd pushes back, and June and I find ourselves shoved to one side. They pass three rows away from us, close enough to see the terror on the scabs' faces and the calm professionalism in the Pinkertons' eyes. Creative obscenities—some of them from June—rocket around, and everyone presses so close that we have little control over our own motions.

Tugs and shoves become punches, and the Pinkertons start laying into the strikers with the butts of their guns. With each impact the crowd grows angrier, blows beginning to fly in all directions. The armored crew's progress toward the factory door is slow but unrelenting. I stumble and fall in the gravel a few feet from the door. Pinprick scrapes dot my arms and knees as strikers tumble over me. The wave of feet parts effortlessly around us, the fallen comrades, part of a long-rehearsed dance. It gives us a moment to get to our feet. June is right near where the scabs are frantically unchaining the door. The Pinkertons methodically push the picketers outward in a semicircle to clear room. It looks like one of the lead guards is saying something, but it's impossible to tell what over the din. Mini presses up against me.

"Come on," he says. "It's your fight now. You gotta push." His expression tells me that any respect he had for me and my grand plan—his grand plan—is gone.

I do as I'm told, and push into the backs of the strikers in front of me. For a second we swell, and those at the front rise as if squeezed from a tube made of bodies and Pinkerton rifles. Then comes a collective stagger and the squeal of the opening door, and somehow the scabs and their escorts are inside. A heavy rod falls behind the door. The strikers pull up short.

The silence blows like a horn after the previous mayhem. June makes her way back toward me. She sports a black eye and a grin.

"It's been on my bucket list to sucker punch one of the Pinks." She checks an imaginary checkbox in the air. "Done."

"Why aren't they trying to break in?" I say.

A striker nearby replies, "The door's too strong. We built that sucker ourselves. It's designed to withstand forces stronger than a dozen carriages being rammed into it."

"Come on, guys," I say, surprised how well my voice carries. "You spent all of yesterday defying physics in order to build as many carriages as you did. If you really want to get into that factory, a little thing like a door shouldn't stop you."

"You don't know those doors like we know 'em," a striker shouts.

Hollers of agreement chorus around me.

"It's a big door, that's true," I say. "I'd even go so far as to say it's the strongest door I've ever seen, even stronger than the one guarding the steel city."

Begrudging agreement. The sounds of whirring machines start up inside the factory.

"But you said it yourselves, you built this door. You built it with just your hands and the tools available to you. The way I look at it, that means you should be able to take it down no problem if you take physics out of the equation."

Murmurs. A couple of the workers put their hands to the door as if testing its strength. I wonder absently where Roland Hendricks got off to.

Mini steps beside me. Sweat and dirt stain his collar, and his overcoat is missing a button. I never noticed that every single person here is wearing suspenders—even me and June, though I can't remember putting them on. It feels comforting to loop my thumbs into the straps, mirroring Mini.

"He might be just a kid," Mini says, "but some of the best ideas ever been had have come from folks too young and naïve to believe otherwise. I say we give him a listen, and do our best to crack that door. Fall in line, gentlemen and ladies."

He turns away from me as he says this, as if he can't bring himself to make eye contact. The strikers shuffle into a line parallel to the factory gates. Before I can shout to start the effort, the workers have moved forward and begun pressing upward. They groan against the heavy bar holding the door in place on the opposite side, but with consistent pressure the door folds inward, bending into a concave shape. As they continue to push, the door curls and, as if on pulleys, rises up over the backs of the strikers, swinging in a wide arc before falling behind them. I stutter step backwards as the now crescent-shaped door crashes into the mud at my feet.

The strikers prepare to charge into the wide-open factory, and all hell breaks loose.

A stream of bullets clatters off the door and through the crowd. I drop behind the door as splinters fly from the heavy piece of metal. Cries of pain rise over the sharp report of gunfire, and five or six strikers fall with blood splattering around them. An instinct yanks at me—*gunshot wounds don't look like that*—and for a second I'm suspended above the scene, unmoored and watching the strikers throw themselves at the Pinkertons in a tide built of martyrdom.

Then I am back in the mud, my ears ringing. June crouches beside me. The nearest gunshots have stopped as the Pinkertons by the entrance have been overwhelmed, and the strikers swarm into the factory. There are obviously limits on creative influence this close to the factory, which is a place usually dedicated to building rather than fighting, since both strikers and Pinkertons follow the primitive rules of blunt objects, rifles, and the occasional revolver. Some of the workers have gotten their hands on the carriage-making equipment, and I get the sense this isn't the first time they've used a wrench in other than a professional manner. June waves for me to come on, rising out of cover.

"Are you crazy?" I yell.

"Come on, what do you think are the odds that you actually get shot?"

I stare in horror at the eight or nine dead and wounded around me. All I can do is point at them.

"Ugh you're so literal," June says, grabbing me by the arm and yanking me forcibly into harm's way.

A group of three strikers is laying into an unarmed Pinkerton with their fists by the front office. June scoops up the guard's fallen rifle and hands it to me. I don't know why it feels comfortable in my hands, but it does, and I feel better being armed. A group of stragglers follows me and June. Guess this is as good a moment as any to create my narrative. As I think this, the number on my wrist rises over *10,000* for the first time.

"Keep going!" I shout. "Don't let them stop you!"

By the shouts behind me I know I've fired them up, and we tear onto the main factory floor. We are met instantly by gunshots from two Pinkertons standing near the central assembly line, and we take cover behind a giant tank I hope doesn't have anything flammable in it. I poke my head around the corner to catch a glimpse of the Pinkertons, but am immediately met by a volley from the two guards.

My understanding of the factory is rudimentary at best, but I do notice that the central area the Pinkertons defend is the final staging area, where a flat platform—essentially an elevator—lowers the carriages down to the paint shop below.

"Hey, you there," I say, pulling a young woman aside. Her hair is purple, as are her suspenders. "Do you think you could take a group down to the paint shop?"

Her intelligent eyes dart from me to the tank, gauging the position of the Pinkertons and instantly catching on.

"We can get down there," she says, "but the Pinks will've turned the elevators off to slow us down. You would ordinarily be able to hear the mechanism working."

"That's okay. I think we can handle it. I'll give you five minutes to get down there, then you be ready."

The woman nods. "Make it three." She and five others sprint off to the stairway.

I count out the minutes on the giant clock on the far wall. Its hands move impassively.

Smoke rises next to me, and my heart flips in my chest.

But it's just June, smoking a cigarette.

"I get bored waiting," she says by way of explanation. "You want?" She tilts it toward me.

"The probability that this tank is filled with some kind of incredibly flammable petrochemical has to be at least three in five," I say. "You're going to turn this whole place into one giant cruise missile."

"Mattison, I'm going to need you to settle down. If the architect of this whole revolution/uprising can't keep a cool head, I don't know if I can continue to be a part of this."

"I didn't plan on being the architect of any of this," I say. Even though there's no breeze in here, the sparks from her cigarette stream consistently away from the tank beside us. Nice touch, June.

"It's been more than three minutes," she says.

Shit, it has. I cock my rifle and focus on the pulley mechanisms governing the elevator, which are locked into place. I'm not entirely convinced they existed before I realized they were there. Either that, or I have an insanely instinctual understanding of the machine. No matter. *Bang! Bang!* With a creak, one side of the platform comes free, and the Pinkertons shout as they slide down the now ramp-like surface into the paint shop. I rush forward with my rifle clutched at my side, the others following behind me. We pull up to the edge. The purple-haired girl and her compatriots have already knocked out the two Pinkertons, who lie in limp piles at the bottom of the elevator well.

We don't have time to celebrate, though, as a tide of metal churns over us, throwing us down into the hole with the guards.

The world rotates. I am unmoored. I fall. Spikes drill into my flesh.

Everything darkens as I cover my face against the wave of shrapnel.

Once again I am unmoored. It is evening. Early spring. I float. I spin. I fall, metal around me.

Do I exist in this moment? In the arbitrary limbo between life and death, where only the sheer luck of physics decides my fate, is there anything that could truthfully be described as me?

When I stop moving, I find myself at the bottom of the elevator ramp, my legs trapped under a pile of scrap metal. My legs have taken the brunt of it, but I can feel cuts against my chest, arms, and face. There are some throaty laughs from above us, as whoever emptied the massive containers of scrap metal runs off. Pain courses through my shins, where a long rod digs into my skin. Every move I make pushes it further toward bone.

"Shitting shit buckets," June says as she extricates herself from the pile. She took a broken wheel spoke to the forehead, and bleeds in a cascade of scarlet.

"Are you okay?" Others around us have come away with similar injuries, though I appear to be the worst off.

"Probably," June says. "Can you move?"

She leans over me with concern.

Reality blinks at me, and it's no longer June above me. My vision is blurry, and my entire lower body feels distant.

"Can you move?"

Shattered glass trickles out of my hair.

Somewhere in front of me is something I cannot comprehend yet. I look down at my hip and scream.

A phone rings. Twice. I move to answer it. On the other end is death and hope.

"I don't know," I say. June puts a warm hand on my shoulder.

She grabs the rod that's holding my leg and yanks it away. She pulls me to my feet.

White lights. White on metal. White on white. Soft beneath me, but pain leering out of my numb body.

"Turns out you can move, I guess," she says.

"I guess." My thoughts are still in the haze between reality and somewhere else.

"If we're going to take this place over, we have to take out the rest of the Pinkertons."

"Why bother taking the factory?" I ask. "This was supposed to be about getting better pay for the workers, not waging war on Hendricks."

"You don't understand," the purple-haired girl says, spitting a small chunk of metal out onto the pile at my feet. "This is our factory, we've put our blood and lives into it. If they hold it for even a second without us, it's like losing our home. Or worse. Losing who we are."

"You're an instigator," June says to me, "but don't overestimate your effect. The workers would've wanted to take this place whether you were here or not."

The purple-haired girl nods. "This one gets it. Shall we go?"

We pick our way out of the scrap metal and scramble up the ramp. I'm surprised to find my leg can hold my weight. It aches deeply, but not in accurate proportion with the wound's severity. Once my mind commits to the fact that I should be climbing, the pain reduces to a level that allows me to climb. Heading up the stairs past the factory floor, we bypass the empty balconies encircling the floor, and push toward the offices above. A crowd of workers has gathered in front of a smashed window. A couple workers with rifles cover the open office beyond. Every so often a Pinkerton pokes their nose out from behind a filing cabinet in the back corner, and is met by a barrage of gunfire.

I take cover next to Mini. He's bleeding from a cut on his upper arm, but has a grim smile on his thin lips.

"That's the last of the Pinks inside," he says. "Almost there."

"What happens when we take the factory?" I ask. I imagine the workers moving into the office and beginning to file paperwork in order to get the factory back up and running.

"Then we have the factory."

A harsh electrical whine tears through the building. It resolves into a familiar voice.

"Good workers of the Carriagemaker's Union, this is Roland Hendricks." A collective groan goes up, and the gunfire ceases. I don't trust this calm. I crawl over to the window overlooking the entrance.

"We have stationed our private security force at all entrances and exits," Hendricks continues. "You have fought only a small fraction of the forces we have available to us. It would be my sincere recommendation that you do not force me to give the order to fire everything we have."

The view from the factory window is worse than I could've feared. Smoke rises over the entire scene, and several carriages and tool carts burn violently, surrounded by the scattered bodies of Pinkertons and factory workers alike. Civilians pick through the bodies, collecting the injured and carrying them to a makeshift infirmary set up outside the range of the fighting. At least two-hundred Pinkertons have their guns trained on the upper windows—on us. The other strikers peer out the window beside me, the office forgotten. Hendricks stands in front of his army holding a bullhorn.

"You have proven your strength once again. Do not force me to prove mine."

A figure squeezes through the crowd, nudging Pinkertons aside to move beside Hendricks. It's Jer, every movement speaking of exhaustion. He puts out his hand to Hendricks, who hands him the bullhorn.

"My people, this is Jer. This carnage has gone far enough. In my thirty-five years running this union, I've never seen this much blood shed for no reason. Stop playing into their hands with this needless violence."

The faces around me do not convey emotions that much different from when Hendricks was talking, but some resigned murmurs have started.

"Come on, you can't stop now," June says. "We can hold out in here. Block the door, start the furnaces. This factory can just as easily be used to make weapons as carriages."

"I don't want to see any more of my people hurt," Jer says. "Please. Hendricks has offered to negotiate, you'll have your jobs back by tomorrow morning."

"Do you really believe that?" June says, looking to me for backup.

Mini shakes his head. "We gotta listen to the boss. I motion we stand down."

"You've been listening to bosses your whole lives," I say. "Where has that gotten you?"

Mini meets my eyes. "Matthew, you've done your best. This is done."

"Come on, we've gotten so far," I say. "If we give up now, it's all for nothing."

As I say these words, and note the approval on June's face, the pain on Mini's, I feel as if I'm falling out of my body. What we've done today, it's beyond what I ever intended. People are dead, all because I advocated this course of action.

I realize that I'm not arguing what I actually believe. I'm arguing what I think June would like to hear, what I think would fit this story I've chosen the best.

"But maybe getting this far was always the point," I allow. "Hendricks has to come to the table now."

The others nod their agreement, and June's look of approval sours. The few dissenters quickly realize they're outnumbered, and we begin filing toward the door.

As we walk out in a ragged line, I half expect the waiting Pinkertons to open fire. But they lower their guns. Jer shoves the bullhorn back at Hendricks without looking at him, and disappears into the crowd. The strikers shuffle off in rows, blood-ied and dejected. Those with families watching don't react to the defeat—no anger at endangering themselves, no celebration that they're alive. Just quiet reunification as they dissolve to their own corners of town. Behind us, smoke rises from the factory.

Worst is the bodies. I don't have a full count on the casualties, but it must be more than thirty. Workers have begun stacking them.

As I pass them I see one who wasn't shot, but rather appears to have had his throat slit. The wound is no longer bleeding, but dark red stains his neck and chest. He's young, barely old enough to work in the factory. A low murmur comes from his throat, despite his lifeless eyes. There's a tune to the utterance. It's hauntingly sweet, and barely audible over the noise of the cleanup around us.

I cannot make out the words, but this young man, already dead with his throat cut on the battlefield, is singing.

Even June flinches at this. My own horror simultaneously pulls me in and pushes me away.

We pass within a few yards of Hendricks, who smiles at me with his strange, crooked teeth. He makes the shape of a pistol with his thumb and pointer, and aims it in my direction.

"Why did you want them to keep fighting?" I say once we've passed the last of the Pinkertons. June is still fuming.

"Isn't it pointless if you stop halfway? We were about to take the entire factory. Why even start if you're going to quit?"

I look back and shudder when I see that the Pinkertons have begun to stack more bodies around the entrance. Wounded are being ferried to the makeshift infirmary down the street. The true horror of what we've just been through is only now starting to sink in.

"People died, June," I say. "It was never supposed to go this far. All I wanted was for their jobs to be a little easier."

"You didn't make them die for what they believed in."

"But they wouldn't have if I didn't push them." I wipe the first tears out of my eyes.

"You pushed them out of their lethargy," she says. "This was the one way they could stop going through the same old motions, the one way people could start thinking differently."

I want to believe it, but I can't convince myself that any of it is worth a single person dying.

"You gave them something to believe in, showed them what was possible," June says. "You gave them a story, which is damn sure more than they had before."

"A story doesn't mean much if you're not around to tell it."

She pulls up short. We're about to turn onto the busy high street. Hendricks carriages roll stoically behind her.

"The Pinkertons didn't have to start shooting. Do you really think no one would've been hurt if we hadn't pushed? Someone would've crossed a line, the Pinkertons would've found some excuse. It would've ended in blood one way or another."

"I don't know."

"Don't be such an obstinate heifer. You're proving yourself incredibly capable of blaming yourself, when the people you should be blaming are the ones who treat their own workers like an invading army when they ask for decent wages. Blame Hendricks."

The throbbing, heartsick sensation in my chest does feel like it could change into something resembling anger. It's true. They didn't have to bring the scabs in. They didn't need the Pinkertons and their guns. Even Hendricks' speech, I'm now convinced, was designed to rile up the workers and instigate a fight.

But I can't pretend all this would've happened without me. I look back at the bodies—many of them with families like Mini—being piled onto carts. What matters to their families isn't how much food is on the table, how large their house is, or even if they can afford an education. What matters is that their mother or father comes home at the end of the day.

Mini walks toward us out of the crowd. At least he's mostly uninjured. Someone has applied a bandage to the cut on his face. He slaps a strong hand on my shoulder. His eyes stare into mine, their intensity nearly overwhelming. I can briefly see all four, as I did when we first met, before they revert to the usual human pair my brain makes of them. Then he pats my shoulder once, hard, and stalks off.

"Do you want to do something?" June asks. "Go flying? I have a meeting with the Armageddeons but it can probably wait."

"No," I say. "I think I need some time alone."

"I know a spot."

Cuppa Café does not have any discernible customers to justify its existence. The single table at the back of the narrow, white-walled space is unoccupied. The barista has an intricate web of tattoos on her arms that forms a single continuous pattern when her hands are joined. She brings me my latte with a smile and a "here you go, babe," but otherwise we don't speak.

The foam on top settles into the shape of a tree, its branches filled out with leaves that rock in a nonexistent breeze. It makes me wish I had tipped the barista more. I don't touch the drink. I worry that if I tried to pick up the cup—white, on a white saucer, on the white marble table—my hands would shake until it shattered on the spotless floor.

My face is covered in bruises, and my pants are torn below the knee. Dried blood clings to the fabric and my exposed skin. I'm wearing a hoodie that was clean this morning, but now is ripped in several places, and stained with grease and dirt. The suspenders that had suddenly appeared in the factory disappeared just as suddenly.

The violence isn't the only thing I need to be alone to process. The images I saw at the bottom of the elevator well won't leave my mind. They're clear in their lack of clarity, indelible even as they're completely elusive. With a surge of pain, I give myself over to the memories—because memories is what they are, I'm sure. Amid the smashed metal and glass is another detail. A stink that covered everything before the world spun and I bounced about like a heavy leaf in a metal breeze. Alcohol. Sharp, pungent. And anger. Rage. Yelling. Fighting. About the smell and something else, something I can't remember now. I wonder if this incident is related to the hospital memory Bailly showed me.

It's too much. I'm sobbing, and I need to pull back. The branches on my latte tree droop, as their leaves disappear into whatever the caffeine equivalent of winter is.

I follow the less painful thread. My hand reaching out for the handset—a house phone, then. Not a familiar one. I would remember it, the way any familiar object in your home feels natural, the way the moment it changes you feel displaced.

It's not just the phone I'm disconnected from. It's the entire image and its sensations. There were strong emotions there, but they didn't feel like my own.

The more immediate horror I've witnessed returns. I thought I'd been creating my own story. A story that ends with this type of carnage doesn't feel worth being a part of.

No, what I've just been through was not a story at all. The less powerful getting screwed over by the more powerful isn't new. It isn't something that requires a narrative. It's the accepted and consistent state of the world. The horror comes not from the tragedy of it, but from the normalcy of it. I should've seen that from the beginning. In my mind's eye, Hendricks' smug, crooked face stands in for the entire oppressive weight of his organization. Blood flashes out from bullet wounds, and I shudder.

On the device that has slumped down my forearm, the blue-white numbers read: *8,102* through a crust of blood and dirt. They're stuck there, unblinking. I shake my arm, trying to get them to change. They stay put. I wish I knew what exactly

they were tracking—most often it seems like a simple pedometer, but at times it rises more rapidly or slowly than could be
explained by just my steps, and always resets after 10,000.

My leg throbs. A few flakes of dried blood have fallen onto
the floor. I bend and sweep them into my hand, but I can't find
a trash can to put them in. I drop them back onto the floor.
This place is clean, well lit, although a little less of both for my
presence. I stare into the swirling shape on the foam for a long
time.

The Carnival - Carl's Estate

"**N**asty business," Carl says. "Truth be told, I've had to employ the Pinkertons on more than one occasion. Really should only be criminals like me doing that, not respectable folks like Roland Persephone Hendricks."

"His middle name is Persephone?" It's the longest sentence I've spoken since Carl's carriage picked me up outside my inn. Almost a week since the incident at the factory, and it's the first time I've been able to bring myself to answer his courier. I had expected him to be inside the carriage that picked me up, paws folded in his lap, but instead it was empty and the driver brought me to a house high in the hills overlooking Valdrada, hills I don't remember seeing on my flight around the valley. It's a striking view, though. Distance gives the city a glisten it doesn't possess at ground level, and the lake at its far edge twinkles.

"Doesn't matter." Carl leans on the metal balcony railing overlooking the interior courtyard of his house. The modern design is at odds with the tweed jacket—elbow pads and all—that Carl wears despite the heat. The whole place has a tropicality to it, as if Florida got scooped up and deposited in the rolling hills. Valdrada's microgriff infestation has not reached this far. It's almost strange to be without them.

"I understand you're probably feeling not mentally all there," Carl says. "After trauma like that, you've got to take care of yourself."

I nod. He leaves space between us, and I appreciate that he doesn't push me to speak before I'm ready. I sip the cold drink Carl offered me as soon as I walked in the door ("Iced tea with lemonade. My one true indulgence. I do hope you won't make me finish the pitcher myself.") The flavor hits me at the critical nexus of sweet, tart, and bitter.

Birds make happy noises in the trees below us. Narrow paths bend lazily around the half dozen fountains that spray mist into the morning air. Each fountain depicts a different comedic scene. Most involve a person, invariably nude, slipping on a wet surface, their face caught in the shock the moment between realizing they're falling and hitting the floor. Carl giggled to himself as he showed them to me. I can't recall ever having met someone who could be described as being "tickled" by his surroundings with such frequency.

"I don't dream here," I say finally.

Carl's face is unreadable. "You don't need to."

"I don't dream, but I keep waking up in strange places. The last three days I've woken up in an office without any idea how I got there. I'm always sitting at a desk, and it's always stacked with folders. I know I'm supposed to be filing them, and I honest to God do my best to. But this guy keeps coming in and dropping more on my desk. No matter how fast I file, he keeps coming in and dropping more. By about thirty minutes in I'm panicking because the pile is only getting higher and higher. I start throwing them into random drawers, but the drawers don't get any fuller. I can stuff an entire stack into the same drawer, and the next time I try again, there will still be space. My hands get tired, and I end up covered with paper cuts. The worst part is, no one's stopping me from walking out. I have no obligation to be there. But all three times it's happened, I've kept going."

The experience was horrifying the first time, and has only gotten more so with each iteration. I begin to wonder if I'll ever wake up in a bed again.

"When I walk out, the rest of the office is empty. The dude with the papers is nowhere to be found. And you know what's the craziest part?"

Carl remains still at the railing.

"The craziest part is that before I leave, I walk through the entire damn office and turn off all the lights. Like it's my job to close up shop for the day. What the hell do you make of that?"

I don't know what I want Carl to say. Maybe I want him to tell me I'm crazy, that my somnambulism is a sign that I've really and truly—finally and inevitably—lost my goddamn mind. What a relief that would be, if someone would just confirm it.

He reaches for the pitcher. He pours carefully, making sure none of the ice falls into his drink.

"The mind goes to tremendous lengths to impose order on the world," Carl says. "As humans we take something disordered, chaotic—I'm referring to life here, to be clear—and try our best to turn it into something that makes sense to our ape brains. Alphabetization. Filing cabinets. Right angles." He motions to the perfect square of the courtyard. "It's all a way of controlling a world that cannot be controlled. If my understanding of humans is correct—and I've found it usually is—the more chaotic, the more unpredictable the world becomes, the more we fight to control it. It's one of the great paradoxes, though, that the more boxes we create, the less tends to fit into them."

"Are you trying to tell me my accidental office job is a manifestation of me feeling that the world has spiraled out of my control?"

"I'm not trying to psychoanalyze you," Carl says. From anyone else it would sound defensive. "I'm just brainstorming. I'm not going to pretend I have answers for you."

I chew on Carl's words for a minute. When I compare him to Bailly, it's something Carl lacks that makes me more comfortable around the mobster than the record keeper: certainty. Bailly always seems so certain of everything.

"More to the point," Carl says, "I do want to emphasize that all those deaths at the factory are not on you. I know you're set on continuing your psychological martyrdom, so I won't keep saying it. But if you're going to keep the guilt around, you might as well use it for something."

"For?"

"To get angry, for one. The world works in ways that screw people over. Why not turn your guilt into useful rage at that fact?"

I stare up at the sky. It's impossibly blue through the palm trees that obscure the upper level of the courtyard.

"I'll give it a shot, I guess."

Carl smiles.

There's a disturbance below, and a flock of birds explodes upward. Four massive shapes tramp across the manicured grass. It's the chickenmen. They weave around the fountains, either chasing each other or running randomly.

"How the hell did they get in?" I say. The courtyard's only entrance is through the house, and there wasn't any indication of the intruders breaking through the glass doors.

"Hey! Gentlemen, find a different playground!" Carl yells.

"We're sorry," one hollers back.

"Not that sorry."

"Much ashamed."

"Rather obliged."

Carl sighs before saying to me, "I don't know why I tell them off. I should've learned by now that they'll do what they please."

"Do you need a referral for better security? I might know a guy."

"The chickenmen aren't subject to the same rules as the rest of us. The other residents of the Carnival learned long ago that it's better to stay out of their way. Besides, they're really mostly harmless."

"Mostly?"

"Idiots can hurt people without trying to." Carl watches as they gallop behind the largest fountain, and disappear. The quiet of the courtyard returns.

"I suppose we should inspect the damage," Carl says. I follow him downstairs. The lawn is covered in clawprints. Carl leans over a divot and delicately replaces it. "I have a piece of information I'm excited to tell you in exchange for your next job. It's a tough job, but I can assure you the reward is worth it."

"Any hints? As you've already seen, I'm dangerously close to a breakdown."

Still crouching, Carl pulls an envelope out of his jacket pocket.

"Your instructions. I've already alluded to the fact that the Carnival has an exit, that there's an Elsewhere. I will give you the location of the exit. I'm the only one who's been to this exit and recognized it for what it is. That's right, not even June."

I have a hard time looking at the envelope, I'm so distracted by this new payment he's dangling in front of me.

"I know all you want is the truth," Carl says.

I nod, although part of me wants to scream at him to stop with the games and tell me everything he knows. I briefly consider the possibility that he may not actually know everything. But if all he knows is the way out, that's all I need.

"I understand, sir. The job?"

"To assassinate Roland Hendricks."

The Carnival - Valdrada

I don't know if me and June are fighting, or if we just happen to have not spoken for a while. She's spent the vast majority of her time on her ambassadorial missions.

I don't tell her about my own mission. I'm still shaken by the disapproving looks she gave me after I allowed the factory strike to end. It annoys me that I care this much about what she thinks.

Whatever qualms I may have, it's not hard to justify killing Roland. He's the primary party responsible for all those deaths in the factory. The Carnival will be better for him not being part of it. Last night I ran into Mini at Night and Dragon, and he informed me that the negotiation resulted in lower wages, since Hendricks argued that the loss of factory property needed to be offset by a reduction in costs.

"It'll never change," Mini said, slurring his words. "Not until someone puts a bullet in one side of his head and then out the other side. Bang!"

I'd always thought him a gentle person. But I guess even gentle people have a limit.

"You're a good kid, though," he continues. "I know it didn't all go over right, but you tried to do your best. That's all anybody can do, that's for sure."

"Thanks, Mini."

He put a sloppy arm around my shoulder.

"You're a good kid. A good kid. A real good kid."

I ended up scraping him off the floor with the help of one of his friends, who dragged him home well before midnight.

The Carnival – Hendricks Manor

The night when I'm supposed to help kill Hendricks finds me once again in a carriage with Alyssa. We're dressed head-to-toe in black, and each carry a pistol with a silencer. She also has a variety of lethal and non-lethal grenades she doesn't let me near. Probably for the best.

Carl's driver drops us off in the middle of a pasture. If all goes according to plan, we'll be back here in an hour to catch our ride home. Using the fence by the side of the road as a marker, we measure out our paces, stopping every few feet to re-check the map from Carl's envelope. The Hendricks have not always confined themselves to carriage-making, and this tunnel used to be one of the primary smuggling routes onto their property. According to Alyssa, one of their operations involved skimming wheat off local farmers' crop, then repackaging it here before selling it in Valdrada.

I find the tunnel when my feet break through rotten wood, and I nearly fall into the hole. Alyssa gives me a *please be louder, I dare you* look, and we set to peeling the moldy boards away. A metal ladder leads into darkness.

The tunnel at the bottom is about six feet high. Though neither of us scrape the top, I have the urge to crouch. The hard-packed dirt has been fortified with wood on either side, but for the most part our feet plod over uneven ground, illuminated by our flashlights. I go first. The air feels sluggish, soupy, like it hasn't moved for a long time and is doing so only reluctantly now. We move as quietly as possible through the empty passage.

At the first fork in the tunnel we take a right. Both branches lead to the estate, but this one will take us more directly. The slope heads steeply downward, and I nearly lose my footing more than once.

Once the tunnel levels out, the hallway becomes more uniformly square, and the walls change from wood and dirt to concrete. The floor is grooved. As we continue, the grooves become deeper, widening to about a foot square—and they are square, I realize, perfectly so. They continue to deepen and widen, until we are picking our way through square holes over a foot deep. In the dim light and shadows cast by our flashlights, it's difficult to make out the floor. Eventually the squares settle on a single size. My quads and calves burn, and I stop to catch my breath.

Panting, with my hands on my knees, I take a closer look at the squares. Their bottoms are completely flat and covered in a thick layer of dust. I try to identify any inconsistency in them, any sign that they're anything less than perfectly symmetrical, but I can't. The roof, too, is composed of exact right angles.

"How hard does it have to be to kill one titan of industry?" Alyssa says.

I smile humorlessly. I'm reminded of the office I've been waking up in, the unremitting squareness of everything. I want to take a sledgehammer and smash the corners of the boxes.

We start again.

"Shouldn't we be going down more?" I say. We're making for an elevator far under the Hendricks estate. No sooner do I say it than the path slopes downward again. The boxes continue, but they rotate with the slope, becoming a set of stairs that quickens our progress. It begins to feel like we're running. It's not just that we're going down, it's that the boxes are moving beneath our feet, like a giant escalator. With the movement comes a grinding, creaking sound.

I stop and almost lose my balance, vertigo threatening to overtake me. Alyssa grabs my shoulder to steady me, and we ride down together. The tunnel begins to level once again, but the walls of the boxes beneath our feet turn precisely, so that our feet get passed off to the next box without catching or being trapped between them.

The boxes stop so abruptly that we're vaulted into a heap on the cement floor. The grinding continues in the passage behind us.

"As far as modes of transportation go, I'd rank that slightly higher than jumping out of a plane without a parachute, and right below riding an escalator where you can only wear open-toed shoes," I say.

"Hendricks wanted to install these all over the Carnival, in the places where carriages couldn't reach. Complete transportation monopoly."

"They never took off," I say.

"No. They were a bad idea. Come on, the elevator is close."

The elevator is right around the next corner. It's another concrete cube. The concrete doors slide open when we step close, and snap shut as soon as we're inside. There are no buttons, but the elevator rockets upward nonetheless.

Alyssa and I point our weapons at the door. We have no idea where this will come out, and no control over where we're going. She nods confidently, but I can't keep a tremble out of my hands.

All of this is starting to feel like a bad idea. But on the other side of it, the union's biggest villain will be gone, and Carl will reveal the location of the exit. I have to press on.

We stop abruptly. The wall behind us opens. Alyssa spins first, expecting a trap, but there's no one there. The doors slam behind us as we step out. We're clearly in a cellar. Large casks line the walls on either side of us. This place shows more signs of use than the smuggling tunnel—a couple dirty cups sit on a barrel that has been set on its end, with a half-used candle melted onto the wood beside them.

I note the labels on the barrels: "Oaky," "Fruity," "Fox fur and vellum," "Very very old," "Not good, drinking not recommended." Old Roland's a connoisseur then.

The entrance to the next room comes out behind a fully-stocked bar. Full bottles of every conceivable variety of whiskey line the shelves, which are lit from below by dim bulbs that give the liquid a smoky glow. We slide over the top of the bar and nearly run into the room's most prominent feature. Spheres the size of bowling balls dot a massive green surface, which falls away into large leather baskets in the corners and at each side. We're looking at an oversized pool table the size of a basketball court. The pool cues, which lean haphazardly against the edges of the raised surface, remind me of tree trunks, and would have to be steadied over your shoulder. We skirt around the edge.

There's something here, something that taps a faint spring of memory. Bending over a pool table as I line up my shot. The crack of the balls as they carom across the tabletop.

"I meant to do that," I remember saying. A goofy face mugs at me. I've lost again.

We climb a wooden staircase, which winds into the main part of the mansion. We creep past a landing opening onto a gaudy foyer with the most excessive chandelier I've ever seen. The stairs continue up to the upper floors—seven of them, to be precise. At every floor the stairway opens onto a balcony overlooking the main entrance, bamboo railings cut into squares that form a dizzying pattern of mirrored levels. There's enough light from the wall sconces that we don't need our flashlights. The floors, which could be brand new for how much wear they show, barely creak under our feet.

Roland lives alone in this house, as far as we know. Without the army of servants who assist him during the day, his nights are spent alone in the expansive darkness. The emptiness is oppressive. I look down over the railing. Directly below the chandelier, there is an ornate carriage of a much older design than any I've seen. It looks much, much more expensive, painted bright blue, with golden seams curling along all sides so that the carriage appears to possess no edges, instead resolving into golden waves that transition seamlessly to the next roiling crest. The effect is that the carriage looks like it's traveling over a blue-gold ocean, even while stationary.

"Almost there," Alyssa whispers as we pull up at the master suite on the fifth floor.

There are two entrances, one at the top of the stairs and the other at the far end of the balcony. Alyssa takes the far one. Carl wasn't picky about who actually takes the shot, but I hope it falls to the person sneaking around the back. I will confront Hendricks directly.

A fire burns in the hearth in the receiving room. A half dozen uncomfortable-looking couches are arrayed in front of it. The space is so inordinately large that even with all the couches it still feels oddly empty. A half-eaten selection of cheese and fruit sits on the low table near the fire, next to an empty wine carafe.

I try to steady my breathing as I creep down a long hallway, my gun level. At the end of the hallway, the sound of running water reaches me. The door at the end is ajar. I pause, trying to make out movement behind the door. But all I can hear is water splashing.

I bite my lip and turn, gun-first, into the room.

The entire room is one massive, square bathtub. Hot water pours in a steady stream from the ceiling. A thin walkway surrounds the tub on each side, slick with water and soap. I can't see anyone in the tub, but the near side is so filled with blue bubbles that any occupant would be completely hidden. Water splashes against the side of the tub, causing me to jump.

But there's no one there. Just variable waves from the waterfall. Blue bubbles could be pleasant, maybe blueberry flavored, but the entire room smells of mildew, and the bubbles form a toxic sheen on the surface.

Beyond is a heavy metal door, and past that, the master bedroom.

Fifty yards at least separate the entrance from the nearest piece of furniture. What appears to be another carriage is, I soon realize, actually a carriage-shaped bed. It's unmade. I move quickly across the space, pulling up short when I see Roland Hendricks sitting on the couch on the other side of the bed. He has his feet up on the coffee table. Two empty carafes of wine lie on the floor beside his bed sheets, which are half draped over the end of the couch. The light from the dying fire casts half of his body—his sloped chin, the hand that holds a full glass of wine, his gray bathrobe—into dull light.

Hendricks' eyes, red-rimmed and bleary, take in my presence without alarm.

"Are you the new cleaning boy?" he says. His words have the measured slur of a practiced drunk.

"In a manner of speaking."

Hendricks makes a gun symbol with his thumb and forefinger, the same he made at the factory.

"Your intentions are not exactly difficult to divine. Don't worry, I sent all the staff home. I'd offer you wine but I seem to be on the last glass. I don't think we should share—I have a cold and I don't want to get you sick. Please, sit."

He's slouched, his pinstriped pajamas poking out of the bathrobe. I wish Alyssa would appear to tell me that actually this is as far as we needed to go, and we can consider our job done without killing him.

I sit in the plush green chair facing him.

"Comfortable, right?" he says, before taking a swig of his wine. "Ah, I do love the Oaky. Smooth, very smooth."

The tapestries lining the walls—all of them depicting carriages in one form or another—swim as he drinks.

"I hope you enjoy that," I say. "It was paid for by murdering your workers."

"Indeed it was. You don't have the stink of a union man." He sniffs the air. "No, you're an outsider. Maybe a savior, who knows. I should ask Bailly. Bailly will know."

"Bailly was the one who suggested I get involved. Doesn't exactly seem like he has your interests at heart."

"Bailly doesn't really do interests," Hendricks responds. "Other than his own. But regardless, here you are, ready to put a bullet through my head. Are you from the Armageddeons?"

"No. Why, do they want you dead?"

"No matter. There are plenty out there that would rather Hendricks ceased to exist. Sad, really, that the Hendricks company will live on without a Hendricks there to oversee it."

I look around the cavernous space. He understands the implication.

"No, there's never been a Mrs. Hendricks. No children—not legitimate ones, anyway. I have everything I could ever want, and what I've wanted has not included a family. Oh there have been some times in here. Mistresses come and go like the expensive jewelry and clothes they're after. We could be here all night picking my favorite." He fixes me with a level stare, and his voice is suddenly sober. "They're dead now, most of them. I had them killed as soon as they started asking for things I couldn't give them. Why do women always feel the need to take more than you can give?"

"That hasn't been my experience."

Hendricks finishes his wine, and my perception spins briefly. The windows change from squares to circles, then oval themselves back out to squares again.

"Experience? Little boy playing adventure with his toy gun. I bet you even forgot to turn off the safety."

I hadn't felt the safety on my way here, but I note it now, and find that it's off. Good.

"I'm not a good man," Hendricks continues.

"You're not, you're a terrible man, and you deserve to die."

"No disagreements there. I've spent the last forty years running a company that depends on the workers making as little as possible, on working in the worst conditions possible. Hendricks profits have never been better. I've done my father and his father proud. As a boy that was all I wanted, to make carriages and to turn those carriages into money, and more money. You want to know the secret though?" He leans forward. Even a good five yards away, the stench of wine is heavy as he whispers, "I have more money than I need. What a headache to spend your time thinking of what to do with extraneous money. It's almost enough to make one decide to pick up politics."

"If you have all the money you need, if your bottom line is so good, why the hell would you be willing to set the Pinkertons on your own workers? Why would you be willing to let them die?"

"We all have roles to play," Hendricks says, "and I've played mine with the gusto of Lawrence of Olivier."

"That's bullshit."

"And your role right now—" The gun shakes in my hand, and Roland smiles "—is an assassin."

Blood spatters the back of the couch as a bullet smashes through his skull. His nearly empty glass falls to the floor. The last droplets stain his disheveled sheets.

The hole in Hendricks' head is a mere pinprick, but as I stare at it, it grows, sucking inwards to form a chasm. Soon the rest of his face has been sucked up into the ever-widening hole.

Alyssa approaches from behind with a businesslike gait, her pistol smoking.

"Boy, but the bastard did love to talk," she says.

I stand. My hands are trembling so badly that I fear the gun in my hands is about to go off.

"Give me that," Alyssa says, yanking the pistol out of my grasp. "We've done our job."

She pulls out a can of spray paint. Thankfully the hole in Hendricks' head has settled. Instead of churning into itself, it is now a still and oddly sterile—if uncannily large—gap. On the couch beside Hendricks' body, Alyssa sprays out a strange symbol, a circle with two sides of a triangle, pointing right, and a line dead through the center.

We retreat from the lifeless body of the carriage magnate, leaving him to his dying fire and his rumpled carriage bed.

I don't speak the entire way out. All is still quiet. I wonder how long it will be before anyone realizes that Roland is dead.

I didn't kill him, but it feels like I may as well have.

Worse, or better, I don't know, I wanted to kill him. Worse, or better, I don't know, he wanted me to kill him. There was nothing but drunken honesty in his eyes. He could have changed, maybe, but if he knew exactly what he was, if he had always known it, then there's no reason to think he would have. He was a despicable man, who lived despicably, in full awareness of how despicable he was. I feel as if I've looked into the deepest chasm of humanity, and discovered a secret at its core.

I don't know if I like the way humanity looks when you take that plunge.

I try to focus on my own ends. Carl will tell me the location of the exit now. The workers will no longer have to put up with Roland's shit. That's two problems solved at once. We take the long route back, avoiding the spinning boxes on our way to our waiting carriage.

But when we emerge from the tunnel, there is no carriage. Instead a pair of Vespas—sky blue and teal in color—is parked in the ruts our carriage left behind.

"You've gotta be freakin' kidding me," Alyssa says. One of the Vespas has a note attached to its handle.

Please refill tank before returning. Thanks!

A low wail begins within the estate house. The earth beneath us shakes, as the wail grows into a high scream. There's a mournful tenor to it, but beneath that is pure rage.

"Let's go," Alyssa says, and I don't need any more encouragement or a reminder that I've never ridden one of these in order to jump on one of the Vespas and yank the throttle. We peel out over uneven ground. My hands shake as I try to keep the front wheel steady in the carriage tracks. The number on my wrist device climbs quickly, seemingly with each turn of the Vespa's wheel.

Behind us, a sound like heavy machinery churning through hard earth rips the air, and something bursts out of the ground.

I chance a look over my shoulder, and immediately wish I hadn't. A bright blue carriage has erupted through the earth. The golden waves at its edges roil, not merely an ornamental illusion, but actually morphing as it blazes through the night. At its head sits a tall, slanted man in pinstriped pajamas and a bathrobe. He has a hole through his head, and his eyes burn the same blue as the carriage. He lashes the reins, and the skeletal horse pulling the carriage surges forward. The horse's existence is fuzzy around the edges, but its blue eyes match its master. Whether this version of Hendricks is living or dead, or something different entirely, I can't say. I put my head down and turn the throttle as far as it will go.

We skid out onto the main road. Golden waves roll off the spectral carriage as it rockets onto the road behind us. Alyssa shouts over her shoulder, but her words are ripped away by the wind and Hendricks' screams of rage.

Bales of hay enclose the road, rising to form a tunnel. We're moving toward the skyscraper, that incongruous structure that forms the primary landmark on the otherwise flat surface of the plain.

Though the Vespas move with uncanny speed, the carriage is gaining with each passing moment. The ghostly horse pulls the massive carriage with impossible strength. It swings its charge wildly from side to side, smashing hay bales into oblivion.

A rain of hay falls around us. It becomes so thick that I have to look straight down to discern the road's edges. When I look up, the air has a cold tinge to it. The hay lashes against my skin, growing finer and finer until it becomes a thick haze of snow. My vehicle's tires, ill-suited to anything but manicured city roads, now churn through several inches of snow, which grows into drifts that already obscure the hay bales.

I can no longer make out Alyssa ahead of me. Behind are two sets of blue eyes, burning in the dark. Hendricks' shrieks have become indistinguishable from the wind.

Absently I notice the goggles that now cover my eyes and offer the faintest promise of visibility. My hands are uncovered, though, and they're already numb. Digits change wildly on my wrist, too fast to read.

Silver shapes spring out of the snow along each side of the road, leaping and disappearing. I catch a glimpse of shimmering fur and vulpine muzzles. The silver creatures are smaller than any foxes I've seen, but have the same lithe build, and follow the chase as if by instinct.

An unsettling sensation grows behind me. Heat. I snap my head back. The horse's face is directly over my shoulder, mouth gaping. My stomach winces, and throttle range I wasn't sure existed gives me a kick of speed. The Vespa whines.

We shoot past the looming rise of the skyscraper. As if they were waiting for us, a half dozen motorcycles dart out of the haze shrouding the entrance gate. They project flashing green lights into the snow, and police sirens join the din.

I swerve as a team of cross-country skiers glides across the road in front of me. Snow sprays as the Vespa slips sideways, then rights itself. The skiers disappear into the night. The motorcycles form up into a semicircle behind Hendricks' carriage. His screams are now in frustration as well as anger.

An annoyingly familiar melody finds me out of the snow. My eyes catch on a large blocky shape, driving on the other side of a snow bank. It churns a deep, non-linear furrow through the fields.

The distinct shape of a soft serve ice cream cone juts from one corner of its roof.

The melody takes me to quiet summer streets, heat rising from concrete. A laconic rush to find enough change on the way out the front door.

The ice cream truck veers suddenly, plowing through the snow bank to my right, and swerving across the road. There's a muted crunch as it lodges itself in the snow bank on the opposite side.

I realize too late that the truck is blocking the entire road, and slam on my Vespa's brakes. I skid. I fishtail. The bike slides out from under me, and I disappear into a soft bed of snow, settling feet away from the crashed truck.

Snow pulls down on my limbs, and I try to rise to face the terrible eyes of my pursuer. But Hendricks' carriage has stopped about two-dozen yards away, the six motorcycle riders parked around it. Green lights flash from them, as the riders approach in choreographed formation. They hold long weapons that vaguely resemble pistols, but which end in circular rings. The rings emit a hum.

White helmets and navy jackets give the riders the look of policemen. To a person, their eyes are shaded by sunglasses. I make it to a kneeling position just as they brandish their weapons. As the hum grows, Hendricks thrashes in his carriage, and the horse rears.

The riders do not slow or speed up. They continue forward, one careful step after careful step. Hendricks is powerless before them. His screams dissolve into the hum.

With one final look at me through raging blue eyes, Hendricks crumples inward, folding himself first into the hole in his head, and then into nothingness.

Abruptly carriage, driver, and horse disappear. The hum stops. Green lights flash through the falling snow. The garbled music of the smashed ice cream truck continues halfheartedly.

The riders form a line in front of me. I can't rise further than my knees. Their features are indistinguishable, and if there's an expression on them, I can't make it out through the falling snow.

I'm a man kneeling before a firing squad, and I can't find anything further within me to escape my fate.

Then they turn back to their motorcycles. With a dull roar, their flashing lights recede. I am alone on the road. The ice cream truck's jingle continues, but after the cacophony of the last few minutes, it sounds like silence. My Vespa lies in a crumpled mess beneath the truck.

I abandon it, skirt around the far edge of the truck, and begin the long trek back to Valdrada.

The Carnival - Valdrada

"**A**re you F-ing insane?" June says. We're at Night and Dragon.

"I mean yeah probably," I say. "But why is it crazy to bump off an evil corporatist overlord? They make movies about that."

June turns me into a piece of satay with her look.

"You can do anything here," she says. "Pretty messed up to use that ability to kill someone vital to the functioning of the Carnival."

"I wasn't actually the one who killed him." That sentence doesn't sit well between us, but I'm in no mood to back down. "You and Bailly act like this is some Garden of Eden. That's not the Carnival I've experienced."

"You're being incredibly childish. Just because you don't know how to tell a halfway decent story—"

"Bullshit."

"Oh, it's bullshit?" Her mug of beer lies forgotten, the foam forming a lattice climbing up the inside of the mug. "Your union organizing got a little complicated and what do you do? Instead of finding a solution, you murder the owner. You do realize that without Hendricks, more than likely the factory will shut down permanently."

"It's worth it," I mutter. The performance on the bar's stage tonight is a single trumpet that blows blue steam as it plays a mournful solo. I stare down at the table.

"Eyes up, Matthew," June says, grabbing my chin and forces me to look into her eyes. There's sweat on her fingers. Is that an edge of panic in her voice?

"Carl has promised me information. About the Carnival. About the Wasteland, the Substratum, and beyond. I'm just trying to gain a little perspective."

"Perspective is overrated."

I'm tempted to get up and leave, but that would feel too much like running away.

"I wonder," I say. "If Hendricks had a little perspective, maybe he wouldn't have repeatedly screwed over his workers."

"Sure, let's play hypothetical games. Great time for it, now that you've probably incited a war."

"You should've heard him. He had no remorse at all for re-peatedly exploiting his workers. The way he told it was like his actions had been pre-determined. He believed he was a bad guy, so he would always behave like a bad guy."

"For the record, he was a bad guy," June says. "That doesn't mean you had to waste the poor bastard."

"Setting aside the fact that it was Alyssa who did it, all I'm saying is that his narrative shaped his reality. That's all. And a narrative without perspective sounds like a recipe for a limited reality."

"You're missing the point. The Carnival is infinite. Infinite perspective? Oh yeah, you're right, we totally need to look beyond that. So limiting."

I give an exasperated sigh. This is going nowhere.

"Carl's meeting me soon," I say. "I'm sure you could stick around for what he has to tell me. Or you can go screw off into your infinite perspective."

We don't have to wait long. Good thing, too, since June spends the entire time with her arms crossed, occasionally making passive-aggressive comments about my intelligence.

Carl slides into the booth beside me, and Alyssa—somewhat rudely—encroaches on June's space on the other side.

"June," Carl says. "A pleasure as always."

"If you say so," she says. "You brought your harpy with you."

Alyssa gives her a smile, revealing pointed teeth.

"I'm sure with a little luck we can all manage to be civil," Carl says. There's real concern in his eyes as he puts an arm over my shoulder. "Are you all right? I know how much I've asked of you, but I'm told the two of you came through with flying colors."

Alyssa mimes firing a pistol. "Straight to the head."

June and I shudder.

"You are to be commended," Carl says. "A lot of people will suffer far less with Hendricks out of the picture. Anyhow, a large favor demands a large reward."

"I thought the reward was the destruction that's about to be unleashed," June says.

"Funny, how June only ever seems to care about things that happen in relation to the struggle between the Armageddeons and the Apocalyptians," Carl says.

"That should be all you care about too," June replies.

"Come on, both of you," I say. I'll have to ask June what Carl means later. Based on the anger in June's words, I sense that Hendricks' death has somehow changed the dynamic between the warring sides. I'm finding it hard to care about that at the moment. "Like you said, now's the time for the reward."

Carl smiles. "I've told you there's an exit. It's not a door, or a passage through the mountains like the Substratum. Fitting, I think you'll agree, that the exit to the Carnival is not something you can just walk out of."

"Nor should you," June says.

"That's not up to me," Carl replies. "There's no door, but I've heard that one could board a Brooklyn-bound F train from West 4th Street-Washington Square Station. That, under the right circumstances, one's train would never make it to Brooklyn."

I don't recall West 4th Street ever being a particularly pleasant station, and that's even true here. The multilevel maze of criss-crossing platforms is not exactly as I remember it—and I do remember it—but it's close enough that I don't have any trouble finding the F platform on the lower level. A drummer is playing a rapid beat on a set of buckets. People line the platform, though not enough for it to be during commuting hours. Sweat sticks under my collar, and when the train clatters into the station and the doors open, the car's air conditioning follows the riders onto the platform.

June and I let four trains go before I climb into the car. We sit on the far side next to a woman with a tiny white dog tucked into a tote bag between her legs.

"Is this it?" I say to June.

"I'm sure all of your questions will be answered by getting on underfunded public transportation." Her glare tells me she's mostly here to see me fail. I had noticed her looking up a few times as we travelled the streets to the station, as if expecting some threat from the horizon.

"Stand clear of the closing doors, please," calls out the train announcer's obnoxiously cordial voice.

June points to the device on my wrist, which now displays three emojis of subway train cars.

The car is clean, one of the newer trains with the light blue seats along the walls. As the doors close I catch sight of the drummer on the platform, a young man about my age meeting his girlfriend by the benches, and a man steering a cart filled with bottles past them.

The train rumbles into the dark tunnel. I feel anticipation building. What's next? I can never remember if it's supposed to be East Broadway or Broadway-Lafayette.

The Carnival is a mirror. Everything here is a reflection of something else. What is this dingy subway platform reflecting?

When we emerge in the next station, I feel dizzy. The signs on the support beams read *W4*.

June laughs out loud. "I guess we never made it to Brooklyn."

"Carl said under the right circumstances," I say. "This can't be what he meant."

"It would be funnier if it didn't involve you essentially murdering someone for this information. But it's still pretty damn funny."

As the doors open, a few people get off. The woman with the dog still sits next to us. The bucket drums blast into the car. A young man meets his girlfriend on the platform as a person pushes a cart filled with bottles behind them.

"Stand clear of the closing doors, please."

We sit for a while, June seeming more and more jubilant at my failure with every passing moment. Each time, the train pulls out of West 4th Street and then moments later arrives at West 4th Street. Even the people on the platform are the same each time. A finance bro takes a last pull on his vape. An older woman wraps her arm around her husband's, as if to protect him from the arriving train. A group of northern European tourists heft their backpacks. A teenage boy offers a pregnant woman her seat, but she turns him down. She's reading a beat-up copy of *The Faerie Queene*.

After the fourth time pulling into the station June gets off, saying she prefers to take the bus. I watch her disappear up the stairs as we rocket back into the tunnel. Good. Her absence is definitely preferable to her presence right now.

I don't know how long I ride this train to nowhere. It's probably several hours, though I've lost count of the number of times the automated voice has told me to, "Stand clear of the closing doors, please." After a while the voice is so drilled into my head that I begin to feel as if he's speaking directly to me. The doors close, a man pulls his bicycle out of the way in the nick of time, and a few people jockey for position on the center pole.

"Stand clear of the closing doors, please."

This can't be all. It's a sick trick. I imagine I could spend a hundred years on this train, riding in and out of this station, and return to find the world unchanged. And if I came back here in another hundred years, the electronic voice above would still remind me to:

"Stand clear of the closing doors, please."

With each return it's as if the train is speeding up, the time it takes to speed underground and re-emerge shortening to nothing.

"Stand clear of the closing doors, please."

"Stand clear of the closing doors, please."

The hope of the last few hours...

"Stand clear of the closing doors, please."

...the horror of what I've done...

"Stand clear of the closing doors, please."

"Stand clear of the closing doors, please."

...evaporates to nothing.

"Stand clear—"

The doors snap shut behind me as I march onto the platform. I push past the young man and his girlfriend, past the drummer, past the person pushing their cart of bottles, and climb back up, out of this awful place, leaving behind its horrible promise.

When I surface, the sky is dark, the streets quiet save for one elf, who turns his crank at a mournfully slow pace, serenading a half dozen microgriffs. For the first time I can't see the stars here, and it feels fitting. I wander alone, over cobblestones and paved sidewalks, having to avoid carriages and at least one trolley lumbering past. But where before wandering revealed wonders both benign and threatening, there is no strangeness here any-more, only a city asleep, restless, slumbering in fits and starts. I walk until the bottoms of my feet ache. Everywhere I go, I see the elves with their pointless boxes, turning their compulsive cranks. It's as if everyone else has been banished from the streets. I walk through wind and calm, and don't stop until I've wound back to my inn.

But rather than leading to my room, the door opens onto a terrace overlooking a courtyard. I look down three stories onto an empty tile floor. Vines entangle terraces in a square around me. This is new. And inconvenient. There's an open balcony directly across the courtyard. Through it I can clearly see my room, down to the polo shirt I left over the back of the desk chair. Unless my observational skills or memory have severely declined, I'm pretty sure my room didn't have a balcony.

As I move closer to get a better view, the air shimmers before me. A clear surface that distorts light extends from the balcony. I study it from another angle. There's clearly a flat surface, at least two feet wide, reaching all the way across the courtyard to my room on the other side.

I look down at the drop. Those tiles look hard. But after everything I've been through today, all I want is to collapse into my bed. The sound of turning cranks reaches me, even here.

I step onto the balcony's ledge.

Whatever the clear surface is made of, it's thick enough to bear my weight. It doesn't even creak as I take a first halting step onto it.

This is beyond disconcerting. I'm walking on a solid structure but when I look down, all I can see is tile, which arrays itself in a consistent checkerboard of black and white. I focus on feeling rather than seeing the surface.

As I near the middle of the courtyard, I notice that the vines that had been confined to the terraces now extend all the way down the walls. Not only that, but they're growing downward. I can't quicken my pace, though I want to. Soon the vines cover the entire tile floor, and begin growing straight upward. I stumble, having to steady myself on one knee. The rapid growth of plant life throws the world into vertiginous motion. I rise and continue forward. The vines curl around the walkway in front of me, for the first time putting the structure into clear relief. My feet slip over the uneven, slick vines.

Plant growth thickens in the air around me. The change is so quick that I barely have time to dodge backward as one of the vines becomes a massive branch and smacks downward onto the walkway. The entire structure shakes. *WHACK*. Another vine has become a bulbous swatting branch. Another catches me across the calves, sending me roughly back to my knees. I get up, ignoring the smashing motion of a now thick branch. The entire courtyard has become a mass of violent green. As it intensifies, I sprint forward, heedless of where the walkway ends and the air begins. The vines are now so thick that I could practically walk on them in any direction. I can still see the window of my room ahead, but it's closing fast. I run, eyes on the rapidly diminishing patch of light, ignoring the scratches and smacks of the vegetation.

I dive over the terrace wall, landing awkwardly on the floor and rolling into the bed frame. The vines dive toward me. I slam the shutters closed, and bolt them into place. For a second there's a battering sound, and I brace against the shutters for dear life.

But then the sound stops. The shutters still. Only my own breathing and the pulse of my heart fill the room. I risk a peek through the gap between the shutters. All I can see is a narrow ground floor alley with a gravel walkway. On the other side of the walkway, a spindly vine grows up the wall. It looks like it could use some water. Its leaves are brown, frail, and motion-less.

I close the shutters. I try to sleep, but at any moment I feel like the windows will shatter in a storm of vines. More, there is an expectancy building in the air, like that preceding a great storm. I can barely keep my eyes closed. Finally, I carry my blankets into the bathroom and fall asleep in the bathtub, expecting to wake up somewhere unexpected.

I wake up in the same bathtub, but it can't be long after I fell asleep—morning hasn't yet pushed aside the dark, and the ground is trembling. I rush outside onto the street, joining crowds of people. On the opposite side of the street, there are now close to one-hundred elves in a single line. They crank faster, in perfect rhythm, and with each turn of their handles the ground shakes. The wall behind them is filled with microgriffs, packed so densely they're almost a single entity. June, her hair a tangle of sleep, appears beside me.

"Stop!" she yells at the elves. "Stop!" But they've lost either the will or the capacity to listen.

"We've gotta get the hell out of here," June says. "The Apocalyptians have come." As if on cue, the microgriffs burst upwards, blotting out the sky with their wings. There is nothing beautiful about them now.

We sprint down alleyways, June leading the way. The ground continues to lurch from side to side, and everywhere the streets are lined with the elves and their wooden boxes. We turn onto a main road and pull back as a beast twice as large as a Hendricks carriage bounds past, plumes of feathers trailing behind it. A crowd of fleeing civilians runs before it. One by one it crushes them with its massive jaws. Microgriffs screech overhead, pecking and breathing their tiny fires at anyone they can get their talons on. Another of the massive creatures runs in long, floating bounds in the opposite direction, as if the bonds of gravity do not apply. We turn back to the alleys.

"What the hell was that?" I have to slap away a rogue microgriff who is trying to peck my face.

"The Apocalyptians have unleashed their entire arsenal on us. Nowhere in Valdrada is safe."

We don't get much farther before a flaming projectile smashes into the house next to us, engulfing its wood frame in flames.

"I thought you were supposed to be negotiating a truce," I say.

"Not much you can do when one of the captains of the Apocalyptians gets murdered and the Armageddeons take credit for it."

"What?"

"Hendricks, you mushy pile of rotting grapefruit. He was a leader and primary financier, and some idiot left the symbol of the Armageddeons at the scene of his murder."

I think back to the symbol Alyssa spray-painted on the couch after she shot Hendricks. But why would she do that? Carl can't have wanted this.

I wish June could fly us away, but we are not in the mountains, places where soaring is part of the essence of the place. Here, we are horribly limited to the blocked and burning streets.

June shoves a burning pole out of the way to clear the path in front of us, and out of the space behind it emerges a giant head with slavering jaws. The creature's moist, scaly hide reflects the burning wreckage next to us. It roars.

I am here, I am not here. I am between the creature's teeth, I am looking on from a hundred yards away.

It lunges, but June is there to meet it, brandishing a flaming piece of wood the length of a shower rod and three times as thick. She slams it into the top of the creature's mouth, and it bellows with rage. Its skin hisses as it burns.

A paw slaps June to the side, almost an afterthought as the creature recoils. June lies stunned against the building, with smoke billowing around her. I charge forward to stand between the beast and June. I am weaponless, without any sort of plan, but I stand there nonetheless, as the monster scrunches its mouth, considering the best way to bite my head off.

I could run. I could abandon June to whatever fate this creature has decided for her. I try to make something happen, to slide beneath the slippery surface of the Carnival, maybe make a weapon appear in my hand, or imagine a passageway out of here. But the more I try, the more I am rooted to the spot, the less powerful I feel, and the larger the behemoth becomes.

The creature pounces with the full force of its tons of scaly muscle.

I feel a wrenching sensation, like I'm being tugged by the spinal cord, and then I am floating above the burning town, directly above the confused monster. With a flash, June floats beside me, still unconscious, her arms splayed at unsettling angles. The creature roars its rage, before bulldozing through the burning house and continuing its path of destruction.

Bailly appears near me, eyes on the destruction below. Ten to fifteen monsters tear through town. Elves flank them with their boxes.

"What are those things?" I ask, breathless.

"The first wave," Bailly says. I can't read any emotion in his voice. "Ah, right on schedule. The Apocalyptians."

If the monsters sent by the Apocalyptians are frightening, the Apocalyptians themselves are a thousand times worse. They march in rows five abreast through the main gate, and though they may have been human once, there's nothing human about them now. Their flesh is molded to sticks and pieces of bark, and from each protrudes a riot of sharp wooden edges. Dark triangles of painted wood have been attached at their brows, shading their eyes. Most wield scythes, which they swing with the grace and determination of an army of reapers. They chant as they cut down person after person.

"We have to do something," I say. I watch as a swarm of microgriffs overruns a fleeing carriage, turning the hard wood into splinters and tearing the people inside to pieces in seconds.

"They began evacuating as soon as the attack started," Bailly says. At the train station, a last group of people is climbing aboard before the doors close. "Everyone who could get out is out. You can't stand in the way of the Apocalyptians and survive."

"What about Mini? Jer? D'Angeline? They could still be down there."

"D'Angeline is safe. I would not let any harm come to her. The others will have to make their own way, just as you have."

I realize we're moving away from the fighting, toward the mountains outside of town.

"We can't leave," I say.

"It's too late."

"It's not—"

The ground, which had been shuddering throughout the assault as the elves turned their cranks, now visibly buckles. The entire circle of Valdrada's walls trembles, and collapses. A deafening grating sound follows, and the earth where the walls once stood gives way. I watch in horror as it falls into a single circular sinkhole, the edges growing to swallow Valdrada whole.

Overhead, a black shape circles. Its wings look almost like fabric, stretched out to a massive width. It's too far away to see its face, but as it flashes past us I catch a hint of pale, blurry features, distorted but human, surrounded by stiff blackness. It observes soundlessly. When it departs, it leaves only more darkness behind it.

Bailly's eyes are transfixed by the falling city. The Apocalyptians are fleeing. They call to each other in harsh cries of fear and anger. They clearly aren't doing this. This is some other force, something much older, much deeper. Almost none escape as the city disappears into the now mile-wide hole. Civilians, soldiers, and monsters alike plunge into the depths.

We float above an empty space. All is silent except for the rush of wind.

I look down into the pit where Valdrada used to stand. Survivors scramble around a cluster of trees rising from the debris. They are tall and nestled close together. The fertile earth holding their roots churns slowly upward, until it is halfway between the bottom of the pit and ground level.

"The Grove." June holds her forehead, but her eyes are clear. "Is this the Unmaking?"

Bailly shakes his head.

"I guess it's only Valdrada," June says. "Jesus Christ, if this were the whole world..."

Past the outskirts of town, nothing has changed. The train with refugees aboard still makes its way toward the steel city, and the river still runs down from the dam in the mountains, past the skyscraper that points up inexplicably from the country road. But where the river used to meet large waterwheels at the edge of town, it now drops into the chasm in a muddy waterfall.

I think I glimpse one of the F trains, torn from its track and smashed. Good riddance.

"That took out hundreds of Apocalyptians," I say.

"It must've been the Armageddeons," June replies. "They got the Grove to act at the precise moment they needed it to."

"It would appear so," Bailly says. "In any case, the war you've been working to avoid has begun, and the contours of the two factions will never be the same. Your work is done, for now."

June's face is pure fury.

"You did well, Juniper." Bailly's soft voice doesn't set her at ease. "There was nothing more you could've done—some stories only have one ending."

"I thought that if I understood them, if I really learned what they wanted, they wouldn't be so goddamned set on killing each other."

"Not everyone is capable of change," Bailly says.

"I don't believe that."

I keep my eyes downturned to avoid her wrath. But when I look up, her fiery eyes are locked on me.

"You know what I did in my first couple of weeks here?" she asks. "I went exploring in the caves in the mountains. There's an aquatic species of people that lives in the underground rivers. Their princess had been kidnapped by a rival tribe. I found the princess, rescued her, and established peace. There were challenges along the way—a jealous brother who was in love with the princess, inter-tribe rivalries, even a swimming contest to the deepest point of the caves—but you know what didn't happen? At the end of it, there wasn't a giant hole where their civilization once stood, and no one ended up dead."

"I'm sorry," I say. "I didn't mean to hurt anyone."

"Should probably tell that to Hendricks, assuming he can hear through the bullet hole."

"I'm sorry."

"Please. You've never believed in this place. You've always thought that you were better than it, that if you found a way out it would disappear. Well guess what? This is real. This is all real, and you're deluding yourself to think it doesn't matter. This is my home. You're not trying to tell a story yourself, you're just trying to destroy mine."

After all the effort she's spent convincing me to stay, I know I've crossed a huge red line if she now wants me to leave. Though a part of me wonders if getting me to stay was ever really her idea—Bailly has been behind her this whole way.

Bailly stands to the side—his posture is so rigid it's easy to forget we're still floating—his hands crossed at his waist.

"I'll go as far away as I can," I say. "Bailly, can you help me?"

"I have a suitable destination in mind. It's still within the Carnival, but out toward the fringes. Is that okay with you, June?"

"Yes. I think I should spend some time in the steel city. The survivors have to be looked after."

"Good," Bailly says. "You will find that the train is still operational. It arrived moments ago at the station outside of town with a full team of rescue personnel."

"Thank you," June says, before turning to me. "Until next time, you giant ball of coagulated—"

June disappears, and I'm left alone with Bailly.

"You are no more responsible for this than anyone else," Bailly says.

"Thanks."

"Carl played you. He knew he could use your curiosity to accomplish his own ends."

"I don't understand why he would do that," I say. "Carl was always kind to me."

"Carl's motives are his own," he says. Not for the first time I catch the faintest resemblance between them, something about the way his strong top lip splays. He scowls as if Carl is a vexation on the order of a particularly resilient rodent infestation. I don't think I could personally bring myself to speak with Carl again, even if he does know a way out of the Carnival. "The Grove would've risen eventually, and when it did, it would have consumed the entire world. You've actually prevented this subsuming process—the Unmaking—from occurring for many years. It will be a long time before the Grove's temper blooms again."

The rescue crews from the steel city have begun rappelling into the gorge. A flock of aircraft, hovering on blue jets, projects searchlights into the depths.

Bailly says, "I'm sorry your entry here has been this dramatic, but you've taken a plunge few would've taken. I hope with a little time and reflection you'll see that there's been some value to this. There's still more story left to be told. A different story."

In that moment I wish for a father like Bailly, someone who will tell me it's not my fault when things go south, who will walk me back from the abyss of my own despair.

I wish I had a father. That wish comes back to me now, not from outside, but deep below the surface.

Other wishes pull themselves up with this thought, like garbage caught in a trawling net. Seething anger rises in me, and images come with it. I'm yelling, telling my father to pull over, that he's not in any shape to be driving. This isn't the first time he's come straight from the bar to pick me up from school, but it's by far the worst. A good drinker doesn't slur their words when they've had a few too many, but he sure as hell did that day. Ironic that the fight was about the drinking, and that it ended with a disoriented wrench of the wheel, an overshoot of the exit, and complete blackness.

When I came back to consciousness, the first thing I remembered was the point I was trying to make. The interruption was so sudden the argument had continued in my mind even as my world had been ripped apart.

"I'm sorry," I say. I'm shaking in fear and recognition as I piece together the images I saw in the factory, and under Bailly's guidance. I can follow them as far back as the circle in front of my high school where parents would wait to pick their kids up. I was alone. He was already late, and I was ready for a fight. Getting into the car and being overwhelmed by the smell of liquor set me off. Things would've been different if I'd let him drive me home, if I'd let mom ream him out instead of doing it in the car, with his already compromised faculties. They were on the way out already. Maybe she'd have left him for good then. At the very least I'd still have someone who I could call a father.

Then I wouldn't need to look at someone like Bailly and wish. A firm hand, a clear mind, not wracked by whatever monstrous anxiety tore at my own dad. And unlike Carl, Bailly's at least not a manipulative psychopath.

"Where can I go?" I say. "I don't want to ruin anything more for June."

"There's a chain of islands far off the shore. They have a few names, but the most common is the While Isles. It's far enough from June, and I get the sense some sun and time on the beach could be good for you."

"I'd like that," I say. The images are fading, but I can still hear my heart hammering away in my chest, each beat like the brass stroke of a tower clock.

Bailly puts an arm around my shoulder. This time there is no jerking sensation, nothing but pleasant calm as we evaporate from existence and reappear on a sandy shore. Gentle waves roll in. I take off my shoes and let them float away on the waves. The cold water is soothing on my feet. The black band on my wrist judders and the number wink out, replaced by *000*. Then *001*.

Across a lapis lazuli sea, there is only a hint of a far shore. A fresh start.

"I must return to my own shore," Bailly says. Thankfully the hole where the city used to be isn't visible from this distance. "But I am close, and know that June is too, should you need her. At some point she will remember that you gave her something no one else could."

I turn my eyes from the far shore, and walk up the beach to where mangroves join the sand. I don't look back to watch Bailly go.

The Carnival - The While Isles

Time passes on the While Isles, but sometimes it does so in slightly the wrong order. My first weeks there are marked by exhaustion. There was a heaviness in my spirit that even meeting the local population and learning their customs couldn't erase. For the most part they let me be—as inhabitants of an island where food is plentiful and conflict scarce, it was no great burden to feed me, put a shelter over my head, and otherwise allow me to roam the island or lounge in the sand as I pleased. They even supplied me with a canoe I could use to paddle between the islands, but during my first week I was pulled so far out to sea on one such venture that the Whileans had to tow me back to shore. No one in these islands can use creative influence to manipulate water, and I'm obviously no exception. The only things that work here are acts of magic that capture something else—perfect facsimiles of faces carved into trees, inscribed tablets that describe historical events in such detail you can actually see them when you read the page—but nothing that changes the existing world in a tangible way. After that outing, I kept my sea voyages to the narrower passages between the three central islands, and let the others remain a mystery.

The Whileans live in circular houses constructed out of driftwood and shaded from the sun with palm fronds. A peculiar pink fungus is omnipresent on the island, growing primarily on the rocks at the water's edge and giving the shore the perpetual impression of sunset. The Whileans use this fungus for almost all of their furniture, padding their beds and chairs with the springy growth, which fades into a reddish brown once removed from its native substrate. Their villages mirror the construction of the houses, forming concentric (and perfectly circular) rings around a central pavilion. For the most part the Whileans spend their time in the pavilion if they're not out fishing or foraging. The While Isles are always hot, and I soon take after the local custom and go without a shirt, keeping only a scrap of cloth tucked into my belt loop to wipe the sweat from my brow.

While they are welcoming, the Whileans take some getting used to. They are prone to disappearing from a conversation, getting lost in thought and only re-emerging minutes later with an answer to a now ancient question. I soon came to understand the reason for this: from birth, every Whilean is required to learn the complete history of an entire era of the Carnival. Every major movement within Valdrada, every development made in the steel city, all the political maneuverings of the mountain cities in the north, and of course the history-making wars of the Apocalyptians and Armageddeons. All of this is passed down through generations, with each person focusing on a slightly different era, so every century has a definitive expert. Debates on historical subjects often go deep into the night as the fire burns low beneath their pavilion.

My first friend on the While Isles is Kereus, the nephew of the island's Provost. Though he's a year or two younger than me, it's often hard to gauge with the Whileans, as their normal growth through childhood and their teenage years is secondary to their historical study.

Kereus and I are out checking the traps in the shallows nearest the village. Most days the traps would catch one or two of the large crustaceans that feed in the tidal area, but today there must have been a school passing, because nearly every trap is crammed full. We already had to go back once for another set of buckets to carry them. As we work, I ask whether the Whileans ever consider leaving the islands for the rest of the Carnival. Kereus gets the far-off look he often does when diving back into the past. Used to it by now, I let the silence pass.

"When we are sent out as emissaries to the Carnival, to live among them and learn their present history, we see everything it has to offer," he says. Even the younger Whileans speak with a grave voice that seems to contain the weight of history. "Some have been tempted to live among them permanently. But life in the Carnival is one lived in the present, a moment by moment unfolding. Whileans are not designed to live in this way. If we do not understand the past in its fullness, we will never be content in the present. Here I can turn to my brother or my aunt and ask why a certain tree is in a certain place, why a village was moved from one location to another, why our boats are built with a flat hull rather than a round one, and I will always receive a true answer. In the Carnival if you ask why a certain dish is seasoned with sugar instead of salt, you will receive a hundred different answers, almost all of which will be incorrect, and the majority of which will amount to 'it doesn't matter.' Most of us cannot stand to live long under these conditions."

"Have you ever left as an emissary?" I ask.

"Only adults are sent out. This ensures that we have already adequately learned our section of history, and are prepared to live on our own if we are displaced."

"Displaced?"

Kereus pulls one of the traps out of the water, and yanks it open with his strong arms. He plunges his hand in, grabbing the crustacean by the midsection—between the spiny tail and the reach of the powerful front pincers—and tosses it to me. This is as close to a game as the Whileans have, and I've gotten reasonably good within the three weeks I've been here. I catch the crustacean in the same spot, only lightly brushing the spines, and deposit the screaming creature in the bucket on top of its squirming brethren.

"Displacement is the thing we fear most. When the temporal hurricanes strike the islands, anyone on the mainland will remain in their current time, while back home, everyone moves forward or backward. Fortunately most displacements are short, but some Whileans have returned only to find that the islands they knew have become the islands of one-hundred years ago."

"What happens if you return to a time where you already exist? Does the universe collapse or something?"

Kereus doesn't laugh. Pretty much ever. But I've never needed anyone to laugh at my jokes in order to keep making them.

"You know Quissea, scholar of the era of The Small Kingdom? He is his own father."

He might not be prone to levity, but Kereus understands how strange this is to me, and smiles. He tosses an empty trap back in the water before saying, "We make it work."

In those early weeks I ask a lot of questions about the Whileans and their customs. But when it comes to the history itself, I find I can't bring myself to inquire about the Carnival's underpinnings. I know there's a Brooklyn-bound F train that's supposed to be the way out, but I'm done asking these kinds of questions. Whenever I do, people die, and the truth feels further away. I consider whether I should see if Bailly would be willing to supply me with more memories, but my most recent plunge into those particular waters brought only pain as well. And something about the While Isles makes me feel that memory isn't so far away.

Sometimes I listen to the stories being told in the pavilion, but for the most part I remove myself. Evening is a pleasant time to be on the shore, where waves wash over the sand, cool nighttime breeze stirs the palms, and mountains of water suddenly rise when one of the leviathans that populates the deeper areas offshore comes to the surface. There is a lot I could be thinking over, especially after the chaos I've witnessed, but I find it easier to set the thought aside. How humane to be as separate from the madness of the rest of the Carnival as the Whileans are, only needing to chart the course of events rather than participating in them. Even the chaotic flashbacks I experienced in the aftermath of Valdrada's destruction have faded into the background.

A good part of my distraction can probably be attributed to Curi. I first noticed her staring at me openly across the fire at dinner one evening, about a month into my time here. She had been investigating me for quite a while, but that was just as I was coming out of the haze of the dissociative limbo I'd arrived in. The green of her eyes was the first pinprick of color in a black and white world, and I came suddenly and sharply into myself, back into a reality I'd forgotten existed. She didn't look away, and I dropped my eyes to my bowl, feeling my heart beating wildly in my ears.

I asked Kereus about her (probably regrettable that I phrased it "what's her deal?") and he responded simply, "That's my cousin Curi, the Provost's daughter. You think she's beautiful, don't you?"

And I did. I got used to those eyes watching me over the coming days, and I returned the gaze carefully. The intense curiosity behind it intrigued me. Besides that, she had a cute, pointed face that in other places or times might have been described as dainty. The active life of the Whileans gave her a strong body, and the short skirts she wore made it difficult to keep my eyes off her long, slender legs. Two long weeks passed after that, and she would pop up in the most random places—improbably gathering driftwood outside my hut in the morning, mending a trap as I came to collect it, and always sitting within view of me at the evening meal and nightly debates. Every time, my stomach would drop into my knees, wobble there for a minute, then come back up to form a nervous lump in my throat. Whether it was the feeling of being watched or the thought that she had deigned to make me a part of her visual experience, it was difficult to say. I found myself thinking about her when I would wander alone, or in my hut at night, thinking about those eyes, fantasizing about what it would be like to be near her.

Every time I plan to talk to her, my throat goes into ana-phylaxis. With my inability to make any kind of introduction, it's several weeks until I finally do something strange enough to catch her attention.

This afternoon, I'm alone on the beach. I spent the better portion of two hours building a scale model of the Carnival out of sand, with intricate buildings and a wall approximating Valdrada, and a ravine for the valley beyond it. I had noted the high tide point, and built my model slightly below it as the water closed in. I've tapped into the one type of creative influence that works here, and the model is far more accurate than I could have ever managed on an ordinary beach.

The water is still several feet from my walled town when I hear voices in the trees. A trio of young women is passing, laughing and chatting with each other. They treat me as an odd but not unwelcome part of the landscape, as most Whileans do. But after the voices have passed, a presence remains at the border of the trees. I look up to see a face watching me.

I could say nothing, let her keep watching me until she loses interest. Momentum tugs me in this direction, toward the eas-iness of silence, but I let words skip the part of my brain that thinks better of it and speak broadly to the tree-line.

"Today's performance, entitled 'The Destruction of the Carnival Due to Time and Being Built Out of Inferior Building Materials' begins now. Tickets are free for those guests willing to sit on sand rather than seats. Our premium tickets have already been sold out, as there were none to begin with."

I sense a pause as Curi evaluates my odd behavior.

"The story we observe today is an old one, and not particularly well-plotted. However, it does present the innate pleasure of watching something it took hours to build get washed away in the matter of minutes. It has been called, by one critic, 'not quite as dull as watching someone else read a book.'"

I bend down and put the finishing touches on my train station. I try to remember how many benches were on the platform, and opt for two side-by-side. They easily come into relief.

I peek back up toward the trees to see Curi standing with her arms crossed, deciding whether I'm completely off my rocker.

"The audience is reminded that standing room tickets require an extra inconvenience fee of $57.45."

This almost gets a laugh, and more importantly it is enough for Curi to pace down the beach toward me. She stops at a respectful distance and sits, smoothing her skirt over her legs. I pretend not to notice her as I continue my work. The waves move closer.

"I would like to lodge a complaint with the management," she says. "The amenities here are subpar at best and the staff is—how do I put this delicately—odd enough that I'm concerned for their safety."

"On behalf of all of us, our sincerest apologies for the behavior of our staff. As an aside, we think it's cute that you think we have anything resembling management."

"This is unacceptable," she says. "I will be forced to pursue a frivolous lawsuit against you in order to secure a refund."

"The show is free, ma'am."

"And damages."

A laugh comes out of me in the form of a snort.

"I think you'd probably win that lawsuit, frivolous or not," I say.

Curi smiles, breaking character for the first time. I take my cue from her, and let my voice drop to a normal register.

"You took me off guard. I usually expect a Whilean to be far more literal." My heart hasn't stopped pounding throughout the exchange, though her willingness to go along with my half-baked theater premise puts me oddly at ease.

"I was being completely serious," Curi says. "Expect a letter from my attorney." But she can't keep herself from laughing.

"I'll be representing myself, of course. Expect to receive approximately double the amount you're asking for."

"I don't know, I think my lawyer's degree was made in Photoshop." She's scooted closer to get a better view of my rendition of the Carnival. The waves creep upward, blotting out the lake and caressing the city wall.

The mention of Photoshop strikes me as out of place. My surprise must register because Curi says, "There's a fully automated city inside a mountain in the center of the Carnival. You think we don't know about photo editing software?"

I slide back so I'm sitting even with Curi, but a few feet away. We watch in silence. The most ambitious waves are now taking chunks out of the wall and carrying them away. Foam roils around sandy bricks. We watch together as the wall begins to crumble, until the largest wave yet crashes through Valdrada, plunging it into a gaping hole as the base of the city erodes. It's eerie how much it looks like the destruction I witnessed in person.

I turn to see Curi watching me carefully.

"Thanks for watching the show, Curi," I say. The sound of her name coming out of my mouth makes me unspeakably nervous, but I roll on my side to offer her my hand. She takes it in fingers much stronger than their slenderness would suggest.

"Thanks for putting it on, Matthew. Although I don't know if I should be talking to you while I watch."

"Why?"

"We are historians here. My area of study is those from Elsewhere, people like—well—you. We don't get involved with our subjects."

"Hate to break it to you," I say, "but by me living here, you and your people are already part of the story."

"I've had this thought," Curi says. She bites her lip then, coming to a decision all at once, she blurts, "Could I maybe talk to you some time, about where you came from, about your story? It would help with my research."

"I'd like that very much."

We watch as the mountains are consumed by the water, washing down into hills, and then flattening into a barren plain, with rills of eroded sand streaming down into the waves.

We began to meet nearly daily, and she would interview me about my time in the Carnival, for the most part letting me tell the story, but jumping in at certain points for more detail. At times her questioning felt uncomfortable. For example she spent an inordinate amount of time on my relationship with June. This was something I myself hadn't worked out, so I frustrated her with a lot of half answers.

On her end I don't know exactly what it was. Was I actually inherently attractive to her? Or was I just an enigma to be unwrapped? At the very least she understood there was deeper she needed to pry to understand me. But there was something between us from the very beginning. Mutual curiosity, maybe. For my part, I obviously found her physically attractive, but past that I quickly fell for her inquisitiveness, her slight awkwardness—so contrasted to June's self assurance—and if I'm completely honest, found I enjoyed being a subject worth studying.

The first time we kissed we were sitting on the pink fungus by the shore, for the hundredth time breaking down the assault by the Apocalyptians, our near death by the beast, and Bailly's intercession. Bailly always trips Curi up.

"He's not exactly one to explain himself," I say. "He sort of just does things."

"There are rules governing the Carnival," Curi replies. "But those from Elsewhere are not subject to the same ones as everyone else."

"Are you trying to say I'm immortal or something? I'm all about that."

"That Bailly felt the need to save you implies that you're not. But he did save you, which suggests you are not subject to the normal rules. Anyone from the Carnival would've either been killed or left to fend off the beast themselves."

"I was having an off day."

"I'm sure under normal circumstances you would have shot a fireball from your eyes and incinerated the creature," she says. "But Bailly jumping in is indicative of a special relationship between him and those from Elsewhere. I believe understanding this may be a key piece we're missing." She says all this without breaking stride, and I laugh out loud.

The power of her eyes stops whatever response I had.

"I think Bailly wanted you to find me," she says quietly, grabbing my hand as if holding on for dear life. "He sent you here for a reason, and now I'm involved."

"I'm glad he did," I say. Her fingers have the rough texture of outdoor labor. "And I'm glad you are."

She darts forward then, catching my mouth almost mid-word. The desperate motion of it contrasts with her usual deliberate speech. I'm plunged into a deep sea. Then all I can feel is Curi's warmth and the softness of her lips on mine.

When she pulls away the fear is not gone, but her expression suggests she's uncovered a new piece of information.

"I think I'm meant to be part of your story, Matthew."

Nothing makes me happier than this thought. Yet every time I think about the story behind me, the deepest part of me screams to stop, to slow down, to look past the narrative and simply exist here and now. But here and now, Curi is pushing me toward the truth. And perhaps the truth is that story. Perhaps my exile here is not to separate me, but rather to provide me a perspective that brings me closer.

Curi kisses me again.

Our romance presents something of a problem for my occupancy on the While Isles. The rules governing the Whileans' relationships with outsiders are at best unclear, and there's no way to spin Curi's romantic involvement with her subject.

Unfortunately, we're probably too blinded by the compulsive need to spend time together to think about appearances.

In typical Whilean fashion, a routine trip to deliver a new set of tableware to an elder villager named Dom—he had recently started mistaking the plates for the discuses he would throw at birds in his younger years, necessitating a more or less steady supply to his hut—resulted in a loud debate between Curi and Dom's assistant Stu.

Stu, a scholar on the history of the Grove, always called my arrival the "return of the Unmade," which to this point Curi had let slide, until he repeated it so many times that it became clear that he wasn't making a joke.

"You know it wasn't a true Unmaking, right?" Curi says, trying to remain casual. But Stu takes the bait and they're off.

"A scholar with little knowledge of the Grove might think that, but in terms of Grove history, an Unmaking is any cyclical disruption of the world heralding a new epoch."

"But we're not in a true new epoch."

"The seat of power in the Carnival was destroyed!" Stu says. "The Grove rose and obliterated Valdrada. There is no destructive action the Grove can take, by definition, that is not an Unmaking."

"Just because something's never happened before doesn't mean that when it does, we have to squeeze it into an existing definition."

"What are you proposing?" Stu scoffs. "That what happened was a Semi-Unmaking? Now you're just making up words."

"He sure came up with that quickly, didn't he?" I mumble to Curi.

"I'm not saying that at all," Curi says. "I'm just saying that your schemas for the Grove are obviously too rigidly defined."

"You're telling me how to conduct my research now."

"Yes," Curi says, "I suppose I am, since your current methods are clearly misguided—please excuse my language."

Stu had been leaning in the doorway with the new set of plates, but now he sets them down on the step.

"Daughter of the Provost or not, I find this highly improper."

"Apologies. Of course, this area is yours, and it is yours to mishandle as you will."

"If ascribing proper terminology to Grove-related phenomena is mishandling, then I'll go on mishandling it as much as I please."

"That's good to hear," Curi says. She seems to remember something, and at the same time I remember we've had a similar conversation before. "Other than of course yourself, who is the primary expert, what other experts would you believe about this?"

Stu thinks for a moment. "I doubt the Provost would be willing to weigh in. But if anyone, I would say Bailly. Bailly would be the one who could settle this—not that I find your angle plausible enough to warrant any kind of settling."

Curi smiles, sensing victory. "It just so happens that I've come across an individual who happened to be by Bailly's side immediately after this supposed 'Unmaking.' Matthew, care to comment?" I had been slowly sidling away. It's a strategy I've learned works very well when faced with a choice between being in a debate with people who are much smarter and more knowledgeable than you, and not being in a debate with people who are much smarter and more knowledgeable than you.

"I suppose I could try to remember how he phrased it."

Usually I don't do well with exact quotes. It took me an embarrassing amount of time to memorize the Gettysburg Address, and half of that is already memorized by default. But things heard in the Carnival make a stronger impression on your mind. Rather than having to go back and access the memory, it's as if you're still in the memory, and just have to look over your shoulder.

But I realize that the look in Curi's green eyes is just as helpful. It's a look that expects whatever I say to be correct and intelligent. It's a look that trusts in a way I can't remember being trusted before.

"He said: *The Grove would've risen eventually, and when it did it would have consumed the entire world. You've actually prevented this subsuming process—the Unmaking—from occurring for many years. It will be a long time before the Grove's temper blooms again.*"

"I guess it is just one opinion," Curi says, "of one person who happens to be the arbiter of truth in the Carnival."

Curi has a grin on her face the entire walk back.

"I really shouldn't do that, you know," she says. "I'm not an expert on the Grove, and it would've been really easy to put my foot in my mouth."

"You didn't, though," I say. "How did you feel comfortable calling him on it? I'm never able to be that direct."

"It's part of our culture to hold each other accountable for the facts. That's what we care about above all else. Besides, I knew I had my expert witness on hand to bail me out."

"I cannot believe you rested your argument on me. That's like building the foundation of your house out of kindling and lighter fluid."

"Oh come on. We make a great team. Wasn't it at least a little fun?"

She stops and pulls me close. I kiss the top of her head and match her mischievous look.

"I guess it was sort of a little bit fun."

An unusual spell of calm weather marks the beginning of my stay on the islands, but with each passing week of good weather, the Whileans grow more restless. The longer they go without a temporal hurricane, the more likely that the season will be a bad one.

Though at first I had been afraid to take my canoe out to the outer islands, under the firm hand of Kereus and Curi, I enjoy riding to the farther reaches. We make a habit of picnicking on the uninhabited outer islands, spending the day on one of the sandy beaches, and paddling back as the sun sets. I had fashioned a bracelet to cover my wrist device, but whenever I looked back at it, I confirmed that it still kept counting upwards. I was being tracked, whether I liked it or not. Or maybe I was the one doing the tracking—the IT Guy did say it was a self-emanation.

"Oruc has a tendency to exaggerate," Kereus says as his paddle slices the water. Oruc is one of the younger adults in the tribe, and will soon be on his way to the mainland to begin charting its history. He tends to lord his new status over everyone else, so I'm glad he's just given us a heading, and isn't actually in the canoe.

"He likes to make things up and pass them off as prophecy," Curi explains from over my shoulder.

"I wouldn't think your people would appreciate that," I say.

"We're not literal, we're knowledgeable," Curi says. "Except for Kereus, he's only literal."

"An insistence on truth helps to keep the world together," Kereus says.

"It also makes the world a gray, musicless place," Curi says.

"Even so."

"What did Oruc say we'd find there?" I ask. Most of the islands are similar in character, though each with its own intricate shoreline.

"He says that the leviathans spawn in the bay, and that their eggs are six feet wide and glow," Kereus says.

"Maybe we can take one of the eggs back. I'm sure those who study the history of the seas would find some value in it," Curi says.

We watch as a leviathan rises to the surface about half a mile away. Even at this distance its wake requires the paddlers to focus in order to prevent the boat from drifting off course.

"I don't know that disturbing their eggs would be wise," Kereus says.

The island we're heading for is one of the furthest, and we carry supplies to spend the night. We take turns paddling, though our progress is much quicker when I leave it to the cousins.

We continue for several hours over calm seas. The sun plays hide and seek with clouds, and a firm breeze blows behind us. A school of flying fish follows us, occasionally leaping out of the water and over our canoe. Curi snatches one out of the air. The fish gives her a disapproving look, and she tosses it back in the water.

"They like seeing how close they can get without getting caught," Curi says. "That one is going to get endlessly made fun of by its friends."

The next time I'm not rowing, I try to snag one of them, but I'm not even close. Curi laughs at my increasingly flailing attempts.

"If you overturn the boat, you lose," Curi says. "That's pretty much the one rule."

I miss another of the fish. "Am I allowed to dive in and catch them in the water?"

"You're welcome to try, but from what I've seen, you're more of a land creature."

Kereus keeps looking over his shoulder. At first I think it's to watch the flying fish, but after a few minutes I realize his gaze is further off on the horizon. I follow his eyes and see a line of dark gray, far off but moving quickly in our direction.

Curi notices too. "I thought today was going to be clear."

"We're due for a storm," Kereus says. "The wind has been steadily rising."

What had been a pleasant breeze has now become gusts, pushing us forward but also bearing a strong scent of atmosphere.

Kereus' worried expression spooks me. "We're still at least two hours out, and I don't want to get caught in a storm on the open water. Matthew, can you add a third paddle?"

Steering is more challenging with three of us rowing, but our pace quickens.

The line of gray clouds soon overtakes us. Behind it is a massive band of orange. Neither Kereus nor Curi say anything, but it seems to confirm their suspicions. The sky quickly becomes entirely subsumed by orange, as if by a terrible, massive—and ominously sunless—sunset. Our oar strokes become more desperate with the first lashes of rain. It's warm on my bare back.

Soon we move almost blindly. The sea, which had been calm all day, begins to churn. We descend through valleys, rise up hills, and then crash down again. Kereus shouts orders for us to shift our weight and slow our paddling, but his voice is lost in the wind. My stomach is a knot of anxiety. I have to keep my focus on my paddle in order to avoid losing my composure completely.

We come up over a high rise, and I can see a strip of land, our destination, much closer than I had dared hope. There might be a chance of reaching it yet.

As we drop off the peak, another wave crashes in from our right, and for a second I think we've gone under. We rise again, wet but still upright. I feel Curi's hand on my back. It's warm despite the fact that we're both soaked. I lean back and kiss her. Brief, salty, and as intense as any kiss I've ever experienced. Then we set back to our oars.

The sound of a temporal hurricane is not the sound of wind. The wind is the most present experience along with the rain and the roiling seas, but the sound is a high wail. We row on, our only thought fighting for the foot of water ahead of us, and then the next foot after that. The song of the hurricane takes on a melody, but I don't possess the ability to describe it. When it hits a high note, an image comes with it, and I'm lifted outside of myself.

I stand in a doorway.

"There's no silver lining."

I step forward into the living room. My mother is on the couch, her back turned to me, her voice quiet as she speaks into the phone.

"I know it is, and thank God Matthew wasn't hurt more than he was." She pauses. "How can you be so practical?"

"Matthew!" Curi's voice comes over the wail of the storm, and I'm wrenched back into the bottom of the boat. My oar has slipped out of my hands. I try to pick it up, but as my fingers scrape it, I'm pulled back.

"Mom?" She spins, startled.

"Listen, Matthew just came in. I'll talk to you later." She hangs up.

"Who was that?"

"My friend Russ. He got you in with Doctor Stevens."

My hip is still a mess. I limp over to the couch and ease into the couch beside my mom.

"Friends in high places. Always good to have." I wince as I prop myself up with a pillow.

"Couldn't sleep?" she asks. Her face has been nothing but concerned for the past three weeks. I catch her eyes drifting to the scar on my forehead. Doctor Stevens said it would probably fade over time. My mom has been diligently slathering vitamin E ointment on it.

"I don't feel like I can really do that anymore," I say.

"Me neither."

She puts her arm around me, gently, as if she's scared she might break something. We sit in silence for a long time. There's been a lot of that since the accident. Silence, weighed down by painkillers and the absence of the person at the center of all this.

"Russ says he could probably get you in with the physical therapist next week," she says. "Usually she's booked months in advance but they were college classmates."

"If you think it's necessary." I'm not super attached to the idea of a full recovery right now.

"Of course it's necessary."

"Then sure, I guess."

I run my hand along the raw skin on my arm. The plastic on the car's door shattered in the collision and carved a jagged line over my forearm.

More silence. My mother isn't used to being allowed to say much, and it shows at times like these.

"There's still time to change your mind about the funeral."

"No."

"I know he made bad decisions, but he was still your father."

"I think you misheard me. I said: No. Not: Okay, I'll consider it."

"It's your decision."

I feel anger rising in me.

"You ever get tired of pretending it's a tragedy that he's gone?" I say.

"Matthew."

"I do. We've been sitting around, saying nothing to each other for three weeks, saying what a shame it is. But nobody's said the truth, which is that things are a lot goddamn simpler now that he's dead."

"Now is not the time," she says quietly.

"Of course it's the time. I know exactly who we're supposed to be mourning. You think it was a different person who would come home and yell at you over petty shit, and who picked up his son from school wasted off gin and tonics? He died like he lived, a drunk asshole."

"It's more complicated than that."

"You act like he wasn't capable of making his own decisions," I say.

"We'd been fighting for years. It wasn't always about drinking. That was a symptom, not a cause."

"I'm not going to let you blame yourself. That's what he would've wanted."

"I'm not blaming myself. That doesn't mean we have to disown him."

I'm in tears before I realize it, and it takes me a second to choke out, "I tried to disown him, but he kept coming back. Persistent asshole."

My mom hugs me more firmly as I cry. I wish the painkillers would put me into some kind of stupor. No one told me the physical pain would be the easiest part, but it is.

Then I'm walking through the halls at school. I'm still limping, but moving more quickly, trying to hide it. Cass had met me outside, and she held my hand all the way in, a rare public display of affection. But she knew I needed someone beside me. There was nothing nasty in the looks. Everyone knows what happens in a small town, and my accident had provided some welcome drama to the end of the school year.

Cass, a light of patience in all of this. She'd watched with resigned sadness as I fell deeper into bitterness, as my conversation turned more and more toward my father, toward my anger, and away from what we used to talk about. What did we use to talk about? I can't remember a time before all of this, because of course before this we spent plenty of time talking about my father abandoning responsibilities or fighting with my mother. But whereas before Cass was an escape—her family was a normal one where they fought about dumb stuff one minute and made up the next—now she's sucked into my hatred. We've crossed some line, and I don't know how to go back.

Sitting in my seat in English class, Cass having left me at the door with a desperate hug, the classroom feels smaller. The copies of *The Tempest*, used by three generations of bored students, feel more beat up, and the words on the page sound less mystical. Mr. Peters does his best to act like everything's normal, but I feel a vortex of attention on me. I get up and roam the halls, a half hour still left in class. I feel like a ghost. Even the security guard who would usually ask for a hall pass lets me by unquestioned. The weight of grief and anger separates me, and before long I find myself alone in the gym, sitting on the half pulled out bleachers.

When the gym teacher, Ms. Hart, finds me there, the first thing she does is call my mom. Then she drives me home, waiting with me in the living room in silence while my mom makes the forty-five minute drive.

There are a lot of therapists and psychiatrists' offices after that. I drop so many f-bombs, I make even a few seasoned mental health professionals flinch.

Nothing helps. School becomes a distant memory. My mom works from home, and I stay inside, drifting aimlessly throughout the house. I snack endlessly but never feel full. My mom doesn't mention the bags of chips that populate the pantry only briefly on their way, empty, to the garbage can. She makes healthy snacks, and I eat without even looking at them. I play more video games than I've ever played before, the fantastic worlds never enough to serve as a real escape. The painkillers provide brief moments of clarity and calm, but I get nauseous the more I use them. I use them anyway, drifting away from pain. But the disappearance is always temporary, and when I return I find myself craving the pain I'd left behind. I take to finding possessions that remind me of my dad and depositing them in a contractor bag. Then I take the bag to the town dump and hurl it into the household trash. I laugh as I do, watching the remnants of his life disappear amid old PVC pipes, mangled bicycle wheels, and broken plastic Tupperware.

I consider killing myself, but decide that my time to follow my father over the river Styx has not yet come, that I will live a full life into old age and only then, dying an old man, will I come back to my father, stepping past Cerberus and into Hades. Then I will come before my father in the form I had at seventeen before whispering, "Remember me?"

I cough, and seawater comes out. I'm cold. The storm still blows overhead, but the boat isn't moving.

"Matthew?" Curi's hands are on my arm, on my face, desperate and cold with fear. "Matthew, wake up." I roll over and can barely make out her face. It's hidden by rain-soaked hair and a bleary mist.

"Matthew, we need to find shelter. The storm will continue for a while."

She helps me to my feet. I stumble over the side of the boat, but she steadies me.

"Come on," Kereus says, leading us up out of the shallow water where waves still nag at our feet. We climb a steep hill. Mangrove roots and sharp ferns cut my legs. We crest the hill. Behind it a small outcropping made out of volcanic rock forms a three-foot wall. We huddle behind it, holding each other close for warmth. We wait out the storm there. It's too loud and we're too exhausted to speak. As the storm continues, I experience more flashes: a wedding, a girl beside me who I don't know and don't particularly want to like, a perfectly rolled joint lighting up the darkness, which I drop to the ground and stamp out with my foot. But as the rain passes, they fade.

We sleep, and when we wake the sun has returned. A litter of snapped branches surrounds our shelter. Curi's head is against my chest, and it feels familiar, right. She looks up at me with sleepy eyes, kisses my cheek, and pulls me closer.

"I'm going to see about our boat," Kereus says. He has a cut across his arm, but miraculously none of us are otherwise hurt.

"Where'd you go during the storm?" Curi asks.

"Elsewhere."

Her expression suggests she was expecting this answer. "You must tell me everything."

I let it all pour out unedited. She deserves to know the whole truth, and I trust in her strength that she can handle it. This time she doesn't stop me until the end.

"This Cass, she was your girlfriend? Is, maybe?"

"Yes."

There's sadness in her eyes.

"If you don't want to be with me, I understand."

I'm taken aback. I hadn't even thought about that.

"I can go back to being your historian," she says.

When she looks at me, I realize why I'd never thought about it. She and Cass have the same eyes.

"The boat will require repairs," Kereus says as he returns, "and we'll need to make another oar. It'll take a while since all I have is my knife. See about getting some food and starting a fire."

The going is slow as we pick our way around the splintered trees with our bare feet. It's not particularly difficult to find firewood, though much of it needs to be left out in the sun to dry.

Food is not an issue. The entire coast is covered in fish that have washed up on the shore and have long since stopped wriggling. We stash several in the cool shallows until we're ready to cook.

As we're dropping the last of them in, Curi says suddenly, "Don't you think you'd have realized earlier if I was Cass?"

"I had the same thought." Every time something has reminded me of my past the experience has been intense, if often brief. Curi gave an impression of familiarity, but it was more like a stranger who has a mannerism similar to your friend.

"But my presence here means something. Some connection to your past."

"You're right, but it's not direct," I say. "It's like I'm one point removed. I've been having this feeling since I've gotten here. At first I thought I'd been sucked into my own mind. But there's nothing here that's completely familiar."

"And yet there are all these pieces, pieces like me."

She says this without sadness.

It doesn't take Kereus long to fix up the canoe and carve an oar, but he spends the better part of the day testing it out in the shallows to make sure it can withstand the rough currents that have persisted after the storm. By the time he deems it safe, it's deep into the afternoon, and we have to stay another night. That night after dinner he turns in early, and again Curi and I walk around the island, keeping to the beaches, which are more passable than the interior with its shattered trees. At the far bay Curi stops and points.

In the shallow water, bobbing with the gentle tide, are massive glowing orbs. The leviathans' eggs were undisturbed by the hurricane. They light the entire bay a dull blue. After the loud rush of the storm, the waves seem gentle, and the light promises a new generation of the gentle, powerful leviathans.

Curi puts an arm around my shoulder, and in that gesture I feel the strength of our bond, of the experiences we've shared.

Her eyes reflect the glow of the bay, and in them I feel safe, and warm, and whole.

We sleep under the stars.

When I awake it's still dark out, and I'm aware of Curi's eyes on me. I can tell she doesn't know how she should be looking at me. I feel the same. I stare back at her for a long time, and eventually reach my arm around her back and pull her close. We melt into each other.

The next morning we depart into calm seas. Most of the journey passes in silence. As our course takes us within view of Valdrada, I start at the sight of the walled city, rising much as it did when I first arrived there. No Grove, no giant hole in the ground, just rows of clapboard and stone buildings, twisting alleys and wide streets. Did the temporal hurricane take us into the past, or far into the future after it's been rebuilt?

Suddenly something breaks the water ahead of us. My first thought is that it's a leviathan or a school of large fish, but the round protrusion is metallic, and as more of it comes into view I can see that it has antennae and other navigational instruments poking out of the top. It surfaces fully. Kereus and Curi back-paddle to prevent us from running into it as I register that it's a submarine. Though the craft is not particularly large, its wake almost tips us over. The noise of the engine cuts through the calm air.

I look between my two companions, but get only shakes of their heads in return. They're just as confused as I am, just as aware that we can't possibly outrun the craft in front of us. There's been no indication of any threat, at least not yet.

A hatch on the top of the sub screeches open. Out comes a hand, shielding the face behind it from the glare. Then I recognize the familiar undercut, the familiar bounce in her step as she climbs the ladder, and the familiar combat boots as she swings them out of the hatch to perch on the railing running around it.

"Hey June." I have to yell to be heard over the sound of the engines, but my voice still sounds weak. Seeing her feels like rolling back all of the time I have spent in the While Isles, as if I have returned to the scared boy trying to plot his escape from this place.

It's an escape I can no longer unequivocally wish for.

"Laundro-Matt, you look so tan!" June says. My stomach curdles. "I just stopped by to say hi."

I expect to see annoyance or even hatred on Curi's face. I've told her a lot about June, and it's hard to say much of it has been positive. But instead I see only fascination. Right. Like me, June is from Elsewhere, which means she's also Curi's subject of study. I'm sure if she had a notepad with her, Curi would be writing furiously.

"Last time we talked you accused me of trying to destroy your story," I say. "Now you want to say hi?"

"How could I still be mad about that? It's been nearly fifty years."

Oh hell. My companions are unfazed by this revelation, but I'm not fully a Whilean yet, and the idea of a temporal hurricane shooting us fifty years into the future is a tough one to stomach.

"Come on up," June continues. "Your friends and/or lovers can come too."

I sigh and ask Curi, "Do you want to come?"

"Yes, for the sake of curiosity, but this feels like a conversation you need to have on your own."

We paddle the boat closer, and June lowers a ladder. I climb up, slipping a few times on the metal hull.

"Good to see you," June says when I'm at the top of the ladder. She locks me in a surprisingly firm hug.

"Has it really been fifty years for you?" I ask.

"Don't I look it?"

She doesn't. Her face looks more careworn, and the cardigan she has on registers as slightly more mature than the band t-shirt she was wearing the last time I saw her, but in terms of actual physical aging, she hasn't changed at all.

"I've got a really good plastic surgeon," she says, then indicates that I should climb down into the submarine. I do, and am engulfed by darkness.

The Carnival – June's Submarine

We sit in the large living and dining room that June insists on calling "the mess." The rest of the sub's interior had all the metal walkways, control rooms, and everything else you could want from an underwater machine, but this room is more like the front of a large-windowed townhouse. As soon as we got inside, June pressed the dive button, so now it is like the front of a townhouse that also happens to be underwater, complete with a view of fish swimming by.

June is on the couch with her feet up on the coffee table, while I take a vinyl seat next to it. She had already made a strong batch of tea, which we drink out of China with a floral pattern running along the outside. Mine is so bitter I have to drop two extra sugar cubes in it to offset the flavor.

"How long has it been for you?" June asks.

"A few months. Long enough to feel like I'm settling in, not long enough to feel like I truly live here."

"Man, you're lucky. Fifty years with only the people of the Carnival for company is no joke."

"I thought you still had so many stories to tell. What with the Armageddeons and all that. Valdrada looks like it's standing again, so things can't have gone too wrong."

June sits up, putting her feet on the floor, then thinks better of it and leans back into the couch. Her boots scrape against the coffee table's natural wood.

"I know I blamed you for what happened," June says, "and while you were obviously a little shit stirring up trouble where you had no right to, there is some important context I may have left out."

"This is gearing up to be a hell of an apology."

"It's not. But you do at least deserve to know where the Apocalyptians came from." She sits up again and takes a swig of her tea, which has to be way too hot to drink in that quantity. "When I first got to the Carnival, one of the stories I told involved an underground city, with a race of people who lived in the waterways beneath the mountains. The details aren't important, but I ended up married to their queen, Dietri.

"I loved Dietri, but most of all I loved that place. I can still remember every waterway, every pool, every cave. It's strange, you would think as a human you would yearn for the outside, where the sun can hit your face and your fingers aren't raisined up all the time, but I never felt anything but content. We governed together. She was the only queen in name, because of course an outsider couldn't hold that title, but we made every decision together.

"At this point I may have screwed up just an eensy bit. You see, marital bliss is wonderful, but even when you're married to perfection itself and even when your sex life is popping off like a nightly firecracker, you can still get bored. I got bored, and I thought it would be fun to start an insurrection against our rivals. Nothing too crazy, just a small rebel group. But I had a little too much fun with it."

I start to feel where this story is heading, but I don't interrupt June.

She continues: "I molded them into something really and truly evil, not bent merely on the destruction of our rival's regime, but also of the world itself. I convinced them that the path to the world went straight through our enemies. I didn't anticipate that they would take to the role with such glee, or that they would grow beyond more than a small force. Boy was I wrong. They soon named themselves the Apocalyptians. That was too on the nose for me, and it was around that point that I checked out of the whole operation. But the ball was already rolling, and before long they had blown a massive hole in the mountainside, and started their war against the Armageddeons."

Our silence is filled with the low hum of the sub's engines. Outside, a school of fish shimmers by, and I wonder how it is light enough to see them.

"What happened to Dietri?" I ask.

"Leave it to you to miss the point entirely." She shrugs, and I've never seen more pain in a single rotation of the shoulders. "She died."

"I'm sorry, June."

"We age incredibly slowly here, the people from Elsewhere. You and me. It was inevitable, and I had plenty of time to say my goodbyes before turning my attention to the Apocalyptians. To what I'd done."

"I'm sure you didn't know what they would become."

June shakes her head. "Of course I did."

I think back to how adamant she was that she prevent war between them and the Armageddeons, how her entire sense of purpose bent around that one goal. I always believed it was just her way of creating a story—I didn't think what the story was about mattered. Maybe that was naïve of me.

A grandfather clock in the corner chimes. Curi and Kereus are waiting in the boat. Whileans have no shortage of patience, but I don't want them to worry.

"There's something else I've learned," June says. Her voice is once again filled with life, as if she has unburdened herself. "The chickenmen, I'd always known they were different, but I found an old account of what they got up to before they were so ... you know ... chicken-y."

I almost laugh. "Their pre-fowl state?"

"Exactly. It's weird, the account made it sound almost like they were actually important guys. Apparently they were originally stewards of the four corners of the Carnival. The story was kind of rambly, but I was intrigued by Rob's part of it. He created a settlement called Riverwood. The entire kingdom was made up of a single town running along a river. Boats, waterwheels, and all that. Lots of the buildings were either built next to the river, or with half their foundation on either bank, so that the residents could tie up boats beneath their house, and paddle up or down the river.

"Rob was fascinated by the process of governing, and encouraged each district to adopt town hall meetings and hold local elections. They called them the Riverwood Debates. The perfect democracy in action. They were actually intelligent, civil, and focused on democracy rather than personal gain. People spoke fiercely, but always recognized that their government was founded on a principle of love and societal improvement. The trick was to get your opponent to see your side of the story, not turn them into an enemy."

"It sounds nice," I say. The concepts she's describing sound ideal, and I am almost positive that part of the absence within my memory contains a lot of time spent thinking about these ideas.

"It does. But it was immediately destroyed because one of the other chickenmen—I think it was Bob, but it doesn't matter—built a warring realm that crushed Riverwood. The resulting squabble was so bad that their combined creative influence reset the Carnival to a null state. Set it back to zero. All that was left was an empty void, and Bailly."

"Bailly?"

"Of course. Bailly is always here, Carnival or not."

"I think I actually see the point of your story this time," I reply, the implications of what I'm about to say chilling me. "The chickenmen seem to be from Elsewhere too."

June's serious eyes tell me I'm on the right track.

"They have just as much ability to create, to tell stories, to set their own parameters," I continue. "If it was long enough ago that the Carnival didn't even exist in its current form, maybe they've aged, just slowly over the course of millennia."

"And look what's happened to them!" June shouts. The sound ricochets around the tight space. She leans forward, her eyes blazing. "I think I'm beginning to understand something important about the Carnival. We can tell any stories we want, but over time, telling stories is just that: telling stories. Now when I try to do some things in the Carnival I feel too powerful. Like I can do anything. And when you can do anything, it's like nothing matters. I have to create my own challenges, and it all feels fake."

This turn from June, the tiredness I see on her face, all makes me extremely anxious. "What do you want, June?"

"I want you to come back with me. To Valdrada. I think if we work together, we can figure out how to..." her voice drops to a whisper "...leave."

I take a long second to gather my thoughts. I know that if I don't, they will come out in a raging river. I need to keep some semblance of calm.

"Do you know why your stories are so boring?" I ask. "It's because you're selfish. It's because all you care about is bending the world to your will. I've seen glimpses of Elsewhere, of the world outside here. And let me tell you, it may not have crazy things like islands that can move through time, but it's full of just as much pain and sadness as the ones you create here. So if you're asking me to leave, to come with you and abandon everything I've made here, my answer is simple. I'm not going anywhere with you."

June doesn't meet my eyes, and in her seething breaths I can tell I have hurt her beyond just rejecting her offer.

Her next words are almost a hiss: "Get off my goddamn submarine."

The Carnival - The While Isles

I barely speak on the way home. At around the halfway point we meet another boat, this one larger than ours and rowed by six men. The Provost sits in the prow. He stands when he sees us, and we paddle to him. He embraces Curi, almost overturning the boat.

"My daughter, when the storm came and you still had not returned we feared the worst."

"Luckily we were close to an island," she says, letting relief show for the first time.

"We'll have a feast tonight," he says. "My daughter brought home to me safe and sound is the perfect opportunity to renew the tradition of the Feast of Lost Days."

The men in the boat nudge each other at the mention of the feast.

The Provost's eyes turn me over. His eyes are as gray as his hair. He doesn't look much like Curi, save for the quiet, insistent spark of intelligence. When he speaks again the warmth has dropped out of his voice.

"I'm glad you are all right as well Matthew," he says. "I imagine your first temporal hurricane was a trying experience."

"I would not have survived without Curi and Kereus," I say.

The Provost nods, and his gaze turns back to Curi, still searching.

Not long into our journey back to the village, a gray shape breaks the water to our starboard. A massive wake follows as the leviathan surfaces. The Whileans stop rowing, each placing a hand in a fist over their stomach in reverence. It glides silently back into the depths, never breaking its motion.

"An auspicious sign," the Provost says, leaning over to speak in a whisper. "The giant knows my daughter is out of danger, and has blessed our passage home."

Preparations begin immediately for the celebration. Boats launch to hunt sailfish—their sails will be used as containers to cook their tender meat. We gather wood for a bonfire. The feast will take place on the beach rather than under the pavilion, and ordered chaos reigns as the Whileans haul everything to the shore. Within a couple hours a long feast table digs into the sand, the area has been flattened out, and there are enough chairs for twice the population of the village. Messengers rowed out to the outer islands, and were followed back by a retinue of guests. Though no one dresses up, many have bathed and braided their hair, and there's rosy excitement on every face.

Curi disappears into her family's hut, explaining that she must prepare for her duties as the Provost's daughter and guest of honor. She kisses me goodbye, in full sight of anyone passing by.

The Whileans are a sober people, but as soon as cooking starts, the liquor distilled from the sugary sap of the island's palm trees begins to flow. I help Kereus at one of the cooking fires, where he roasts a sailfish over blazing coals. He drinks dutifully from a cup of the palm liquor, taking no apparent enjoyment from it. I feel it would be rude to turn it down, but I feel a slight twist of revulsion every time my nose dips into the cup. I take some comfort in knowing where this feeling comes from. It's as if putting a name to the cause somehow makes me, if not a master of it, at least an active participant.

The liquor is strong. A flush comes over my face after a couple sips.

By the time we sit down to the table, there's laughter everywhere. The younger members of the community carry food out on large platters to raucous applause. Following tradition, everyone serves the person on their right, carving the juicy fish and setting it atop a bed of seaweed on their neighbor's wooden plate. The meat's sweet scent rises over the entire beach.

Before we begin, the Provost rises. At this simple motion, the entire table—over two-hundred people—falls silent.

"Thank you all for being here," he begins. "For as long as there have been people inhabiting these islands, we have gathered together to celebrate our unique perspective in time, to restore old friendships, and strengthen old ties. Traditionally these ceremonies have been held after the first hurricane of the season, that most powerful beginning of the hardest season, after which it is most necessary to celebrate our mere survival.

"I know most of you are aware that the lateness of this first storm means we are likely in for a series of frequent and powerful storms. With hard times ahead, it seems fitting to return to our old ways, to the old traditions that have united us."

Servers carrying smaller trays filter between us, placing long spindly objects at each plate. They're the bones from the sailfishes' sails, retrieved from the cooking fires. The Provost raises his cup.

"Today we drink the strong liquor of weak trees, trees that fall in the storm but grow back when the wind dies. On this one day we intoxicate ourselves in recognition of the oblivion of the passage of time, and the pain and confusion this causes. We drink also for pleasure, acknowledging that oblivion itself is tempting, that the cycles of displacement and loss can be seductive."

He takes a long drink, and everyone else at the table does the same. A couple of the younger islanders cough as they take bigger sips than they can handle, prompting knowing laughs from the elders.

"The meat before you symbolizes our connection with the ocean, as the source of our strength, but also as the source of the destructive power that rules our lives. We choose the sailfish, whose shape evokes a ship borne by a strong breeze. This breeze brings a sense of freshness and life once the storm passes. We also choose it because of its danger, because of the poisonous fish it consumes, which must be carefully removed from the stomach before it is edible. In this way it also represents caution and moderation, the requirements of living as we do."

He lifts a fork holding a small bite of the fish. He pops it in his mouth and chews thoughtfully. I follow his lead along with those around me, savoring the deep sweet flavor of the meat. Kereus smiles at the obvious pleasure on my face.

"Finally, we have the sailfish's spines." Each is about a foot long, and brittle after its time in the fire. "A straight line, more or less." A few people chuckle as he holds up a crooked one. He smiles, but continues in a grave voice. "Linear time, proceeding from beginning to end, every point connected to each other. One logical route." With a violent motion, he snaps the spine in half. "We break the spines to remind ourselves that our world does not operate in this way."

The sound of snapping bones fills the air. Mine takes a couple tries, but when it breaks, juices trapped inside pour out, releasing an overpowering smoky aroma.

"Finally, the selfish part of the celebration," the Provost says. "My daughter, caught out in the storm, has returned." He points toward the tree line. Curi is framed by bright torches on either side. She looks beautiful, but in a regal, powerful way I haven't seen before. She wears a crown woven of ropes and palm fronds, and a flowing dress of blue-gray, like the ocean on a cloudy morning. She walks along the table, and stands at her father's side. Maybe it's because I know her so well, but I can see the slight lanky awkwardness in her stride, even as she moves with measured steps. The effect—the dichotomy between her normal state and the rigors of ceremony—is striking.

The Provost puts his hands over his daughter's shoulders, and she smiles at him.

"If time permits it, and if you choose to have her, one day she will be your Provost," he says. "One day she will stand at the head of this table and pass on our traditions, just as I have." He offers his cup to her. She puts her hands over his, and drinks deeply. The ritual of the moment passes. He embraces her. For a second she is just a girl hugging her father.

"Are you ever going to let them eat, father?" Curi says once the hug ends. This gets a cheer out of the crowd.

"She has a point," he says. He puts his cup down and raises both hands.

Then we eat.

It's deep into the meal, and I'm both full and somewhat lightheaded. Kereus turns out to be a lot more fun when he drinks, and entertains me with stories from his historical period. One king of the Carnival decreed that cat ownership was a crime punishable by a harsh jail sentence. The resulting riots consumed the city for a period of weeks, only ending when a man who didn't own a cat, but worried a dog ban would be the next logical step, took matters into his own hands and kidnapped the king, promising to let him go if he retracted the law. Seeing an easy way out of the madness he had created—he hadn't felt particularly strongly about the rule anyway, and had only really put it in place to keep his mistress happy—the king relented, and soon cat ownership was legal again throughout the Carnival. His mistress would go on to become the leader of a minor but vocal rebellious faction who later tried—and failed, it wasn't even close, to be honest—to depose him. All of this trouble could've been avoided, Kereus tells me, if the woman's father had not allowed the family cat to play in the children's room when they were young, and if the cat hadn't enjoyed tormenting the poor child, thereby instilling a deep-seated hatred of both felines and masculine authority figures.

When the story ends, I'm immediately sucked into another one, this one told by a man who appears to have been imbibing more than the others. He's listing names of various historical figures throughout the Carnival's history, followed by a brief—and often disturbing—account of their death. From the detail of his accounts it's evident that he's spent a good deal of time studying the gruesome intricacies. He's just finished recounting the decapitation of one of the more widely known political martyrs when a woman who appears to be his wife cuts him off and suggests the conversation be allowed to return to something a little less gory.

The Provost makes the rounds, shaking hands with each person at the table and exchanging a few words. He appears at my shoulder. I can tell from the cant of his eyes that he has been indulging in as much palm liquor as anyone else, but his stare doesn't waver.

"Matthew," he says, "I hope the food is to your liking."

"It's delicious, thank you sir."

"Please, call me the Provost. Or Provost for short." He chuckles. "I had a name once, you know. I wasn't always the Provost. Do you want to hear it, my name?"

"Sure," I reply. Something about this joking tone feels threatening.

He opens his mouth, and the sound that comes out is an intense silence, like he's opened a door into the sky. Out of it streams emptiness.

The Provost shuts his mouth and laughs again, this time without humor.

"Becoming a Provost is not easy. We lose our names into the void of time. We are still the same person, yes, but the process fundamentally changes you. It requires you to make difficult decisions with incomplete information, or easy decisions with far too much. You must see very far, and also very near."

"It sounds like a challenge," I say.

"It is certainly a challenge," he says. "One day my daughter will take over this burden. I am sure our people will appoint her. She is wiser than me already, and well-loved. The older islanders will appoint her out of tradition, and the younger ones will appoint her out of loyalty, as it has been for almost all our rulers, as it was for me."

"She'll be more than capable."

"She will be, if all goes according to plan." In his increasingly intent gaze I can feel a protective anger beginning to crest. "For one as wise as she is, she's still young. And the young are prone to mistakes they misread as the will of their hearts."

I narrow my eyes. The Provost's smile drops along with the pretense.

"I know my daughter better than anyone," he says. "I know when she's fallen for someone. I believe you are a good person, and I can see why my daughter likes you, but an outsider cannot possibly support her through this process. It's going to start soon, this transformation, and when it does she will need someone beside her who understands what she is going through."

"What are you saying, sir?"

"I'm telling you that if you care about her, you won't continue this."

Alcohol-infused honesty lies heavy on every fierce word.

"I'm your guest here," I say, "and want to respect your wishes. To be honest, though, you don't know your daughter very well if you think you can control her."

"She respects her heritage. She will understand."

"She understands, but that doesn't mean she'll listen."

A chorus of laughter rises from the group next to us, as they raise a glass and chug an entire cup of palm liquor in unison. I realize that Kereus has heard this whole exchange, even though his head is bent over his food.

The Provost seems to realize he's spent too long here, and that other guests are waiting.

"I promise I've heard everything you've said, and will do my best to honor it out of respect for your hospitality," I say, as he turns to leave. "That's all I can do."

He lifts his cup to me, and then puts it to his lips. I return the gesture. He departs down the row, but even as he speaks with people farther down the table, his focus never leaves me. Any festiveness is gone, falling into the abyss like the Provost's name. I look down the table at Curi, who is chatting with the elders. She's drunk just enough palm liquor to have a slight glow. Eventually she rises, and just as they did for her father, the crowd falls silent.

Her voice doesn't command the space in the way his does, but I still don't have to struggle to hear.

"History is everything to us. It is traditional, near the end of The Feast of Lost Time, for a chosen guest to tell a story, both to share knowledge, and to prove the rigor of their study. In other words, to make sure I haven't been slacking off. If I can have your full and undivided attention, if time allows, and if you can strain your ears above the sound of the storm, I will begin."

As Curi concludes her story, she takes a gulp of water, followed by a sip of palm liquor. The story she told was similar to the one June so recently told me about Rob, the man from Elsewhere who built a kingdom comprised of a single town on the river, only to lose it when one of his friends built a warring kingdom next door. In Curi's version there was much more emphasis on the woman Rob fell in love with. She lived in the kingdom of Riverwood, and Rob fell for her after meeting at the River's Bend, a bar built right onto the water so you could always feel a light mist coming off the water. It also happened to be the sight of some of the most spirited political discussions, and this woman was the fiercest of all debaters. Things were complicated by the fact that Rob had created Riverwood, so he had by extension created her as well.

The story ended on the somber note of Riverwood's destruction, as well as the question of whether Rob's love was real, or simply the result of him having created the perfect partner in his own image. I suppose it doesn't matter, since the end result of Riverwood's demise was that the entire Carnival reset to a null state. What happened to all the Carnival's residents when their home reset?

"Here concludes 'The Story of the Four,'" Curi says. "I hope that the winds did not carry away my words, and that they have found fertile minds in which to grow their meaning."

Curi's serious expression breaks, and she smiles as she leans back in her chair to exchange a word with her father. The crowd doesn't react. For Whileans, a pondering quiet is the greatest compliment you can give a storyteller. After a few moments, some return to conversation with their neighbors. It strikes me that in most situations a crowd two shades past drunk off palm liquor might not be the ideal audience, but these stories are so baked into the Whilean society that not even the children who had been running behind their parents' chairs and crawling under the table made a sound.

Though most people stick around, enjoying the remainder of the palm liquor and telling stories of their own, I can't stay any longer. I need space to process all I've learned today. I knew I was like June, but hearing that the chickenmen are the same, that they have been here so long, is something I need time to unpack. Through all of this, though, June's turnaround on the Carnival might be the most troubling part.

I find Curi on the path leading back to the village. She looks exhausted under the torchlight.

"That was incredible," I say, wrapping her in a hug.

"Thank you," she says. "I hope you don't mind that I re-hashed some of what you'd heard from June. I hadn't thought about it in a while, but it was fresh on my mind."

"No of course not, it was perfect. You're perfect."

She smiles and looks at me like she thinks I might have overindulged in palm liquor.

"You've obviously done the work to understand us, those from Elsewhere," I say. "But there's something I have to know."

"Of course."

"If I understand the meaning of the story, with the Carnival resetting because of simple animosity between people who had formerly been friends, this whole place doesn't move forward. It just spins around in cycles and cycles, returning to the same place. Why do you bother studying it?"

Curi takes a deep breath. She pauses and plants a dry kiss on my lips. "June knows this story too, knows its lesson. Why do you think she bothers trying to save the world when she knows the same thing?"

I don't have an answer, nor has Curi actually answered my question. Or maybe she has. I wonder if I will be here long enough for the Carnival to reset, for me to lose everything and everyone I've known within it. But the anxiety this thought might provoke feels as lacking in urgency as worrying about the sun turning into a red giant and swallowing the Earth.

There's the hint of a smile on Curi's face. "You like her," she blurts. "June."

"I do. Other than you, she's the only person who never feels like she's trying to deceive me."

We'd only had a brief chance to debrief on my conversation with June, but Curi obviously recognized how much it troubled me.

"You should watch out for her," Curi says. "I've studied her for long enough to know she's not—I don't know—safe..."

"Not safe? Despite accidentally creating them, she does have the fairly worthy goal of saving us from death by Apocalyptian."

"There is a cloud of coming dread around her," Curi says. "That's all I know."

"Then good thing I've got you to protect me."

She nods once, then turns and leads me by the hand off into the woods. We leave the torchlight behind.

My first temporal hurricane left me shaken, but with each following one I find myself more ready. For one thing, when the next few hit I'm not out on the open water. We hunker down in one of the underground storm shelters. Though these storms are not as strong as the first, each brings the same temporal disruption, and with each I experience a quick flash of memory from Elsewhere. When I come to, my counting device is freaking out, alternating between numbers and symbols I can't read.

First I'm at a wedding. I'm pissed off—again with this? We're nearing the end of the toasts, but I'm stone cold sober of course, and with no better judgment because of it. The microphone still has Aunt Jessica's sweat on it. She's just finished telling everyone how Russ pulled Dee out of the hardest time of her life, and how he's been a godsend who provided order and gave home a new meaning. I wish I'd saved the grape tomatoes from the salad, because they would've been fitting projectiles to complement Jessica's speech.

I see my mother's face go cold when I stand, but Russ is smiling, egging me on. He's younger than her, though he doesn't act like it except when he's trying to earn new dad points.

"It's crazy to be here," I start, and the room falls silent. I'm not holding a glass, so I have no idea what I'll toast with when the time comes. "I know I'm lucky to be. That I could walk up here on my own is some sort of small miracle. If you're bored and looking to try out being in a car crash, I can tell you I would not recommend it." Was that a joke? Neither I nor the audience knows. "Ten out of ten would not recommend having your deadbeat drunk-ass father drive his car off the road with you inside. No sir, not a vibe. Not a vibe at all."

My mom's glare at me is both priceless and makes me feel like the piece of shit I am.

"Sorry, it's hard to talk about. It's especially hard to be here when our family is missing someone. And we are missing someone. Even if what's missing didn't provide much, even if it drove us crazy and hurt us, it's still gone. I've been listening to you all talk about addition. How Dee and Russ are going to join their families. Combine. Add together. But you can't cover what's missing up with something else. Russ, you seem like a fine dude, and if you have a pulse there's a ninety-eight percent chance you're a better person than my dad.

"Anyway, I don't have some grand advice, and I don't feel like saying you're going to set everything straight. It takes more than putting a band-aid over a wound like that. Believe me, I would know. Ha. All I can say is, be good to me and my mom. Or I don't know, just be good to my mom."

The applause starts halfway through the word mom, pushing me off the stage. I pass the microphone on to second cousin Cheryl, and disappear toward the bathroom.

I don't cry. I never cry. Everything feels too empty for tears. I lock myself inside the bathroom. I run a hand through the potpourri on top of the toilet. The smooth surface of the dried roses alternates with the rougher cinnamon and allspice.

The celebration has chosen to move on without me. I hear claps as the next toast concludes, then footsteps and a sharp knock at the door.

"Go away, mom," I say.

"It's Russ."

What the hell does he want? He's probably going to ask me for an apology. Good luck with that.

"What can I do for you, Russ?" I ask, opening the door.

He looks sharp in a blue tuxedo. Nothing is out of place, even though his belly has a middle-age roundness to it.

"I came to see how you were doing."

"I was enjoying my shit in peace, thanks for asking."

"Listen, I understand how you're feeling. It's too quick for me to come into your life. Your world has been shaken up, and I'm one more shake. I know a wedding is the last place you want to be right now."

"I don't have anything against weddings, in theory."

"I don't know if this helps, but I tried to talk your mother out of having it so soon. I don't care about all the ceremony of it. All

I care about is being with her. But as hard a time as you're going through right now, you have to realize she's going through just as much. It might be painful, but this will help her. I can help her. Don't you want her to feel better?"

"It doesn't. Help, that is. But thanks."

Russ has been leaning on the door and shifts his position slightly, angling himself more directly toward me.

"I'll be here for this family no matter what," he says. "You can always talk to me. Even yell at me if it makes you feel better. I'm not your father, so you owe me nothing."

My stomach twists. I have to know if I really can ask him anything. It's a sick test, but I'm in a sick place right now.

When my voice comes out, it's little more than a rasp. "Was she cheating on my dad with you?"

Russ' face betrays nothing, and not for the last time I wonder whether he actually does experience emotions, or if the only emotions he does display are a conscious choice.

"Yes she was. Not for long, but yes."

I run my hand through my hair. It's long and slicked back with a metric shit-ton of mousse.

"Guess I can't blame her," I say. "Compared to my dad you're practically Jesus H. Christ himself."

"I'm sorry."

"Don't be. Just give me a minute, okay?"

"Okay."

The door closes and I look into the mirror. The sight of myself yanks my consciousness outward. I look into my eyes and instead of tears I see a cascade of water. My face dissolves into a muddy bank, and I am back underground, shaking. Curi's warm hand on my chest holds off the last dying gusts of the storm.

"That was a bad one," she says. "We might've been displaced hundreds of years."

I can only nod. Words haven't returned yet.

When the next hurricane hits, I'm out on the beach checking the traps, caught by surprise. I've heard about this variety of storm. Instead of a solid bank of clouds, it comes in rapid green bands. Each one hits like an earthquake, smacking me back a step and deluging me with a seconds-long wall of rain. Instead of a prolonged memory I get only flashes with each thrash of the storm. After the first few I am lying on the beach, helpless as wave upon wave of water and memory smash into me.

I step down off the stage after receiving an award for school service and see my mom smiling. Russ sits beside her, giving me a thumbs up.

"...it could be a good thing to try," my mother is saying.

"It's not part of the Plan," Russ says. "Let's stick to it, right Matt?"

I'm driving and for the first time I don't imagine what would happen if I drove myself off the road.

An essay, edits inserted in neat rows above each line.

"We're so proud of you."

A female voice: "He's the smartest idiot I know."

Another: "I think he's more the dumbest smart person."

Foam pours from a bottle of champagne, and my eyes are cold as I watch the glasses pour.

There's fighting in the air on a warm night. Cass loops an arm around mine and tells me that she's almost at a breaking point. I tell her I'm so far past the breaking point I can't even see it behind me.

Spreadsheets upon spreadsheets, rows upon rows filled in, check marks for each task accomplished. I run a sort function and the table resolves into even more ordered rows, grouped by color and with a satisfying squareness. The world makes sense until I close my laptop.

I'm running soccer drills, my legs burning. I can't sprint anymore, but somehow I do. My personal records fall, and I tumble to the muddy turf.

The page refreshes, but still nothing. Dozens of entries, all between 98 and 100, line up. I refresh and almost throw up when a 94 posts at the top of the page.

I'm drinking coffee after dinner, fighting exhaustion as page after page of practice tests collapse beneath my pencil. A shadow in the doorway urges me on: "You got this."

After the first thick envelope, it stops being a surprise when each letter starts with an abrupt *Congratulations!* Everything outside of me points to elation, but I feel...

...I feel nothing as the choice stretches in front of me. I put it all in a spreadsheet, pros and cons. There's a party. Cass says she's proud of me, and Russ asks her if she doubted me.

We fight. Or rather, she fights, and I stay silent. She threatens to break up, and I wish I could tell her it's the best thing for her. That would be part of the Plan. She's been a distraction, and she clearly knows I think of her as one.

I've come through months of rehab, both physical and emotional, but something is cracking more every day. Out of it leaks a cold emptiness.

Amid this comes another disappearance, this one external, unexpected. But as its impression flashes through my mind, I know already that I am in no position to receive it as anything besides another event, another brick in the wall that makes up the story I'm telling.

This ordered world will not allow pain. I'm free from it, just as I'm free from everything else.

Freedom is its own chain.

There's a long break in the storm, and I catch my breath. But then the last spasm of wind strikes and I hear Cass' voice in my ear, painfully empty of life and hope: "I thought I had you back."

When the storm passes, I am unable to rise from the sand. I wish the wind would carry me away with it.

"It's never been done before, but there's no rule against it as far as I know," Curi says. We're watching a group of youngsters play by the water. It's one of the least strenuous jobs on the island, since most Whilean children behave like tiny history professors.

They're gathered in the shallows, where one girl explains the rules of the game they're about to play. I catch something about one person playing the role of the hurricane, and trying to trap everyone else in a temporal displacement.

"Is this because of your last vision?" Curi asks.

"You get taken out of your old life, and there's an assumption that you'd want to go back," I say. "But what if there's nothing to go back to?"

"What you were describing was an incredible recovery. You showed amazing courage in that old life."

"Courage or not, what did I have to show for it?" I ask.

"It sounds like a good college, warding off depression, reintegrating into society. You're right, sounds like nothing to me."

I watch as one child wraps up another, starting an elaborate dance as she sends her hundreds of years into the imaginary past. Salt spray splashes around them.

"I looked at those spreadsheets, at all those checkmarks indicating accomplishments, and you know what I felt? I felt like the only thing that was real was the spreadsheets and checkmarks. They could've said anything, and all that would've mattered was that they were filled in, sorted, and color-coded. I could just as easily have been solving world hunger as massacring political dissidents, and all that would've mattered was the box that said it was done."

Curi is about to respond, but sees that I'm shaking. She pauses, then puts an arm around me and pulls me close. I lower my head, hiding the tears that now roll down my face. The children pay no notice, continuing to laugh and splash.

"I can't go back," I whisper. "I can't go back." I wrap my arm around her, and past the edge of her chest I catch a blue-white number on my wrist, rising every few seconds like a sum function growing as you add more rows to the spreadsheet. I have a brief flash that, more than even the memories, the useless device is the thing most tying me to my past life. A self-emanation indeed.

Curi wipes my tears and puts a hand to my cheek, forcing me to lift my head.

"If you can't go back, then it sounds like you should stay here and become one of us."

"That simple," I say, laughing despite my tears.

"That simple."

Of course, it's not that simple. I've spent so long either actively seeking a way out of the Carnival, or hoping one would reveal itself through the Whileans. But if what I've glimpsed of my past life is true, there's nothing for me to return to. I've made a life here. I've met someone incredible. The particulars may be strange, but I can say with certainty that I'm happier than I was at any point I've seen in my previous life. I remember Bailly's insistence that I tell a story in the Carnival. I finally begin to feel I've told the right one.

Life settles into rhythms that begin to feel normal. I help out as much as I can with fishing or harvesting mollusks and crustaceans from the shallows. There is always work to be done, always huts to be rebuilt after the storms, or food to be prepared. When I have free time, I spend it with Curi. We never travel as far as we did on the day of my first temporal hurricane, but we do circle the inner islands by canoe, searching for the most beautiful unoccupied beaches we can find. We eventually settle on a favorite. It lacks the pristine sand of some of the more popular ones, but the rocks on the shore have worn down over the years, until they are smooth, white, and almost all nearly perfectly elliptical. They are difficult to walk on, sliding about under our feet, but they remain cool during the day, and at night they seem to catch the entirety of the moon's light, reflecting it in all directions so the shore gleams bright enough to see without any other light source.

The Provost is the least pleasant part of my stay on the islands. He always seems to find me and Curi at the exact moment when I am provoking a silly reaction from her, catching her in the middle of a laugh that he obviously considers undignified for the future Provost. But he hasn't said anything further since the night of the feast, or explicitly forbidden me from seeing his daughter. I haven't forgotten what he said about Curi's responsibility, how if I truly cared for her I would let her go.

But every time I look at Curi, that thought vanishes. Her smile is now as wide as the sea between these islands to me. When I see it, nothing else matters.

So despite the Provost's watchful eyes, despite the occasional temporal hurricanes that bring flashes of my past—flashes of how lost I was, how empty in that still mostly opaque world outside the Carnival—I begin to feel something in my future. An ease, a calm. A life that is just ... being lived. Nothing more.

We haven't had a storm for almost three weeks when a boat appears on the horizon. Its sails cut vicious brown triangles out of the sky. Almost the entire village meets the launch boat on the beach. At the oars are six creatures with bark protruding from their limbs, and vacant faces displaying no discernible effort as they row. These are unmistakably Apocalyptians. They disembark and pull the boat ashore. A shorter figure steps from amidst them, leading the company forward.

June may have the same face, the same long, sure stride, but in every other way her presence is different. She wears a black cape held at her neck by a metal clasp with the texture of tree bark. On her head is a circlet made of sticks and twigs, which jut menacingly in every direction. Her black boots churn the sand as she walks directly toward me. The cape sparks an image in my mind of a coat unfurling itself into wings. A dark figure flying over the chasm that had once been the city of Valdrada. But it remains rigid, barely even flapping.

"Mattila the Hun, still a Whilean after all this time," she says. She wraps me in the coldest hug I've ever experienced. She holds me at arm's length and looks over at Curi, who is staring at her with a mixture of dutiful curiosity and fear. "Still with the biographer? Interesting. I'm happy to see you've discovered a sense of your own narcissism in my absence."

"Why are you with them, June?"

She waves a hand and the Apocalyptians form themselves into a crisp line. Her creations, obeying her command

"It's been a long time for me. You'd be surprised how much your perspective shifts in two-hundred years."

"Two hundred?"

"How long has it been for you?" She studies my face, as if trying to match it against an old memory. "I was fifty years ahead of you last time."

"It's only been a few months since then. For me."

I'm somewhat heartened to see that I can still inspire genuine surprise in June. It falls away quickly.

"I've come to speak with the Provost," she says to Curi. "Your daddy around?"

"You are welcome here," the Provost says, stepping forward, "for now. Come." He leads the way to the village. June winks at me, and her retinue is swallowed inside the ranks of the Whileans, many of whom have picked up whatever approximation of a weapon they can get their hands on.

There is no grand feast in the pavilion for June and the silent guests, only a small plate of smoked fish and jugs of fresh water. June looks with disdain at the non-alcoholic drink before swigging from it anyway.

"Here's the chase we're going to cut to," June says when most of the townspeople are seated. The Provost has taken up his usual position in the heavy wooden chair on the platform overlooking the central open area. The Apocalyptians sit in an indifferent row behind Junes. Their eyes are even more disconcerting up close—their pupils and irises are bleached almost as light as the whites of their eyes. They aren't blind, but the vacant eyes, along with their lack of movement, give them the feeling of existing outside the world rather than being active participants in it.

"I have a lot of respect for what you guys do here," June says, "I really do. Your histories are the lifeblood of the Carnival. I truly mean that. Not to mention that your islands are a beautiful place for a vacation. If you weren't so damn serious all the time it might even be a fun place to hang out for a few dozen years.

"But what make you unique, let's face it, is your relationship with time. Temporal hurricanes don't happen anywhere else, which makes this place quite the anomaly."

"What interest do you have in this anomaly?" the Provost asks.

"I find myself the elected leader of a storied organization. We have a strong interest in this anomaly for reasons of our own. I don't think you will like those reasons, but I think you can probably guess their nature."

"Nothing ends the world quicker than a change in time," I say.

"Did he get smarter? I think he got smarter. Are you responsible for this?" she asks Curi, who is muttering to herself, repeating every word as if to inscribe it on her mind.

"Out with it," the Provost says. "What do you want?"

"It requires almost no investment on your part. All we would like to do is run a small wire from the mainland to one of your outer islands. This will allow us to study the anomaly without being taken along for the temporal ride. At least in theory. That's all we're asking. We'll supply our own team of scientists. Think of it like what you do, studying us for your grand histories. Nothing more intrusive than that."

"Except you will use whatever knowledge you gain for a truly evil purpose," the Provost says. "It's not like what we do at all."

"One man's yam is another man's rutabaga," June says, weighing imaginary produce in her outstretched hands.

"And if we refuse?"

"Oh no, that wouldn't be very smart at all." June's light tone doesn't change as she continues, "if you refuse, we will destroy your civilization so thoroughly and with such systematic brutality that there won't even be islands left to study."

Over the next couple of hours the Whileans disperse, leaving June to pace in the pavilion. I think of when I first met June, when she was so in love with the Carnival that she scoffed at the idea that I would want to leave. I find it deeply sad that that June is gone. As the Whileans deliberate, Curi and I watch the intruders from the doorway of my hut. She's quiet. It hurts to see the fear on her face. If the Apocalyptians decided to attack, there's nothing they could do to stop the destruction of their society. My society.

Eventually the waiting is too much, and I walk back into the pavilion. June is tossing a wooden bowl up into the air, watching it spin, and catching it absentmindedly.

"Come to catch up, Mattattee?" she says. "Good. These guys are loyal but boy are they boring company."

"Boring, bent on the destruction of the world, covered in bark. You've got to work on your friend selection."

"Funny, that's what everyone said when I was hanging out with you."

"Given the circumstances I'm not really in the mood for your jokes," I say.

"This is a new version of you. I can see why the island girl is so awkwardly aroused."

Even after two-hundred years, the only strategy that works with June is to ignore her. "You can't go through with this. If the Whileans don't let you do your research, you have to leave them in peace."

June gives me a skeptical tilt of her head.

"I don't have an alternative offer," I say. "There's nothing here of value I can give you. All I'm asking is that you have the basic human decency not to screw up an entire society because of some crazy whim."

"What makes you think it's a whim?" June asks. "You're assuming I don't have a serious rationale."

"Well, do you?"

One of the Apocalyptians bristles behind me. I keep my focus on June.

"Of course I do," she says. "You think I would bother to show up here, threaten death and destruction, and carry out a rigorous scientific experiment that probably won't even work without a concrete reason?"

"It feels like the kind of thing you would do."

"You wound me."

"How are you okay with hurting all these people? I don't believe you're dumb enough to have bought into the Apocalyptians' whole thing. You created them for Christ's sake."

"Of course not. You're acting like Armageddon—sorry, Apocalypse—is a permanent state. But from every death there's a rebirth. It's that rebirth I'm after, not the death itself."

"That's a pretty flimsy justification for killing people." I feel venom in every word. I've never spoken with June like this before, even when she was at her most difficult during our time together. But she's changed, and I have too.

"People? Your blindness astounds me."

"Your lack of morals astounds me. I don't understand. You love the Carnival."

"A lot changes in a hundred and fifty years."

"And apparently not for the better," I shoot back.

But something in how tired June's face looks, the lingering sense of dislocation in her eyes, feels familiar. It's the same way she looked back when I was on her submarine. When she so casually floated the idea that we might leave the Carnival behind. But how could that possibly relate to the end of the world?

June's expression is unreadable, but two of the Apocalyptians stand and flank me.

"Perspective is a double-edged sword. It's easy to forget how you used to see things."

"What the hell does that mean?" My voice shakes as one of the Apocalyptians puts a cold hand on my shoulder.

"My recommendation would be that you leave the While Isles for good. If the Provost refuses, we will turn this whole archipelago into a wasteland."

The Apocalyptians are not rough with me, but they move me firmly ahead of them, out of the pavilion and back into the light of an island afternoon.

I feel as if I'm floating in the clouds, only realizing when the ground begins to come closer that I've actually been falling the whole time. Should her offer be refused, I don't have any doubt that June will torch the island and everyone on it. But I won't leave. I have to stay and fight if necessary. These are my people now.

The Provost refuses June's proposition not an hour later. June and her entourage return to their boat, escorted by more than two dozen men from the village. Before they board their dinghy, June stands facing the center of the island, looking around almost wistfully, taking in the soft sand, the pink moss, and the first rows of houses through the trees. Her eyes fall on me, and time becomes briefly slippery. But if there's a hidden message in that stare, I can't decipher it.

That night Curi and I curl up in my hut. Neither of us can bring ourselves to sleep. She pulls close against my chest and hugs me so tightly that I feel my own heartbeat echoing off her. Her soft breath next to me, the warmth that melds with mine, these are the only things that matter.

"You're calm," Curi says. Her voice when she's this close is so gentle, and is for no one else besides me. It moves me more than even the voice she uses as a master storyteller.

"Am I?"

"You're obviously scared, but yes you're calm. It's really helping me not to have a full-on nervous breakdown."

I stroke her hair. "There has to be a solution that works for everyone. June's a reasonable person, despite appearances." I'm not so sure though. This is not a June I know.

"I don't know, Matthew," Curi says. "If it comes to a fight, it won't even really be a fight."

"It won't come to that."

Curi pulls even closer. All is still outside. It's a warm night, but even when sweat begins to pool between our skin, we don't let go.

The first shouts of panic start about an hour later. We blearily take in the chaos of moving villagers. The shouts all say the same thing: *Fire!*

Two of the huts on the outskirts of the village are ablaze. By the time we arrive, a bucket line has already formed. The huts' occupants are dazed but safe, their faces covered in ash.

There hasn't been a fire here since I arrived, and by the panic it instills I guess it's not something the Whileans are accustomed to. A third hut, its palm roof dry and ready to catch at the slightest spark, goes up in flames. Kereus is there, shouting along with the others. He calls us over.

"We have to move quickly," he says. "If this reaches the inner ring, the houses there are too close together to stop it from taking down the entire village. Take whoever you can and start dousing the roofs and floors, anything that might catch and is in the fire's path. We need to put as much water in the way as possible."

"Understood."

We run back toward the center of town, having to battle the tide of people moving toward the chaos. Curi tries to recruit as many as she can to make for the inner ring.

In the brief interstitial zone between the inner and outer rings, there's an area of shade. The only light comes from the blaze behind us, and with the number of people moving through the space, I keep getting bumped into. Just as I momentarily lose sight of Curi, there's a sharp crack, and a few cries of pain. Shapes stagger through the darkness.

"Curi?" I call out as I trip over a prone figure. I skid painfully onto my side and immediately feel blood pooling from my scraped knee. I catch sight of a young man on the ground. I recognize him, but don't know his name. He is unconscious, a gash carved across his forehead. I stumble to my feet as more shouts come from the trees around me. I follow the areas with the most motion, fumbling blindly.

What I see are two large, inhuman shapes. Their knotty shadows make it seem like the trees themselves have come alive and begun attacking us. A smaller shape thrashes between them.

I rush toward them, now able to make out Curi's shouts of panic.

I spring toward them, trying to knock one's grip loose enough for Curi to escape.

Instead I am met by a woody fist and a roar of pain. My body is flung back nearly ten yards, all wind taken from it. The

Apocalyptians chuckle in their throaty voices as they lift Curi between them and disappear from sight.

I try to follow, but I can't even get to my feet. Pain shoots through my entire chest. *Curi.* I rise, my limbs requiring inhuman force. But then nausea tears through me. I retch and collapse back to my scraped knees. My vision is blurry. I feel hands on my back and shoulder.

With the trees framing his head and dim light cast from behind, the Provost's face is even more severe than usual.

"Are you all right, Matthew?"

"They took her."

"I know, I know." His eyes are lit with rage. "I've sent the strongest men available after them. There's nothing more we can do."

I want to get up and sprint after them. I want to pick up a spear and send it through the heart of each Apocalyptian—if they even have them—but my body isn't responding. Curi is a prisoner of these monsters.

"They won't harm her," her father says. "They need her for leverage. She is my daughter, after all."

I know, even in the daze of pain and smoke, that in theory he's right. But I don't trust anything about the Apocalyptians. And I don't trust June.

By the time the fires are out and some semblance of order has returned to the village, three of the men who went after Curi have come back wounded, four huts have burned down, and a sense of dread hangs heavy.

Deliberations begin in the pavilion, but even the Provost cannot maintain order. Dissenting voices from all sides crowd out any logical discussion. I leave after fifteen minutes. I don't care what the most prudent move is. I don't care whether Curi's status as a captive is temporarily keeping her safe. I just want her back, and I'm not about to sit around waiting for everyone else to decide whether or not that's an option.

Kereus has been one of the loudest voices insisting that we act immediately, his calm demeanor disappearing along with his cousin. I pull him aside.

"They'll argue over what to do even after the Apocalyptians have killed her," Kereus says.

"Is there any chance that they actually give in? I thought Curi was supposed to be the next Provost."

"She is. But they also aren't convinced that the Apocalyptians won't harm her if we accept their demands."

"Now that we've pissed them off," I say.

"Precisely."

"Then I vote we take matters into our own hands."

Occasionally the Whileans will venture into the deep caves underneath their islands. Reaching these caves requires swimming several hundred feet down from shore, and then paddling through an intricate, completely submerged system of passages. Given how difficult these passages are to navigate, even for experienced divers, the Whileans have developed a number of tools to assist them.

The only problem is that they're all a little gross, since they're derived from the anatomy of sea creatures. Kereus offers me a breathing device made of a fish's lung—you have to put your mouth over an opening at one end, and then allow the gills and the rest of the mechanism to render the air breathable. It's like biting into a piece of aquatic haggis. They also use bioluminescent eggs—smaller than the leviathans' but otherwise similar in appearance—to provide light underwater. These are squishy, and you have to be careful not to squeeze them too hard, otherwise they explode and leak viscous blue fluid. We wear them in thin nets around our necks.

The Apocalyptians' boat is anchored half a mile offshore. We each carry two spears strapped to our backs, as well as an extra breathing apparatus in case we accidentally bite through the membrane.

As soon as we plunge into the shallow water, navigation becomes a challenge. Even through the bay's clear water, light doesn't travel far, and the eggs and the glow from my wrist device create only a dull haze. We have to keep poking our heads above the waves to get our bearings. The saltwater stings my eyes, and every time I think we've found a rhythm in a consistent direction, I raise my head, only to realize we've gotten turned almost all the way around. A few times a large fish or squid swims suddenly into view, and my heart jumps out of my chest. As much time as I've spent in these waters, there's still fear in their depths. But the thought of Curi on the Apocalyptians' ship drives me forward.

Kereus stays close. My ribs still ache, but the pain is significantly less than it should be. I've recovered quickly—not a surprise when I consider that none of the bumps, cuts, bruises, and abrasions I've acquired in the Carnival have stuck around more than a couple of hours. It's almost as if the moment I forget I should be feeling pain, I stop experiencing it.

I'm startled as we come up almost directly underneath the boat. I duck my head back below the surface, hoping I'm not as noisy as I feel.

We can't hear anything going on aboard from here, but there are lights in the rear cabin. I nod to Kereus, and we take out our breathing apparatuses. The fishy flavor lingers. We begin to climb the anchor rope. It's harder than it looks, and the slippery rope creaks with every movement.

We slow as we rise near level with the cabin. Voices are becoming more distinct within. We dangle from the rope, listening to the familiar voices inside as we try to stay out of sight.

"...too bad you're clearly not having as much fun as I am," June is saying. "Don't worry, though, we won't hurt you unless we absolutely feel like it."

My heart races. Only when I hear Curi's soft voice do I breathe a momentary sigh of relief.

"It's fitting that it's me you would kidnap," Curi says. "I now have inside access to this pivotal moment in your story. It's like having your biographer hanging out with you when you're about to have your big break."

There's a short gap in the conversation, along with the sound of someone moving around the cabin.

"I'm not sure how comfortable I feel with having a dedicated biographer," June finally says.

"I think you would find it more comforting if you behaved in a less objectionable way."

June's harsh laugh drops off quickly. "You of all people should understand me well enough to know why that's a stupid statement."

"Enlighten me."

"Not sure that's such a good idea."

"Suit yourself."

I risk poking my head above the window frame. June sits at a low table, which is strewn with the remains of a meal. Only Curi's leg is visible, sticking out from behind the column in the center of the room that she appears to be tied to. June is apparently alone with her. I try to determine logistically how I could throw the spear while dangling from the anchor line, but even if I could get enough force behind the throw to reach June, I don't know whether my wooden spear could break through the window. More to the point, I don't know if I'm capable of harming June, even with this turn she's taken. She was my first friend in the Carnival. I don't believe she's lost for good.

For the moment, I'm stuck in indecision, and the conversation continues above me.

"It must be lonely spending all your time with the Apocalyptians."

"To the contrary, someone who has no desire to talk is the most fun to talk to. It's all June all day, baby."

"I don't think you've convinced yourself."

"You'd be surprised." Once again June's voice has become harsh. "But as usual you're missing the point. The Apocalyptians aren't my people. They're merely a means to an end."

"That end being the end of the world."

"Obviously."

"You should be in control of the Apocalyptians. Instead you're a parrot for their propaganda."

"I created their propaganda," June snarls.

"Exactly."

"Goddamnit. Honestly, if I had any idea you'd be this annoying, I would've picked a different captive."

I find myself blown away by Curi's restraint. It also makes me realize just how well she's studied June.

"You're actually this dense?" June asks. "Jesus Christ. What happens after the end of the world?"

"Presumably another world, if history is any guide."

"But before that world, when everything has fallen back to a null state..."

"Ah. Null. Nothing. No-here."

June gets up and paces in front of her hostage.

"It took me a while to figure it out," June says. "The Carnival can make it difficult to see these things clearly. But of course those of us from Elsewhere are different. When the world ends—when the null state is reached—there will be nowhere for us to go."

I nearly lose my grip. So all of this is just so she can have an outside shot at getting out of the Carnival?

"Or you'll enter a null state as well."

"That makes no sense," June snaps.

"It's a big risk to take," Curi says.

"I have to take it."

June begins haphazardly stacking the plates on the table. Any second she could call in her guard, and if that happens our opportunity will have passed. I prepare the only desperate plan I can think of. I'm going to launch myself spear-first into the window. Hopefully I'll only take a few cuts in the process.

"Ugh it stinks in here," June says. A stroke of luck hits. June is making for the window. She'll see me after she gets it open, but in the moment between those two events...

I brace myself.

"My people aren't fighters," Curi says, and I recognize the authority of the storyteller from the Feast of Lost Days. "But you may find that your conventional means of warfare don't work as well here."

June pauses with her hand on the frame. "They seem all right so far." I have to fight myself not to jump too early.

"I am tapped to be the next Provost," Curi continues. "Do you know what that means?"

"It means you're going to be exactly as boring as your father?"

June lifts the latch on the window. I hold my spear tight with one hand, and bend against the rope with my other.

"It means certain advantages have been afforded me while I'm still in the waters around the islands."

June turns, startled to see that Curi is standing. Hadn't she been shackled? She shows herself in full, and for a moment she appears much older. Then the room shrinks, minimizing itself in a circle around Curi. June shrinks with it, as does the window, and my arm is sucked into the vortex.

The room squeezes into a single tube, and everything around Curi—me, Kereus, June, and even the rest of the islands—form the walls. I am a small piece of a two-dimensional image arranged in a panoptic circle. But Curi, at its center, remains fully three-dimensional and fully herself.

I struggle to keep my hold on the rope as the third dimension returns.

When I look back into the cabin, June's back is to the window, and Curi is gone.

My hands scrabble at the rope. Not at. Through. I fall, and memory engulfs me before the water does.

Bubbles stream up from my mouth, disappearing into the darkness above. The brackish water has a viscosity to it, as if the silt that blocks the sun from reaching more than a few inches down has a physical weight. It's not seawater, and it's a long time until I'll find myself on the While Isles.

I kick up from the bottom—my feet sinking into a squelch and a half of mud as I do—and emerge, shaking water out of my hair.

I've let it grow long, far from the close-cropped trim of a would-be politician.

With some effort I climb over the side of the kayak, dripping muddy water into its bottom. A breeze stirs around me. Though the sun still blazes, this breeze portends fall. It feels crisp, clean. It is an omen of nothing, besides maybe mulled cider and the beginning of the high school soccer season.

I unhook the oar from the side of the kayak, and reorient myself so I'm facing the far end of the lake. I've always thought the trees down there resembled a disapproving male face, perhaps some old god of the lake who saves or drowns teenagers who have the audacity to swim in his still waters alone, depending on his mood and whether they've committed some crime of vanity.

But yesterday I approached the grandfatherly bulge of those trees, only to find the area beneath a clear patch of pine needles, more a picnic spot than the feet of a mighty nature spirit.

Or perhaps the lake god has smiled upon me.

My oar breaks the water's surface silently. The quiet here is so profound that, lake god's favor or not, it would certainly be bad luck to break it.

When I first came to the lake I measured the distance from one end to the other, and put my distance swum—calculated by number of laps—into a spreadsheet. Two and a half miles. Three miles. Four. As I did, I watched the sinew in my arms grows, felt the cords of muscle in my neck and back. I noted these changes with passing interest. After all, what really mattered was the accumulation of data in the spreadsheet and the personal records I was breaking.

But something happened during the second month of this long summer. I wish when I say *something* that I could chart a specific event, but I can't. It didn't happen when I told my mom I needed to defer for a year before entering college. It didn't happen during the ensuing screaming match with Russ. It didn't even happen when Cass hugged me after I told her the decision, and for the first time in six or seven I-can't-even-remember-how-longs I noticed how warm her forehead was, and how it crinkled at a slight angle when she smiled and really meant it.

No, what happened was that I was swimming backstroke, and got so wrapped up in the crisscross patterns of two banks of clouds that instead of continuing to paddle I found myself floating. Absence is hard to identify, but at that moment I became acutely aware that the voice that usually tells me *pick it up, go faster, you're slacking* wasn't there. The drillmaster in charge of tracking my progress and pushing me forward had forgotten to show up.

Well shit, I thought. *What do I do now?*

And what I did then, at that exact moment, was float.

A couple times my mom has questioned me coming out here on my own. What if I hit my head on a rock and drown? What if a storm comes and I get struck by lightning?

I remind her gently that if those things had happened two years ago, I would have welcomed them.

The icy water around me is salt. I sink down down down. There's no bottom to push off of.

A breeze blows across the lake, sending gentle waves drifting against my boat. I flow with the current, increasing the speed of my strokes. Soon I splash forward, moving too quickly for so kind a breeze to slow me.

Russ told me that to abandon the Plan was to abandon myself. With each stroke I imagine a counter, linked to a device that feeds the data about my movements directly into an app, from which I can then export a CSV file. So versatile, those CSVs. Separating the entries with commas hides the barriers between them, but the actual spreadsheet they produce makes the separation more than apparent.

During that fight with Russ a part of me returned, the exact part of me he warned me about. It was the same part that railed against my father on countless therapists' couches, the same part that caused me to boil over when classmates would mention how they had driven home buzzed after a party.

Is this air in my lungs, or water? I struggle against the ocean, but I can't tell which way is up.

But the anger I feared would take over never did. It's as elusive—and irrelevant—as the answer to the question of what to do now. I row back to shore, my strokes strong but unhurried. On the shore, I dump as much water as I can out of my kayak, and pack up the rest of the gear I had left there. I grab the handle at the bow, hoisting it so the interior curve of one side is over my shoulder.

I am not always alone here, but today I am. The lake god at the far end watches me impassively. I take in the last moment of calm. The path ahead of me is open, not exactly clear, but certainly no more brambly or overgrown than any other path in this forest.

Suddenly all of the lake's water rises into the air. Then it comes crashing down, and I am engulfed.

The depths I sink into are so cold I can feel my heart fighting to keep pumping. Pressure builds in my ears and sinuses, and I wish I could scream at the pain.

I thrash in a direction that feels like the surface, but see no indication of a change. I search wildly for my backup breathing device, but my hands find only an empty space. With my breathing apparatuses gone, my lungs begin to scream.

I am going to die here, crushed under the weight of the water surrounding these gentle islands.

I pick a direction. My mind returns to the contentment and calm I felt seconds ago. For the first time I could see a future that was not either pain or emptiness. I need to fight.

My arms churn through the water. They're not as strong as they were that day on the lake, but desperation pushes them well past their usual limit.

Warmth overcomes me. I kick, I struggle, I surge.

A soft surface rises against my stomach, and I splay out as a curved mass pushes into me. I fold into it, unable to fight anymore. We move toward a shimmer, accelerating faster than I have ever traveled through water.

When we crest, I am launched fifteen feet into the air, coming splashing back down in a painful face and belly flop. I gulp air, choke, and gulp again. I've never been so grateful for a simple breath. I look back and see the telltale dorsal fins of a leviathan breaking the waves. I never see its face. The beast is gone, and I am alive.

Arms close around me, and I hear Kereus' voice: "I thought you had drowned."

"Not quite," I splutter. His face is pale. Only now do I have time to think about what we just witnessed Curi do. "Let's go."

Kereus gives me an apprehensive look, like he doubts I'm up to the trip, and then breaks into his stroke.

In the pause before I follow him, I notice an absence on my wrist. The device that had been counting upward since my arrival in the Wasteland is gone. Is it still counting as it descends to the depths? I feel unaccountably free. The IT Guy in the steel city said it was a self-emanation, that my mind was creating it somehow. Does being free of it mean my mind has changed? The freedom feels the same way as my memories in the lake. But fear quickly overrides that freedom. What did Curi just do? Is she safe?

The swim back to the island is a mad dash. Curi has just bent even my understanding of the Carnival. For all the time I've spent with her, there have always been parts of her I didn't know. Now I think she kept these parts from me for my own safety.

But more pressing even than that, I've unlocked a new truth in that memory. With each stroke I'm reminded not of the emptiness of the past, but the openness of the future. There has always been another world outside this one, but for the first time I am certain it's the one I belong in.

Whatever we find back on the While Isles, I am beginning to think it will be the last time I will return.

"Kereus," I say as we reach the shallows and begin wading our tired limbs up onto the beach, "what the hell was that?"

"Think of it like a temporal hurricane. Only instead of the whole islands moving in time, only Curi did."

"She can do that?"

"It didn't look exactly how it was supposed to."

"So something went wrong?" I ask. The wind is cold on my skin, but it's a relief to no longer have salt splashing into my eyes.

Kereus shrugs. This is clearly beyond him as well.

The village is still gathered in the pavilion, but the energy is different. The buzz of panic and debate has been replaced by a calmer, more resolved feeling.

Curi sits in the center of the pavilion, exhausted but un-harmed. I expect her to be making some grand speech, or weighing in on an issue of policy, but the public forum has dissolved. Everyone is just present, supporting each other and speaking in familiar tones. The Provost and a couple of Curi's aunts and uncles fret over her, and one of the grandmothers winds her way through the crowd serving tea. I run to Curi and wrap her in a hug.

She gives me a look—grateful, exhausted, slightly amused.

"I thought I saw someone in the window," she says. I squeeze her tighter. "Come on," Curi says, "we need to talk."

We walk together, keeping to the well-lit and populated area right outside.

"How much of that did you catch?" Curi asks.

"Enough. Whatever happened in those two-hundred years has changed June. She always had a hard edge, but this is different."

"I know that even better than you," Curi reminds me. "But you're right, this is different. June has always loved the Carnival. There's been a willingness to her presence here, unlike you and the Four. She loves this place. Loved."

"Do you think she's right about what will happen? The null state?"

"I want to hear exactly what you think it is that she thinks will happen," Curi says. It takes me a second to realize why.

"She thinks destroying the Carnival will allow her to leave. To return to Elsewhere."

"And?"

"And what? You think I might go off and help her?"

"You and June are now aligned in the one goal you've had since arriving."

I see the hurt on her face. If I leave, I'm leaving her.

"The goal I *had*," I say. "It stopped being about that a while ago. If I'm honest, it stopped being about that pretty much as soon as I met you."

Yet my most recent memory breakthrough tugs at me. The prospect of the life I fought for. I had thought there was nothing to go back to, but I know now that's not true. My memories had lied to me, as if selected to make the most compelling case for me to stay. Curi's temporal disruption showed me the truth.

Curi looks at me sadly. "Matthew, what you saw tonight, my power…"

"It was incredible. It makes me think we might have a real shot against the Apocalyptians."

"No. Even that relatively small act took everything I had. I'm not sure I could even do it again."

"Well, you're not Provost yet."

"That's not the issue," she says. "My family's bond with these islands runs deep. But that single bond is not enough. I have to have a partner to amplify my powers. Someone from the islands."

"I'm not following," I say.

A long silence passes before she says, "I finally understood my limitations, and how much more powerful I could be. If I stay with you, I will never be able to reach that potential."

Shit. "Shit."

She lets me steep in this information. I'd wanted to stay with her to help her defend her people. I'd wanted to be by her side through whatever new storm came our way.

I feel like my insides are being scooped out by giant salad tongs. I want the life that was promised, a life of simplicity on these islands, with this amazing young woman. But the one thing I can't do is keep her from becoming what she's meant to be. And maybe this was never going to be simple.

"Curi, how much are you willing to lose to keep June from hurting your people?" I ask.

"Everything."

"Even me?"

The pain in her face breaks my heart, but I need her honesty.

"Yes, even you."

"You're risking a lot on a hunch," the Provost says.

We're alone in the hut he and Curi share. It's no smaller or larger than any other villager's, the same airy construction, the same minimal assortment of belongings—a low table with a wooden cup, plate, and fork for each person, fungus-stuffed mattresses, and a couple of handmade dolls from Curi's childhood.

"You've already lost your daughter once," I plead. "Don't let it happen again."

"We would find a way to defend ourselves."

"No, you wouldn't. The Apocalyptians are a force of pure destruction. If they decide to eliminate your civilization, they will succeed. But even if I fail and you allow them to conduct their research, it could be hundreds, thousands of years before they can master the temporal storms and carry out their final plan. If ever. Isn't that time worth more than the short days you'd have while you fight off an invasion?"

"I suppose. But the secret of the temporal hurricanes is ours alone. For an outsider ... we're not supposed to be this involved."

"I understand. The final part of my offer is this." I steel myself. "No matter what, I'll leave the While Isles behind. I'll return to the mainland and live out whatever time I have left there. I'll allow Curi to live the life she needs to live, with someone who can support her as she becomes Provost."

I only register that I'm crying when the first tear reaches the tip of my nose. The Provost stands still. A gentle breeze shuffles the roof's dried palm leaves.

"I think I may have underestimated your generosity," he says.

"You've been nothing but generous to me. It's time for me to return the favor. Please, don't give me more time to reconsider."

"Have you run this by Curi?"

"I'm doing this because I care about her. She'll understand that at least."

The Provost extends a slender hand to me. I shake it, feeling streaks on my fingers where I've wiped away my tears.

"I came with an offer."

I'd rowed out on one of the Whileans' rafts, holding a white flag. I still thought the Apocalyptians were about to tear me to shreds when I climbed aboard June's ship.

"I don't really see you as the 'having anything to offer' type, no offense," June says.

"You'd be surprised," I say, and then I roll the dice. "So you want out too, huh?"

Her eyes go cold. "What do you mean by that?"

"I'm gonna go ahead and ignore the bullshit. The only reason you're looking to blow everything up is that you're hoping that blowing it up will allow you to leave. The null state?"

"You're assuming a lot."

"I'm right, though. What, two-hundred years here get a little boring or something? You showed me there are infinite possibilities. You were the one who tried to convince me that I didn't need to look for answers, because there's no reason to leave. Infinite possibilities!"

After a long pause she says quietly, "When there are infinite possibilities, things stop mattering." Her expression holds both the weight of the long years and a childish vulnerability. She may have changed in all those years, but there's still the same person underneath, who wants to love this world wholeheartedly. She can't anymore though, and I need to use that fact.

"Destroying the Carnival may send us home," I say. "But this null state business sounds ridiculously unpleasant, and I think it's more likely we'll end up stuck in an empty void surrounded by middle-aged men riding chickens. They didn't leave the last time it happened, so it's no guarantee we'll be able to this time. Either way, the people who live here don't deserve to die."

"You act like they're real," she says.

"Of course they're real. They're as real as anything I've ever experienced."

"Strong words from an amnesiac."

"Even so. My offer is this: You allow me to go back with you, and together we try to get out of here without hurting anyone.

If that fails, the Provost will let you do your research. Neither of us will stop you."

"One try," June says. "One try your way and then my way?"

"Yes, just one try."

The Carnival - Valdrada

The journey back to the mainland gives me way more time than I could ever possibly want in the close proximity of the silent Apocalyptians. June stands astern, eyes trained on the receding horizon. The creatures do not breathe, or at least not in the normal rhythm of humans. They raise the sails and pull up the anchor, but they do so without a word and without any apparent effort. Every once in a while one will make a wheezing sound as if expelling a large quantity of air.

The While Isles have begun to fade behind us. With them departs the only home I can fully remember. I wonder what history Curi will record from my departure. That I saved her people by cutting a deal with the enemy? That I failed spectacularly and doomed them? I wonder if she'll carve a space for herself in her own history, or if she'll simply recount that I met an island girl, that I fell in love, or something close to it, and that I left. Will she stop as she tells the story, turn to her audience with a knowing smile, and say, "And as you may know, that girl was me."

A touch too theatrical for Curi, if I know her. But none of that matters. If I succeed, I'll be gone for good. I feel a pang at the thought that I won't be able to hear whatever story she decides to tell about me.

The boat slows as a massive surge rises in front of us, and the Apocalyptians hurry to furl the sail. One of twelve ventral fins rises out of a twisting slab of glistening gray.

"Holy heck those things are big," June says. We wait for the leviathan to finish its slow acrobatics. The Apocalyptians obviously see the sea creature, but their faces register no emotions. I sidle up beside June.

"The Whileans refer to them as the Sea Shepherds," I say. "Not because they shepherd other marine life, but because they shepherd the sea itself."

"Interesting," June says in the least interested tone she can muster. "I refer to them as Large Fish because they are large and are fish."

"You were always clever."

"Glad to finally be appreciated in my own time."

The beast's long, ridged tail disappears under the surface, and the Apocalyptians raise the sail again. I wonder if that was the same creature that saved me. We surge forward through the turbulent waters.

Part of me wants to keep my head down and just get this over with, but I have to know.

"How did this happen?" I ask. "You, the Apocalyptians?"

"I'm not sure I appreciate the implication behind your question."

"Imagine it has none, then," I say.

June catches my gaze, and for a second I think I catch the trace of a wrinkle underneath one eye. She pulls a cigarette out of one of her half dozen pockets and lights it with a match, which she tosses into the ocean once she's done with it.

"When Valdrada was destroyed, I'd been working on the negotiations for so long I didn't actually think it could happen. Failure was never a possibility. So when the two parties finally succeeded in blowing each other up, I had no idea what to do with myself. Also didn't help that the majority of the Apocalyptians were killed when the Grove decided to do its vanishing act on Valdrada. The Armageddeons are ruthless, but at the end of the day they're flaky assholes who are really only in it for the fight. No Apocalyptians, no fight."

"Sounds positively boring," I say. "Albeit at the expense of hundreds of lives."

"Peace always has a price, even here." The wind catches her cigarette smoke, blowing it into my face. "I did try to help with the rebuilding, you know. I had a grand idea for a city in a pit, houses carved directly into the walls. The Grove would serve as the central meeting point, things like that. But I don't know. There was something missing in it."

"Bloodshed?"

"Sure. Bloodshed, stakes, whatever you want to call it. Point is, it took me years to track down the remainder of the Apocalyptians. They were hiding out way to the north, in the part of the Carnival that's still a little squishier. There's not much more to it than that, at least that's worth discussing. Squishiness is a great feature when building a society, and it didn't take long before we had a pretty bad-ass one."

"A society of Apocalyptians. Take two."

The shore is in sight now. Gulls fly over the port, and a few miles inland I can make out Valdrada, rising much as it did when I first set eyes on it.

"Is there something wrong with me?" I ask, hurrying before June can make a snide comment. "Why is it that you and the Four, everyone from Elsewhere, come here and immediately want to create some crazy society, while I don't have any desire to. Scratch that, I don't even feel like I *could* build a society."

"Lack of imagination?"

"Maybe. It's like, I don't know, we go in with different assumptions about what the world is. I go in thinking that it exists already, and you're out here assuming it doesn't and that you can make it up as you go along."

June flicks the cigarette over the side of the ship and lights another.

"I don't think creating the world we want is such a crazy impulse," June says.

"Maybe not. I just think it's weird to assume that it belongs to you."

"As sad as that statement is, and as much as I'd like to continue to delve into your inability to dream big, I feel it's my duty to remind you—and I want you to say it with me: 'June is not now, nor will ever be, my therapist, social worker, or any other type of licensed psychiatric professional.'"

"Don't take this the wrong way, but you would be an awful therapist."

"The only person who would be remotely qualified to be a therapist in the Carnival is Bailly," June says, "which reminds me, he's demanding to see you before we do anything."

"What if I say no?"

"He'll probably be waiting at the gates of Valdrada, ready to hit you over the head with his decency and wisdom."

I twist my lips to one side, thinking. Bailly had been right about the While Isles being a good home for me, but with every memory that arrived without his intervention, I felt a growing suspicion of this allegedly benevolent man.

"We're not exactly on great terms right now," June says. "I think he wants you to convince me not to blow up the entire Carnival."

"I mean, that is exactly what I'm planning on doing."

"Just say you'll go along with whatever he wants. That way we can work this out without his interference. I do think he's genuinely worried about me."

I meet June's eyes. The breeze is rippling the waves of hair that fall across her cheek.

"I'm worried about you too," I say, so softly that I'm not sure she can hear, and turn back toward the main deck.

It's not so much the differences that make returning to the city a disconcerting experience, but the sameness. Similar walls confine it, and the twisty streets are still easy to get lost in. There's also a market square, though now it's at the center of town rather than the entrance. The citizens look similar, but with a higher proportion of fully human shapes.

The differences are mainly in the architecture's style. More of the buildings are stone and brick, and they are taller and closer together than the older wooden structures. Particulate matter clings to the air, and I notice a few carts of coal being brought into houses. A persistent fog rises from metal pipes in each building, and everywhere there is a clanking of gears and engines.

"I see heating technology has been rapidly advancing in the last two-hundred years," I say.

"What's wrong with a little grime, sweetie?" June says.

Cobbled side streets take us deep into Valdrada. Porters pulling rickshaws weave between pedestrians, all moving as quickly as they can down the narrow roads. True to form, carriages are still the dominant mode of transportation, though they've been joined by a number of other vehicles. A couple times a hulking metal contraption, with a spherical nose and spewing steam out of its rear engine, barrels down the street with no apparent regard for any traffic laws. There are still microgriffs, though fewer than before.

I rely on June to guide me, since this version of the city is entirely unfamiliar. At times I think I catch a familiar intersection, or a narrow building with high bulbous windows will strike me with a pang of déjà vu, but for the most part the landscape eludes me.

We stop outside of a large wooden door with a brass handle. I had my doubts about meeting with Bailly. He's always been quick to talk me out of leaving the Carnival. And there's a part of me that does still want to be talked out of it. Maybe I can't be with Curi, but that doesn't mean I can't ever see her again. There still might be a life on the islands.

I instinctively glance down toward the device on my wrist, which used to count down instead of up every time I got close to Bailly. But there is only an empty space there, wispy hairs growing over a slowly disappearing tan line.

The breezeway is the same as I remember it. High walls on either side, a rickety picnic table. I pick my way around a leather case splayed to show the tools inside. A wheelbarrow lies upside down on a sawhorse, one new wheel attached, another propped against the wall. Ivy grows in the cracks in the stone.

I don't get far before a gray cat slithers out from under a stacked pile of firewood. If it's the same cat I saw last time I visited, he's grown a lot—he comes up nearly to my knees, and his orange eyes glow eerily. I tentatively scratch one of his ears, and he tilts his head to give a better angle.

When he mews it's a deep, rocky sound. He opens his mouth to yawn, showing off rows of long, pointed fangs.

"Very good boy," I say as I try to extricate myself from the interaction with as little biting as possible. Bailly already stands leaning against the doorframe.

"Matthew, welcome back." He shakes my hand. I'd forgotten the warmth he emanates. He looks essentially the same, his salt and pepper hair cropped close, his beard trimmed over handsome features.

There's already a café con leche on the end table in the living room. I sit and sip, allowing myself to enjoy its richness. It's perfectly warm.

"How are you feeling, Matthew?" He leans forward the way a lot of my therapists and psychologists have over the years, expressing their attention through intentional body language. "The While Isles is one of the kinder places in the Carnival, but I understand the islands can present their own variety of disorientation."

"You know, after being flung hundreds of years backwards or forwards in time a few times, you sort of get used to it."

Bailly smiles. "I hear you became close with the Provost's daughter. I'm happy for you."

The bottom disappears from my stomach at the mention of Curi.

"The Whileans are good people," I say. "They showed me nothing but kindness. It was a good suggestion." With every word my mind swirls. How much do I owe this man? Can I trust him? Everything about him makes me want to. He's never done anything that wasn't in my best interest, and even showed me glimpses of my past. None of the awful things that have happened in the Carnival have involved him directly. Yet I can't help feeling that he could've stopped them if he wanted to.

"What are your thoughts on June's change?" he asks.

"I always thought becoming the leader of a pseudo-satanic cult was the obvious trajectory for her," I say.

No smile this time. "June is working things out in her own way. With the timeframes and possibilities available here, these changes are taking longer for her."

"So this is a natural part of late puberty? I don't recall reading about that particular two-hundred-year period in Health class."

"Growing up is different here. But I didn't ask you here to discuss June. I want to know how you are with it."

"So you know about..."

"Her intentions to destroy the world? Yes."

"And you're okay with this?" I ask.

Bailly pauses, almost long enough for me to think he's actually worried. "Sometimes in order to be truly happy you have to test the limits of your existence. You hear about people who have near-death experiences, and it makes them want to live every day to the fullest. They start organizations that help others, or run for elected office, things like that."

"Speaking from the context of my own near-death experience, I can tell you that sometimes you don't come out of it with an appreciation for life. Sometimes you just come out of it angry. I flew off the side of a highway one day and came out of it one alcoholic father poorer and one burning hatred of the world richer."

Bailly sets down his café con leche. The spoon rests gently against the side of the ceramic cup.

"I'm so sorry, Matthew."

"I don't feel angry anymore. I don't know if it's time, or love, or something about this place, but when I think about going home, all I can think is how nice it would be to see my family again. Every time a temporal hurricane hit, I saw a piece of home, and in the end it seemed like one I would actually want to go back to."

Again, Bailly pauses.

"Oh Matthew, I'm so sorry," he says.

"You mentioned that already."

"No, I'm sorry I didn't warn you about the temporal hurricanes. The Whileans aren't affected by them, and I thought maybe if you were with them you wouldn't be either. But people have been known to see things. They've been known to hallucinate. The storms are too powerful for the human mind to understand, so your psyche will fabricate traumatic narratives to match the traumatic subjective experience."

"Hallucinations?"

"Yes. Let me guess, your mind gave you images of some horrific experience and its aftermath—family drama, pain, and ultimately a path to healing?"

"Yes." My throat closes over the word.

"Being in Whilean society primes a person to think in terms of narratives. What more comfort could your mind provide than to acknowledge the trauma it's experiencing in a recognizable form, and then to offer you the boon of recovery?"

"You're saying everything I saw, everything I experienced during the storms, was a lie? None of it was real?" I try to take a sip of coffee, but my hands are shaking too badly. I put the cup back down, rattling the saucer.

"You've seen how the Carnival creates these kinds of stories," Bailly says. "The temporal hurricanes are no different, just a more extreme form."

"I don't know what to say," is all I can respond.

Bailly picks up his empty cup and takes it back into the kitchen, leaving me alone with my thoughts, surrounded by leather-bound books. The breeze through the open window interrupts the comfortable mustiness of the house.

When Bailly returns he's holding a fresh cup of café con leche in one hand, and a bowl in the other. Inside is a grapefruit, sliced around the edges and gently warmed in the oven. Even before I taste it, there's something in the smell that takes me out of that room. The citrusy bitterness of the grapefruit is tempered and sweetened by the heat. The smell is warmth and comfort. It reminds me of short breaks in long nights of homework, Saturday mornings rushing out the door to catch a bus for a Model UN trip, and the reassurance of knowing I had family who would take care of me no matter what.

But here the smell unsettles me. I am not at home. I am sitting across from a handsome middle-aged man with aggressively good intentions, and an unspeakable amount of power.

"I brought you here first to make sure you were okay," Bailly says, "but second to offer you something, something that I alone can offer."

I nod mid-bite for him to continue. The perfectly warm, perfectly sweet fruit grows cold in my mouth.

"I want to offer you your own section of the Carnival, far to the north. It's blank right now, but I'd be more than happy to help you fill it in. It could even just be a landscape, whatever you decide you want. You can create Swiss mountains or Scottish moors, wander alone or build cities of gold. The point is that it will be entirely yours." He gives me a meaningful look. "It's outside the range of where the Apocalyptians can reach. Not even June can travel there if you don't want her to."

"I didn't know such places existed anymore."

"Just one, and it's yours if you want it. Your happiness is all that matters to me."

"What happened to telling my own story? You were all fired up about me being some sort of union organizer."

"Whether you build it in someone else's world, or within your own, a story is a story."

My own story lies behind me. Not the wild fantasy of the Carnival, but the one I discovered during the temporal hurricanes. It's a story of loss and redemption, bookended by disorientation and new love. Yet if what Bailly says is true, then this story is no more or less important than any other. It's a fabrication of my mind to make sense of the world's chaos. But maybe that's what all stories are?

"Is there a reality within the Carnival that doesn't involve stories?" I ask.

"The Carnival itself *is* story. It's in the very fabric that makes up this place."

Flashes come back to me, both from my hurricane-induced memories and from elsewhere, in the part of my mind I still can't access. Wind rattles autumn leaves against a cerulean sky. A pang of loneliness strikes me as a car pulls out of the driveway.

I steady a full cup of coffee in both hands as I step onto the porch, into the mist of a summer morning before the world has awoken. And Cass waits for me on a subway platform, the brightness of the future alive in her smile.

There are no stories there. Yet all of it is real.

I wonder what Bailly sees as he waits for my response. Am I real to him, or merely part of one of his stories?

Whatever he is, Bailly is no record keeper. The lie of the Carnival is that it's neutral, that it allows you to exert your will upon it. But I see now that the Carnival itself has a propulsive force behind it, and I'm almost certain that force comes from Bailly. I think about the memories he showed me before I left Valdrada. They now seem so carefully curated. I can't say why it was important for Bailly to show a positive interaction with Russ, who I now know was my stepfather and the architect of the Plan, but I can guess why the second memory was meant to show my former self's desire to escape into a different reality. So much was orchestrated not just to keep me here, but to make me believe it was my choice.

"I have some ideas," I say. "I've always pictured a town on a river. You know, with wooden houses sort of integrated with the landscape, so wherever the river turns, there's another house. Maybe even some that go over the top of the river and have doors on both sides. That way you could take a boat directly from your back porch out onto the gentle water."

"That sounds lovely."

"I'd like there to be people there. But I want them to be good people. I want them to care about their society and how they're governed. They'd have spirited debates in the town hall, and make decisions based on the wisdom of compromise and consensus. Civility would be the norm, even during spirited political debates.

"And this type of society would need to have a lot of places to gather. I'm thinking town halls, meeting houses, plenty of front porches overlooking the river. Oh, and maybe a few taverns for the more informal conversations about the concerns of the day. I'm imagining one on a big bend in the river, so that the water sprays up into the air when the windows are open in the summer."

The joy at the start of my description is quickly leaving Bailly's face as he recognizes the story of one of the chickenmen, and the civilization he created long ago.

I finish: "I'll change my name to Rob, we can call the town Riverwood, and then someone can blow it up so we can do the whole goddamn thing over and over again."

I stand, leaving the grapefruit half finished and still warm.

"Matthew..."

"What tends to happen when you give away wholesale pieces of the Carnival? How does that usually go?"

"You're different, Matthew." Bailly is on his feet as well.

"I'm not. I want you to understand that as deeply as I do. I'm not different."

A sound worse than the inside of a temporal hurricane rips through the house as Bailly raises his arms. Suddenly we're in the middle of nothing—a blank gray space in all directions. Faint green stains the horizon.

"You want to look your gift horse in the mouth?" The change from his usual calm is terrible both for its suddenness and its savagery. "Well here it is. Inspect its teeth, make sure there's nothing rotten here. I assure you, it's been well cared for."

He begins looking around, and out of the gray nothingness, dozens of structures burst into existence, mismatched and floating with no ground to support them. There's the swooping multi-layered roof of a Japanese castle. There's a skyscraper so tall I have to look directly upwards to see the antenna at its top. A fleet of fighter jets cascades overhead, chased by an airborne snake a mile long. In our immediate vicinity, straw huts morph into brick colonial houses, grow the columns of plantation houses, and then flatten out into the modern designs of Frank Lloyd Wright.

"Or maybe something more natural?" Bailly shouts. The buildings crumble, shaking the earth around us—and there is earth now, a layer of rough young rock. To one side a massive volcano launches lava into the sky. As the lava flows downhill, it turns into ocean waves that crash around us but never quite touch us. We stand on a narrow island, surrounded by green water. Sandbars jut out every few feet like a serrated knife. A skirt of rocks encircles the island, sending spray from the waves skyward. Then the waves and the island itself rise even higher, and all the rocks on the coast disappear entirely. The sandbars have grown with us. Fifty-foot spines stab upward out of each one, bending in the same wind that raises the waves. The spines join together to form a canopy, their tendrils growing and clasping like hideous woody fingers, until the gray of the sky disappears entirely.

A sudden cleaving sensation pushes me into a sitting position, and we are rising aloft on a giant red mushroom. It grows larger by the second, pushing up into the canopy. The spines part as we near, and soon we're above what had been the roof moments before. All around us a sea of mushrooms has bloomed—red, orange, green, and pink—tearing through their covering like birds violently freeing themselves from eggs after too long in incubation.

We are both sitting, and for a moment everything is still. I tremble with the raw power of it all.

"Matthew," Bailly pleads. "This is the type of thing you could do every day. But you wouldn't have to. You could form a stable society like Riverwood if you wanted. That's the point. It's all yours. No one is dictating the terms. You already have this power. I'm offering you the opportunity to use it."

"What makes you think that's what I want?"

"What is it to be human, but to want to create? To control your environment and suit it to yourself?"

I look out over the mushrooms. Even with their violent ascent, they are arranged in perfect formation, concentric rings of fungus with concentric shapes on their caps. While trying to create a chaotic and disordered landscape, Bailly couldn't resist the urge to position his creations in a perfectly ordered fashion. I stare at the man across from me. He's sitting cross-legged, but somehow neither leg is on top of the other. His fitted brown T-shirt has a single ruffle running evenly across his trim stomach. I can't find anything at all uneven on his face. Not his beard, not his eyebrows. I bet if I counted his eyelashes the tally would come out the same on each side.

"You said I already have this power," I say. "I don't doubt that you think this is a generous offer. But June is waiting for me, and we have a train to catch."

I am not as powerful as Bailly. But the Carnival bestows power as appropriate to the location, and in this place Bailly intends to give me, I feel I could do anything. All I want is to get up from my chair in his living room, and leave.

So that's what I make happen.

Without the rending sound and with no change at all in the light, we return to Bailly's living room. I take one final swig of café con leche as I make for the door—it is delicious after all—leaving a film of milk and a sprinkling of leftover grounds in the bottom of my cup.

I find June outside, petting the massive gray cat, who looks at me disapprovingly as I step into the street.

"Done already?" she asks.

"I think we hit all the key points."

The West 4th St.-Washington Square station is a ten-minute walk away, and as usual the houses around the entrance do not in any way resemble the West Village. We make our way through the urine-thick humidity of the station, and past the turnstiles. My MetroCard gives a balance of $999.999 even after tapping it twice. June hops the turnstile anyway. We walk down three floors to the Brooklyn-bound F platform.

At the bottom of the stairs, Carl is sitting in a lawn chair next to a shopping cart filled with plastic bottles.

I pull up short. He's wearing the same button-down shirt and khaki pants as usual, no different than when I saw him overlooking the courtyard on his estate. His paws are folded in his lap.

"Matthew, I was hoping you'd show up eventually," he says.

I thought the next time I saw him I'd sock him in the face. He set me up to create Armageddon by having me help assassinate Hendricks. He turned me into an accomplice to murder responsible for collapsing this civilization. But that anger is gone, just like the anger at my father.

"You told me I could board a Brooklyn-bound F train, so here I am," I say.

"Here you are, at the edge of the mirror."

"Will the train take me out of the station this time?"

"I think you know the answer to that," Carl says.

June waits impatiently, but I feel I have to make some acknowledgement of the truth I've recognized about Carl, about Bailly, and their place within this world.

"Sometimes in order to be truly happy you have to test the limits of your existence, right?"

Carl beams. "Exactly."

I hug him, give his cart full of bottles a rattle, and follow the sound of the arriving train.

The train gives me the worst kind of déjà vu. I fear being swallowed in the same cycle of leaving and returning, never getting close to Brooklyn or even exiting this damn station.

"Remember, if this doesn't work, we'll have to do things my way," June says.

"If this doesn't work then there actually is no way out," I reply, "so you can do whatever the hell you want." But I still think of the Whileans. It has to work.

The station fills with the rush of air and the screech of brakes.

"This is a Brooklyn-bound F local train," the female train announcer says as the doors open. The drummer plays his buckets in the background. We step onto the train beside a man pulling in his bicycle.

"Stand clear of the closing doors, please," the male voice says.

The man pulls the bicycle out of the way just in time.

I grab the same pole as a group of European tourists.

The pregnant woman with her copy of *The Faerie Queene* remains standing as a young man offers her his seat.

I look out and see a young couple meeting by the wooden benches. *The Carnival is a mirror. Everything here is a reflection of something else.*

Something's different. The doors have snapped shut, but the train doesn't move. Time has been coated in a thick layer of molasses. June gives me a *what the hell* look. Anxiety burbles in me. This is where I need to be. If there's one thing I trust, it's this. We're not whizzing into the tunnel, not re-emerging on the same platform, not watching the same people crowd onto the train on their way to lower Manhattan or Brooklyn.

An inconspicuous man sits at the edge of one bench, his arm wrapped around the pole. The empty seat is light blue beside him. He's probably in his fifties, and I don't remember seeing him on this train before. He's not the kind of person I would tend to pick out of a crowd—not like the woman with the Gucci sunglasses and the tiny poofy dog across from him. He has a close-cropped beard, graying hair, and a bit of a belly. He's handsome in a tired way. Not world weary per se. Experienced. He's lived life, life has lived him, and they've come to terms with their mutual arrangement.

But the fact that strikes itself in bold letters across my mind is that this man looks exactly like a combination of Carl and Bailly, both in his look and in his mannerisms. I watch him, and recognition continues to raise alarm bells.

"Stand clear of the closing doors, please," the automated voice says. The doors are already closed.

I focus on the man. His gaze is between the heads of the passengers in the opposite seat, through the thin slit of the window behind them.

One of the European tourists bumps me with his backpack, and apologizes profusely in accented English. I barely acknowledge him, instead following the man's gaze to the platform. There, a young man and his girlfriend are embracing by the wooden benches. I've watched this scene a dozen times, but for the first time I really look at it, matching the intensity of the middle-aged man. It's a neurotic, anxious intensity. He's either made a decision, or is in the process of making one, based on what he's seeing. I strain for recognition.

Shit. I can't tell from here. It's not. It shouldn't be.

She can't be here too.

"We have to get off the train," I say to June. The doors open.

"Stand clear of the closing doors, please."

We push our way out onto the platform. I'm running toward the young couple. They're locked in the close embrace of young lovers too long apart. He pulls her back to arm's length and plants a slightly self-conscious kiss on her lips. I approach from behind the boy, and as they pull away I see the young woman's face in full, crinkled in a smile, mouth still half-puckered.

The lingering smile speaks of absolute joy. Before, I had focused on the station itself, how the train and the people inside it fit into the story I was telling—or maybe being told. But the truth of that smile unlocks the rest of the woman's face, and I almost have to take a step back, I'm hit so hard by it.

It's unmistakable. The knot of short brown hair, the slightly pointed chin. Cass is wearing the same white safari shirt and high-waisted, baggy jeans she wore when I met her for the accepted students' event at NYU. I remember commenting on it while we were sitting in Union Square, her launching into a comprehensive summary of how the style of pant fit is a never-ending cycle of changing tightness. I remember the sun glinting off her sunglasses, how my own expression of love put me in awe.

She's slightly different, though. There's a sharpness to her eyes, and her figure has almost an exaggerated curviness compared to the woman I had been—am?—dating.

"Matthew," June shouts from behind me. The train is leaving the station, its high wheezing progress filling the platform and nearly blocking out the sound.

I don't turn, but the young man does without quite dropping his hand from Cass' hip.

The boy who stares back at me is both me and not me. He has the goofy smile I recognize from the mirror, the same shaggy hair and haunted eyes. But each feature is slightly off. My ears are smaller and don't stick out from the side of my head, my annoying cowlick is non-existent, the freckles on my cheeks have spaced themselves evenly.

A sneer blots my doppelganger's face as he looks back toward the rushing train. I follow his look and know it's directed at the man watching from the train, that the sneer is just for him.

"June, get over here," I say. I grab her hand.

My doppelganger's attention settles on me. He doesn't say a word, studying me as if cataloguing the same differences I had. I reach out, slowly, and he doesn't pull away. My hand closes over his arm. Through it I feel the moment I'm pulling him out of, and the force of it flows through me. We're a closed circuit of joy and expectation, alive with expectant energy.

We're rocked by the sound of a thousand trains entering the station at once. Every line of every subway in Manhattan converges on this one spot. The ground shakes, and I want to cover my ears from the devastating cacophony, but my hands have melted to June and whatever version of Matthew this is.

The rumble becomes a shriek, and a shape rises above us. A black winged form consuming the entirety of the station's ceiling. Out of its jagged edges bursts a face with blurred features. It stares down on us, and as the sound builds I can't tell whether it's coming from the dissolution of the world, or whatever floats on those terrible wings.

The sound becomes so loud I can no longer hear it, and the world exits stage left.

The Hall of Echoes

"It's dark in here."

"You should start a detective agency," I reply. "With those kinds of observational skills, you could have dozens of noir-ish misadventures."

"You could be my socially challenged sidekick," June snaps back.

It's not pitch-black, just dim after the intensely fluorescent subway station.

We're in a perfectly circular room, marble along the floor and the walls, with a glass dome. The floor slopes slightly down into a circular depression about a dozen yards wide at the center. Tiny indentations too small to read line the walls.

The dome lets in gray light from outside. The winged terror is gone.

Cass and the other Matthew are nowhere in sight, though I can still feel Matthew's skin against mine. I know how the hairy flesh of my own forearm should feel—warm, slightly dry. The sensation I just felt was all wrong—almost hot, completely smooth. Too pleasant, in summary.

"We're not in the Carnival," June says. "This isn't how the Carnival feels."

"What is this place, then?"

"I don't know. But I've been in the Carnival long enough to know when I'm not."

I tread slowly toward one section of wall. My footsteps reverberate around the space, like those of the sole visitor at an art museum who's about to be shushed by an overworked docent. I can see the markings more clearly as I near the wall. Words are carved in a miniscule font. It's the same typewriter-mimicking font film scripts are written in. My eyes are naturally drawn to one sentence with a slight glow around it, as if it was recently pressed into the marble with a hot iron.

As the subway pulled away into the dark tunnel, I couldn't shake the expression on Matthew's face. He was departing not only from the train, but also from my guidance. He was a young man alone, and completely unprepared to face the massive ATM that is New York City.

I can't read more. Queasiness overcomes me, and June has to steady me.

"What the shit is this?" June says.

My chin is trembling. I know whatever words come out next will not be kind. I haven't felt this angry since right after my accident.

June takes a cigarette out of her pocket. Her match briefly illuminates the space, casting moody shadows over the words on the walls. She touches the flame to the end of the cigarette.

Nothing happens. The match stays lit, but the tobacco and the paper around it don't catch. The flame doesn't even continue burning down the length of the match. It hangs, as if in limbo.

"Ah screw it," June says after repeatedly jamming the flame against her cigarette. She drops it and the match on the floor, and stomps her boot on them.

I draw forward to the last sentence. This isn't the first time I've heard someone refer to New York as a massive ATM, and though I can't say why, the cliché touches a conflict in my past.

I put my hands on the words.

I'm back on the subway platform.

A train is pulling in, as it always is.

I watched him spring out of the seat beside me, give a little wave, and step off the train. In front of me a few European tourists were bludgeoning those around them with unnecessarily large backpacks. It looked like they were going on a camping trip.

"This is West 4th St.-Washington Square," the female subway automaton said. "Transfer is available to the A, B, C, D, and E trains."

The expression on his face when he saw Cass by the benches was like watching a dog being proffered a slimy tennis ball. That Labrador energy Matthew always has—as usual directed in stray directions.

Cass had been a problem from the beginning. She and the Plan were incompatible. If he wanted to achieve the heights he wanted, the relationship would be a necessary casualty. His unwillingness to take my advice had brought him here to NYU instead of Dart-

mouth. With proper guidance he possessed limitless potential. Without it, he had a remarkable ability to exuberantly take every wrong turn offered to him.

I watched the two of them embrace. Cass was in a ridiculous outfit, New York having made her "fashionable."

As he looked back over his shoulder, Matthew's expression sent a chill down my spine. His smile was replaced by a flash of sneering victory, and he was sure to catch my eyes as he gave it.

I had been suspecting this breaking point for some time, but that look confirmed it. He was raising a giant, middle-finger-shaped flag in my direction. After everything I poured into him.

I got off at Broadway-Lafayette and waited for an F train going in the opposite direction. Fifteen minutes until the next one gave me plenty of time to consider the betrayal. Never mind how indicative it was of Albany's criminal mismanagement of the MTA, the usual corrupt cronyism that meant rich donors got richer, and the people of New York had to wait on stinking subway platforms to board decaying trains, assuming the signal switches from the 1930s didn't send them careening into another train first.

I got out at 14th Street, and turned west. [REDACTED] lived in the nebulous area between Chelsea and Meatpacking, on [REDACTED] between [REDACTED] and [REDACTED]. I could always find the apartment—it was the third time there after all—though every time I tried to imagine the inside of it, I could only conjure a vague image. I'd written down the address the last time, but within an hour the ink seeped out like I'd dropped it in water.

The front door appeared as if out of nowhere, atop a flight of three steps. I rang the buzzer, and the door snapped open. The fifth-floor walkup was a strain on my legs, and I was panting heavily through the city's swampy humidity by the time I reached the apartment.

I knocked on the door, though I couldn't remember for the life of me if it was brown or black, if it had a knocker, a buzzer, both, or neither. I simply remembered a door, the door opening.

"You're back," said a throaty voice from inside. Its source was indistinct.

"[REDACTED]," I said. "I need your services again."

"Please, come inside."

My head hurts. I'm leaning against the wall, cold marble against my back. June has her arm around me.

"Don't ask if I'm okay," I say.

"Of course not."

I feel the weight of the mysterious powers we've just seen. Terrifying power emanates from the voids in Russ' memories. I can't tell if they're too strong for human comprehension, or if they've actually torn the fabric of memory, carving at the edges like a dull knife, excising their own presence without a thought or care for the tissue around them.

"Matthew," June says.

"You run out of nicknames?"

"I didn't think this would be a good time to call you Manilla Wafer."

"That's a good one," I say.

"Everything's been pretty screwed this whole time, huh?" June says.

"Yes. Screwed beyond screwed."

"We can go back to the Carnival. We can forget about all of this."

I get up, shakily. "No we can't."

I scan the words on the wall. There are so many, some higher up than I could possibly reach.

"He was really upset with you," June says. "It was like you'd kicked his favorite pumpkin or something."

"Screwed beyond screwed. You know what's even worse? That's not at all how I remember it." Memory is still a slippery concept for me, but the reference points of specific events help. "I looked back to say bye, not whatever it is he saw. I wasn't running away from him, I was just happy to see Cass. She's my girlfriend for Christ's sake, shouldn't I be allowed to be happy to see her?"

"Of course."

"It wasn't some big revolution. It was a mildly memorable day because I was visiting my new school."

June nods. "You're right, we should keep going. Let's ease into it though, I think we should find an entry point that doesn't involve either of us."

"Agreed."

June picks out a spot.

The comforting tick of the clock counted down until five. The filing had been completed for the day, the last patient's folder tucked away into its alphabetized cabinet. My office had always been a domain I could say was entirely mine. When the nurses came in looking for a chart, it would be laid out and ready for them. When they returned a file, they knew it would go in the right place. All of these patients had diverse and at times menacingly complex and messy issues, but within their folders, diagnoses were defined, boxes were checked, and prescriptions were noted.

"Come in."

Dr. Lamotte opened the door. He was a hot-shot young orthopedic surgeon. I'd heard rumors that his technique put some of the twenty-year veterans to shame, although he always came in with an air of frazzlement that belied his lauded status.

"Hey Russ, sorry to bother you so late."

"No trouble at all, Pete." I made a show of stacking papers on my desk. As if they hadn't been organized for hours. "What can I do for you?"

I would recognize this room anywhere. I've woken up in it a dozen times in the Carnival. But those stacks would always overflow rather than comforting me. I try to find June somewhere in the ether of memory, but I can't pinpoint her.

"I'm so sorry. I think I misplaced Ms. Washburn's chart. It had my post-op notes. I'd hate to have to redo them." Not to mention that I'd have to report the chart missing.

"You're all good Pete. Marcia dropped off the chart an hour ago. Said she knew you were running into a consultation and might not have time to make it down here."

"Oh my God, thank you so much." Dr. Lamotte's expression of relief almost made me laugh. "Marcia's a peach. As are you, sir."

"No trouble at all, we all have to look out for each other around here."

"Thanks again, I really appreciate it." Dr. Lamotte disappeared around the doorframe. The kid would be fine as long as he learned to pick up his head off the operating table every once in a while. Add a little structure to those natural gifts.

I arrived home to find Cass in the living room with Dee, a half-eaten plate of hummus on the floor by their feet. For some reason, since Matthew's disappearance Cass had continued to show up uninvited. The fact that neither myself nor Dee was her parent and that there were no children her age in the house was somehow irrelevant.

I am bodiless in these memories. I have no form. Yet I try to swim toward Cass, to call out, to let her know I'm here, just behind the eyes of my stepfather.

"Cass!" I shout.

"She can't hear you." June's formlessness pulls close to mine. "This already happened."

"She's right there."

It is really her too, though all of these memories are duller than any memory I could possibly have of Cass.

"Hi, Mr. Georgeson," Cass said. Always a chill in her voice. She'd come around the office asking me questions after Matthew didn't show up for school, but there'd been nothing concrete to tie me to the boy's disappearance. Still, she persisted in treating me with an odd formality in contrast to the easy manner she had with Dee.

"Cass was telling me that Matthew's fund hit thirty-thousand dollars this week." Dee's face was proud, though whenever any subject related to Matthew came up, there was a grimace beneath it. *What was the fund for again? Something around alcohol counseling or rehab, I was pretty sure, but I couldn't remember the specifics.*

"Incredible," I said. "A lot of that was your work, I'm guessing?"

"I organized the event, but we have a whole team."

"She's being modest."

I scream into the void, prompting cries of protest from June. Cass doing all this work on my behalf, under the impression I'm gone forever.

"Patience, Matticus Finch," June says. "Hold it together otherwise we won't get to see anything."

She's right. Every time I thrash against the memory it grows weaker, distorting with the strength of my emotions.

"How great that his memory is living on like this," I said. "He was truly lucky to have you in his life."

"Still is," Cass said under her breath.

"Cass, are you staying for dinner?" Dee asked.

"I should be getting home." She paused, seeing the hint of desperation in Dee's eyes. Sometimes I wanted to shake Dee and tell her that Matthew was perfectly all right. In fact, he had a better life than any of us. She would become unstuck from her self-pity eventually. "I'll be by after school tomorrow. I promise."

I lunge forward. I can't watch her go. Cass' presence calls out to me, and I can't let her walk out that door. I can't let her cross the grass to the driveway, climb into the driver's seat of her navy

Honda Civic. I can't let her sit for a moment before closing the door, staring at the house where her boyfriend used to live, and where she still feels oddly at home.

I lunge. Something tears. It's like a tear in my own body, but my body encompasses the entire room.

"Ow, goddammit!" June screams.

We rip out of my childhood home. For an instant we are back in the hemispherical room, yanked along the wall to another point, before everything goes dark and a car screeches to a halt in a hospital parking lot.

The headlights fell over a woman, and I yelled at her to get out of the way. But this wasn't some random office employee. My ex-wife Van, hands splayed over the hood, looked up at me.

I rolled down my window, and Van came around.

"My God Van, you could've killed yourself," I said.

"Don't worry, my plan has always been to be killed by a van not a car. I decided long ago that there needed to be at least four puns in my obituary."

She looked, I couldn't deny, really good. There had been a nervousness to her when we were together. Worry about June, about our finances, about her friends in the neighborhood, all sapped her appetite and kept her fifteen to twenty pounds underweight.

"What are you doing here, Van?"

"I came to talk to you."

"In the parking lot?"

"Not here, idiot." She walked around the front of the car again, opened the passenger door, dumped my briefcase onto the floor in

the backseat, and buckled in. "McSweeney's." As if I were a cab driver.

I sighed and pulled out of the parking lot. McSweeney's was only a short drive.

It being a Tuesday night and still relatively early, the only occupants were a few grizzled regulars clustered at one end, and a couple young women preparing for their shift behind the bar. McSweeney's possessed a flickering fluorescence that occasionally passed for dive bar charm, and had a yeasty smell throughout that would've been almost acceptable if it were confined to the bathroom.

Van steered me to two empty seats at the bar.

"Shot and a Miller, two for each of us."

The bartender was a bearded man of indeterminate age, who gruntingly went about filling our order, before smacking two cans and two glasses down on the bar in front of both of us.

"Shot first." I hadn't taken a shot in six or seven years. The plastic bottle whiskey didn't give any credit to the variety of beverage. "I'm buying, don't worry."

"That wasn't my main concern."

"I heard about Matthew. It's a real shame, June always said he was a sweet kid."

"We haven't given up yet."

"Like you haven't given up on June?" The hatred in her expression cut much deeper than I thought it could.

"We haven't given up on her, either."

"You've got to be the most unlucky man who ever lived. First your daughter disappears without a trace, then your stepson goes

the same way? Most people don't even get one mysterious disappearance."

The beer did its best to wash away the flavor of the first whiskey. Van had already finished her second.

"I've been thinking about those odds a lot myself, believe me," I said.

"Your disturbing calmness has been noted. Drink your damn shot."

I dutifully tossed back the second shot. The first was starting to sink in, but if anything this one was even worse. I'd have to remember to take an extra dose of my acid reflux medication when I got home.

"I've been thinking a lot about those odds too," Van continued. "I know if someone doesn't actually see you stuffing a person's body into a dumpster you're not technically guilty, but damn if Occam's Razor isn't directly positioned over your balding head."

This time it isn't me disturbing the memory. Ripples of emotion come from June, ripples she had obviously been trying to control.

"I'm here with you, June," I say into the void, unsure if she can hear me.

"I love both of those children dearly," I said. "How dare you imply I had anything to do with it."

"Oh yeah that's right, you've always been a damn saint when it comes to your kid."

"There was a reason she picked me after we broke up."

Van looked like she was about to try to flip the bar. "You orchestrated that so well, didn't you? Always the puppet master pulling our strings. Sometimes I even think my leaving was part of your grand plan."

"How could you possibly say that? I gave you and June nothing but love. You were the one who walked out the door."

"I'm not having this argument," Van said. "It never goes any- where."

And yet the argument did continue, in more or less the same vein, for the better part of two hours. A few customers filed in, a few filed out. We closed and re-opened our tab when the shift changed, and I descended deeper and deeper into the pit of drunkenness.

"I don't know how, but I'll figure out what happened," Van said.

"This is obsessive. Let it go."

"She's your daughter, he's your stepson. How can you be psycho enough to let that go?"

"It's not psycho to have successfully grieved."

"It's crazy," Van said, draining the last of her beer. "I've done so much work on myself over the last few years. I've come right with a lot of things. I've built myself back up. But being in the same room as you, it's like stepping into a time warp where I'm back to being this weak piece of shit."

"You're acting like I made you that way." I prepared to launch into a tirade of my own, but Van was already putting money on the bar.

"Of course you did, Russ. I'm calling a car. I suggest you do the same. Or don't. You're allegedly an adult, you can make your own decisions."

That night, my nightmares were far more vivid than usual. I kept returning to one of my recurrent locales, an underground city with technology far beyond our own, like a Martian colony out of a sci-fi novel. But a great earthquake kept shaking the mountain, bringing down a rain of steel shrapnel. I would wake up as a piece of it struck me, only to return immediately to the dream, to being crushed under a different shard of flying metal.

June is sobbing when we return to our bodies.

"That bastard," she mutters. "That goddamn bastard."

"I'm so sorry June," I say. She sits with her back to the wall, shoulders shaking. I put my arm around her and she leans into me. With everything we've seen, the realization that I'm hugging my stepsister hasn't had a chance to sink in.

"My mom never talked to him like that, ever," June says. "If my dad told her he needed something, she did it. If he told her that her friends were acting jealous, she would stop hanging out with them. But in that memory she was so..."

"Strong?"

Though puffy, June's eyes have the same quickness as her mother's. The same rigid lines define her jaw. She wipes her nose on her sleeve.

"I never would've dreamed of describing my mother as a feisty bitch," she says. "But I think she proudly holds that title."

"I like it."

"Bro, we have to keep going."

"I don't know."

"Yes, we're continuing. We're continuing now."

She pushes my arm away, and gets up. She surveys the walls, finding a point higher up than any we've previously touched. I follow her finger to the word *Larry*.

"Let's see what the chickenmen have to say," she says, the end of her sentence drowning in the sound of a subway.

Larry was more draped around the subway pole than leaning on it. We were on a northbound 1 train and wonderfully drunk, having passed around a fifth of Smirnoff on the way to Village Vanguard, and had not held back in our use of the wad of cash Rob had swiped from his dad's "emergency" stash. Now we were on the way back to Rob's family's apartment on the Upper West Side. His parents, thankfully, were out of town on vacation.

"It's not that it's dangerous per se," Larry was sermonizing. "It's just that there's nothing going on. Why would you go out to Brooklyn when you could as easily find things to do in the Village?"

"It's also dangerous," Bob said, mid-hiccup. "Dangerous like me."

Bob was on his way to a free ride at UVA for basketball. Saying an adjective and then insisting that said adjective described him was one of exactly three jokes in his arsenal.

"Larry, just because you're going to NYU doesn't mean you're an expert on the city," I said.

"There are nice parts of Brooklyn," Rob said. "And there are less nice parts. It all depends on your perspective."

"Your Daoism is getting everywhere," Steve said.

Rob leaned toward him and wiggled his fingers. "Ooooh watch out! It's going to infect you! You're at risk of becoming a decent person!"

"Ew never," Steve said. "You can keep the Peace Corps, I will use my business degree to plunder the Earth as I see fit."

"Charming."

I was having fun, but every mention of my friends' future path held an unspoken counterpoint beneath it. That while they moved on to great things, I was staying put. They had momentum, purpose. They weren't staying home and working towards an associate's degree.

The sound of the train magnified as the conversation drifted away. I became acutely aware of being underground and the speed at which the walls were racing around us. My friends' faces all merged into one. Each was a stinging reminder how far behind I was.

It wasn't jealousy. It wasn't like I had tried and failed to get into an Ivy League school, or had planned a year-long trip in Patagonia only to have it fall through at the last minute. Those things had simply not been options.

I had felt this when the college application process started, subtly at first, but then growing stronger and stronger over the months. My friends were drifting away, and they would only continue to do so.

"Guys, what the hell," I said. "We completely forgot about the Apartment."

"The speakeasy you're always going on about?" Larry asked.

"It's late dude, let's just go home, have a couple drinks in my apartment, and pass the hell out," Rob said.

"Come on guys, it's our last night together in New York," I said.

The rest of the guys exchanged looks, then shrugs, and finally agreed.

After changing trains, it took the better part of an hour to get south, and I had to keep insisting it would be worth it. I'd planted this seed nearly three weeks ago as a contingency, but if I'm honest, since I first learned about [REDACTED] I knew I'd probably need to use her services.

It wasn't hard to get them inside—tell someone a door is the entrance to a speakeasy and they'll go pretty much anywhere.

[REDACTED] stood in the doorway of her apartment at [REDACTED] and [REDACTED], surveying the cluster of young men on her landing.

"All of them?" she asked.

The apartment is still indistinct. The space swirls. Time feels like it does at the heart of a temporal hurricane, insistently present but difficult to grasp.

My head spins with flashing images.

Rob and Steve have already disappeared.

"Where the hell did they go?" Bob is yelling before he too disappears.

Then it's Larry alone, and I'm telling him to be calm, that they're going somewhere even better than a stupid speakeasy.

Whirling, swirling, and I see myself.

Matthew's hands are bound, his eyes scared.

"It won't work as well," [REDACTED] is saying. "He's too unwilling."

"What the hell do you want me to do?" I ask.

Time jumps again.

Then June is sitting on a red velvet couch in front of us.

"You understand the implications of what you're agreeing to?"

She nods quickly.

"Guess it's out in the open now," June says, and her voice pulls me out of the room. I feel carved words on the wall beneath my fingers. I've just seen my own unwilling entry into Russ' mind, and somehow that's not the most disturbing part.

"You chose to be here," I say, disbelief shading my voice. "Why?"

June shakes her head. "Someday we'll talk about it. But it's still too painful."

"It's been two-hundred years."

"Don't be an ass. You know it hasn't really been that long."

"You're right. I'm sorry. Whatever was bad enough for you to want to be here, it's none of my business."

"Another thing I'm right about: It doesn't matter how we got here. We need to get out. All of us."

I cock my head.

"Oy!" June shouts. "Chickenboys!"

A thundering like a herd of horses runs around the perimeter of the room. The marble wall on one side shatters, and through the hole come Rob, Bob, Larry, and Steve on their giant birds, spraying dust and debris across the room.

"We've been called," one says.

"Haven't been here in some time."

"The Hall of Echoes."

"Not our favorite."

"Beats the Wasteland."

"Less sand."

"It's too coarse."

"Not like here."

"The Hall of Echoes."

"Always sounds better than it is."

"The echoes, you know."

"Boys," June says. "We're leaving. Or, at least trying to leave."

The four men look at each other, as if confused by the concept.

"Point of clarification," one of them says. "You are leaving. We are not."

The others nod. The collective understanding on their faces surprises me. If I have the story right, they were also placed here against their will. But they clearly understand something else: they've been here too long, become too much a part of this place to ever leave it safely.

They are now as much a part of the Carnival, of the mind containing the Carnival, as Valdrada or the While Isles.

June sighs, but doesn't protest as she walks around the edge of the room, disregarding the massive hole the chickenmen have blasted—outside I can make out only a gray void—keeping her eyes on the tiny letters. "Here."

I step up behind her, and see that there's a blank space by her ankle. But the space doesn't remain blank. Words slowly trail themselves across it:

...time drifted on toward the end of the day...

June smiles at me.

"What happens at the point where memories are being written?"

"I'm not sure."

"That's called life," June replies, grabbing my hand and shoving it against the wall, which is only empty for a second.

The Superstratum

Time drifts on toward the end of the day. My back stiffens and I switch positions. I'm waiting on one more file to come in before I can head out.

My eye twitches. That's odd. I haven't been especially stressed, and I think my electrolyte intake has been more or less normal. There it is again. I'll have to get some extra sleep tonight.

Nothing strange happens as I close up shop and head out to the car. I wave to Janice at reception, and keep my head down as I pass the entrance to the ER. But even on this bright, brisk but still comfortable day, I can't escape the feeling that there are eyes on me. I turn around more than once in the parking lot.

By the time I've dropped my keys while unlocking my door, I'm thoroughly unsettled. When have I ever dropped my keys before? It's like my hand moved of its own accord.

June, did you...?

I think so. I don't think I can do more without your help though.

Now my hands are fully shaking. There's definitely something wrong. Am I having a stroke? A heart attack? I think there would be pain somewhere. The smell of eggs? I just have to get home so I can lie down.

I keep to the speed limit. Once, my hands spasm so violently I nearly veer over into the other lane. I correct, then crank the radio, trying to drown out my anxiety with pure sound.

Now.

Without my consent, my foot jams on the brake. Horns sound as cars race past. Then my car speeds back up until it's tailgating them. Control returns, and I slow to a normal speed.

"Hello, dad," says a voice. It's not the typical narrator of my thoughts, but it can't be coming from anywhere other than inside my mind.

"Hello?"

"Hey Russ," says another voice, this one male and familiar. A chorus of somewhat indistinct hellos follow.

"You're not supposed to be able to do this," I say.

"Weird, right?" says Matthew. I'd know that voice anywhere, even in my own head. "We got a tip about a Brooklyn-bound F train and we took it."

"Get on a train and you never know where you might end up," June says. "Maybe even Brooklyn."

Good one.

Shut up.

I'm still in control of the car, at least for now. They don't have full control over my actions.

"What do you want, kids?"

"Out," says June.

"That's simply not possible." I put my blinker on to turn off the highway, but find that I can't turn the wheel.

"That's not our exit," Matthew says. "Head to the city."

"That's a two-hour drive in this traffic."

"Drive fast," June says.

"I don't know what you think you're going to find."

"I know you remember how to get to [REDACTED]," June says. "She told you it could be undone, that it would be painful but possible."

"You have access to whatever life you want. Anything you dream is yours."

"Not really," June says. "The rules aren't the same as the ones out here, but they're still there."

"And you're the one making them," Matthew adds. "That's a definite downside."

"If I say no? You can't control me all the way to Manhattan."

"You're driving seventy miles an hour," Matthew says. "We only have to make one move and you end up inconveniencing everyone with a tragic accident."

"You're bluffing," I say, but I don't think they are.

"We're not, unfortunately. Desperate times, et cetera," says June.

We drive for the better part of half an hour. I do as they say and keep up my speed, passing slower cars slightly dangerously and all the while fearing a sudden involuntary movement will send us off the road. I have one last idea, but I need to seem like I'm remaining obedient.

Did I hear that right, one last idea?

This fucking guy.

I keep the thought out of my mind. Eyes on the road. Hands on the wheel. Voices in my head.

"I didn't have to create the world I did for you," I say eventually, as we're turning onto the maze of overpasses leading onto the George Washington Bridge. "I could've left you in the Wasteland, or the null space. You had free reign, an entire sandbox to play in, larger than the entire real world."

"You're a real stand-up guy, huh?" June says.

"You wanted this."

"You conned me into wanting it."

"Don't be a child," I snarl. My jaw clenches painfully shut against my will.

"For the sake of argument," Matthew says, "I would like to mention that I was technically abducted."

"You were better off."

There's a long pause. We slow down as we join the traffic getting off the bridge.

"Damn," Matthew says. "You actually believe that."

Street parking in Chelsea is predictably a nightmare, and we end up six blocks away from [REDACTED] Street. After stopping the car I reach for my briefcase. But I feel resistance.

"I'll need my wallet if I'm going to pay her. She's not cheap."

The resistance gives way, and I open the case partway and rummage around inside. My hand closes over a small tube of plastic with paper around the outside. With the automatic, thoughtless motion I've used hundreds of times, I open the bottle and pour five or six—maybe eight—pills into my hand, and pop them into my mouth.

I hear indistinct shouting as June and Matthew panic. I've reached for my anxiety medication, which cause extreme drowsiness if taken in too large quantities.

As I try to guide the pills back into my throat, my tongue becomes unresponsive. I struggle against the forces holding it in place, trying in vain to push the tablets the rest of the way into my esophagus.

What happens if he...

Best not to find out.

There's a surge of bile as the pills trigger my gag reflex. I use every muscle in my mouth in the fight, muscles in my cheeks, gums, and roof of my mouth that I never knew I had. All meet resistance. Until I twist spasmodically, and let gravity take over.

The effect isn't immediate. We sit there in my body in complete silence for a few minutes.

Then I feel my eyelids grow heavy, and neither I nor my captors can fight them as they fall.

The world we float in is not one we've been to before. It's an in-between place, composed mostly of void. I am fully Matthew again, no longer inhabiting Russ' perspective.

"Is this the null space?" I ask June. She floats upside-down beside me, though by the way her clothes hang naturally I suppose that gravity is affecting her differently, and to her, it's me who's

upside-down. "The one you were trying to get to by blowing up the Carnival?"

"Perhaps. I didn't think it'd be quite this wonky."

I watch as a river of light flows a hundred yards to my right—as if any unit of measurement has meaning here. Every few seconds an object will float laconically past our heads and feet; first a skull, then a corgi puppy, then a baseball mitt wrapped with a rubber band and with a ball in the pocket.

June reaches out and pulls the glove out of the air. A spilled jug of orange juice passes us.

"You every play ball, Ted Mattiams?" she says, taking the rubber band off and smacking the ball into the glove.

"At least through middle school. Russ wouldn't have been around for that."

June hurls the ball away from us. It proceeds in a straight line, not arcing at all, and disappears from sight.

"Nice toss," I say.

"I played Little League too. When I was little I thought softball was dumb—why is the ball so damn big? But when we all hit puberty, the boys turned into baseball ogres, and all I got out of it was boobs."

"Not super useful when it comes to baseball."

A cartoon bear licking honey out of a pot drifts by. He roars at us.

We're both clearly stalling. I'd thought escaping the Carnival, then the Hall of Echoes, would be enough. But the void on all sides offers no promise of a way out.

"*During my last conversation with Bailly, he told me that the fabric of the Carnival was stories,*" I say. "*For all that a lot of random shit happens there, it all fits into an overarching whole.*"

"*As far as I can tell, where we are right now is exclusively random shit.*"

"*That's my point,*" I say. "*This must be what the Carnival looks like without the stories.*"

That thought sends a chill through me. I'd rather be back in Valdrada, surrounded by the elves with their wooden boxes, or getting fire breathed on me by microgriffs.

"*What about the stories we've brought ourselves?*" *June says quietly.*

We begin rotating, slowly, until we're face to face, reunited by the common tug of whatever passes for gravity here. Her eyes have none of the resignation I saw when she was leading the Apocalyptians.

"*Matthew, you're a story, ain't you?*" *June asks. She puts out her hands, palms turned inward. A gap appears between us, and in it are three vertical lines.*

She points at the spaces between them, starting on the left.

"*Here's your birth. Let's call it M Day. The day of our Matthew. We proceed from there.*" *Her hand traces a pattern toward the second line.* "*Look, you learned how to walk! Uh oh, kids weren't so nice on the first day of school? That's okay, you made your first friend! Oh wow, college, a somewhat lucrative job out of school. It appears you're now happily married with three kids.*"

"*I thought you said we brought these stories with us?*"

"*Potentiality, Mattre D. These stories travel with you, whether you've experienced them or not, whether you* will *experience them or not. Oops, looks like you're now happily divorced." She frowns. "It's okay though, you guys figured out how to support the kids, and you're dating one of the moms from school whose husband passed away. She's cute too, no midlife crisis for you." Her hand hits the center line and keeps going, barreling on toward the third and final point. "Retirement agrees with you, but you wish you saw the kids more. The perils of having successful children, right? You fight going into the assisted living facility, but it's nice enough, and yeah, Marcy could use the extra help since her hip surgery. You circle the drain, lucky enough not to be doing it on the raft of Alzheimer's, and to be doing it together."*

June's finger hits the third line, and I feel my own death viscerally.

During her story, something became more solid in the world around us. There's still nothing, but the nothingness feels more present.

Holy shit. June's creating the Carnival. Or some equivalent of the Carnival.

But June's finger passes through the line.

"What's past the end of my life?" I ask.

June smiles, and in it is all the mischief I remember from the first time I met her, when she sat atop the waves in the Wasteland and complimented my swimming.

"It appears we've encountered a bit of an issue," she says.

"Oh?"

"Yeah, your body is in the ground, more or less dead, but you also appear to be summiting Kangchenjunga! You're living out your seventeenth summer as a Sherpa. But you're also swimming down the Thames. Wait, now back up it again.

"You've come back to life and are haunting people, but they're not people you or your family have ever met. They have no discernible relation to you. They didn't even do anything particularly good or particularly bad, yet you're haunting them all the same. Because remember, you're dead."

"What the hell, June?"

Nothingness shakes around us. The stream of miscellaneous objects is quickening, becoming almost as fast as the river of light. A "Wrong Way" sign rotates like a Ferris wheel.

"Are stories supposed to make sense? Are they supposed to proceed from beginning to end?"

"Yes, generally."

"I heard of a great warrior who lived in ancient times," June says. "He was renowned the world over for never killing a single foe or winning a single battle, and his sword gleamed with rust."

We're spinning now.

"What if the world isn't in order, what if there is no beginning and no end?" June asks. "What if none of it fits in a box?"

"I think I'm going to hurl."

"Good! Hurl nonsense into the void. Better yet, reach into the void and pull nonsense out, because it's already there!"

The shaking grows, but we continue to spin. The world moves violently around us.

*"How can we reach into the void if we're already in the void?"
I ask.*

*"Yes! I like that," June replies, reaching her hand into the blank
space ahead of her. It disappears and reappears closer to me, so
her hand hangs on its own, spinning along with us. The objects
around us have begun to undulate, some breaking out of line and
careening in all directions.*

*A manic grin crosses June's face as our rotation becomes so fast
that her edges blur.*

"Quick, Matthew, make me a spreadsheet!"

*In the air in front of us—though I can't tell whether it origi-
nates from me, from her, or some combination of our combined
lack of sense—appears a six-foot tall spreadsheet.*

*"And what will you fill those boxes with?" June asks. "Check-
boxes and sum functions? Will you create a pivot table?"*

*"No," I reply. "I think I'll draw a picture of a squirrel. There
will be no data validation involved."*

*June's laugh is a wild force of nonsense. With painful disregard
for the rigid lines, I begin to draw. I've never been much of an
artist, and an average person would be hard pressed to identify my
creation as what it's supposed to be, a squirrel holding a beach ball.
Every time my finger crosses one of the spreadsheet's lines, it feels
like it's breaking something. The cardinal rules of this medium
break down in the face of my awful drawing.*

*When I begin to draw the squirrel's tail, and it crosses all the
way off the grid, that pushes everything over the edge.*

We stop spinning.

The world is solid blue.

No river of light cascades past. No stream of miscellany flows.

We're alone, barefoot, our toes sinking into a substance that feels like paint. We sink further and further in, first to our knees, then to our torsos.

Fear rises in me, but as June's head disappears into the paint-like blue, I catch her smile.

Now we're at the center of a network of glowing threads. Flashes indicate where the network is active. I poke at one of the threads and watch as light courses away into the distance.

"Cool," June says, then yanks as hard as she can on the largest thread.

The effect is catastrophic. Our world lights up. Pure lightning pulses through our bodies. I feel my skin melt off, my bones shatter, my muscles turn to soup.

Last to go are my eyes, which are now just stray eyeballs attached to an optic nerve. I watch my own brain liquefy. It's gorgeous and horrifying.

I vomit violently onto myself. The pills come out more or less whole, along with the last remnants of the chicken salad I had for lunch.

My brain feels like it's on fire. Random impulses course through every part of my body. I've never felt more awake.

Did the pills not work?

"Goddammit!" That's June's voice. "You're going to literally poison yourself to keep us around? What the hell is wrong with you?"

My visitors are still here. My will deflates.

It takes me a while before I've recovered enough to speak, but when I do I say, "You'll regret this forever."

"I'm willing to live with that," Matthew says. "You, June?"

"Absolutely."

I've never experienced a longer six-block walk. Through beautiful, trendy Chelsea, past happy faces on their way home from work or walking their dogs, I am the image of death and uncertainty.

It's practically Shakespearean, the level of drama.

I'd say the level of drama is more reality TV than Elizabethan London.

My sense memory guides me. Matthew and June's excitement is palpable.

At the corner of [REDACTED] and [REDACTED], I ask for the last time if they're sure. There's no response, only an itch in my toes, a shove at my back.

I press the buzzer. The last time I climbed these stairs my legs burned. This time, propelled by the presences inside me, they feel weightless. The door on the fifth floor is already open and the blur that indicates [REDACTED]'s presence waits in the doorway.

"This cannot be good," she says. I shake my head, and she opens the door wider. "I suppose you should sit down. A cup of tea to calm your nerves. That's just the thing."

I feel eighteen years old again, leading my friends to a fake speakeasy. There's no condemnation in her tone, but I feel the same guilt I felt then.

"Please, have a seat," [REDACTED] says. "All of you." She titters to herself as I sit on the dusty couch. It was probably bright orange at some point, but has settled to a rusty brown. After a few minutes in the kitchen, she appears with a pot of tea on a tray. The crockery features the kind of vague rose-like flowers found on dinner sets at tag sales everywhere. She pours one cup for herself, and then proceeds to fill three more cups. I take one in shaking hands, keeping my eyes fixed on the cups rather than the blurry hand holding the pot.

"You've guessed why I'm here?" I ask.

"It isn't a guess, sweetie," [REDACTED] says.

"Can it be done? I don't know if they'll let me live if not."

"That would be rather inconvenient for them if you were to die!"

"May I have a moment alone with you?"

She settles in the chair across from me. The action has the disconcerting effect of making the middle of the chair disappear. "Yes."

The Hall of Echoes

We're sitting in chairs in the middle of the circular Hall of Echoes: me, June, and Russ. The wall the chickenmen had destroyed is back to displaying pristine scrawling text. Between us stands a nightmare.

The creature is about four feet tall, and every part of its body is a black so vivid that it feels as if the very idea of light is being sucked into it. Its oblong head has no eyes or face, and a gap where its mouth should be. It speaks in croaks and groans.

Russ must understand the sounds because he says, "I would prefer if it were private. Yes, of course."

The creature waddles forward on its wide legs, and opens its mouth unfathomably wide. Russ doesn't flinch as the mouth widens over the top of his head, growing until it engulfs him to his neck. June and I sit there, listening to the muffled sounds of the creature's hideous voice, and what is apparently a long monologue by Russ. We're both far too unsettled to speak. The ten minutes the conference lasts is not nearly long enough to get used to the sight.

Russ emerges with a determined expression. The creature waggles over to us. I feel myself shrink back, but it shifts as it moves, straightening and narrowing, until it resolves into the shape of an old woman. She is tall and wrapped in the folds of what appears to be a black men's pea coat. The fringes of the coat flutter, and I realize that it ends in feathers. Her body is so narrow it couldn't possibly be contained underneath the coat—in fact, the woman's body *is* the coat. When she speaks to us her voice is kind and thoroughly human.

"Your father—stepfather to you of course, Matthew—has not budged. He has in fact asked me to send you back to the Carnival where he can exercise better control of you. I told him that would be unwise. But he's a stubborn man, and the process to remove you won't work if he's unwilling."

"We got him here," says June. "If he resists, we can keep messing things up for him."

"I told him that," she responds.

Russ watches the exchange. The set of his mouth tells me both that he can't understand the conversation, and that he's petrified we'll figure out a loophole.

"Could I ask a small favor?" I say. "Would it be possible to send me back to the Carnival for only a couple minutes?"

The woman's feathers flare.

June starts, "Matthew what..."

The Carnival

A train is pulling away as I appear on the platform of my favorite subway station. Even with this brief absence, the entire scene has a hazy, unreal quality, like walking inside with sunglasses, if those sunglasses also changed their prescription in response to less light.

I make straight for the other version of Matthew, who is moving toward the exit with Cass.

"Hey, Matthew!" I shout. Both turn, and I run to catch up. "Sorry guys, don't mean to disturb your pleasant day, but I need to borrow Matthew for a second."

"What do you want him for?" Cass asks, staring at me as if I'm an existential threat rather than a replica of her boyfriend.

"I need his help with something. I promise it won't take long, and you can have him back once I'm done."

She and Matthew exchange a glance.

"I guess I should probably go," he says. "It does sound like he's desperate."

"Fine, go then," Cass says. "But don't be too long, we've got an orientation at two."

"Thank you." I take the other Matthew by the arm, and we leave the station behind.

The Hall of Echoes

"Ah okay," June says as we reappear. She blinks out of sight.

In my absence the woman has reverted to the ill-defined creature, which remains in the background as I lead myself by the elbow, straight to Russ.

"Russ, the Carnival is an incredible place," I say. "I don't know if it's unique or not, but either way it's a place where amazing things are possible. I appreciate having had the chance to experience it."

"Then why on Earth would you ever leave?" Russ asks.

"I'm not designed for this. I don't think anyone is. Human beings—real human beings—have to exist in the world. If we don't, a part of us is always missing. It's like being on vacation all the time. For a while you lounge on the beach, read a book, order room service. But after you're there for a few days it's too easy. Nothing matters. You could disappear off the face of the earth and nobody would care. We don't go on vacation so we can fall out of existence. We go so we can come back to reality."

"The vacation comparison completely ignores the fact that you're not doing nothing here," Russ snaps. "You can tell any story you want."

"But sometimes we don't need to tell stories. Sometimes we need to just be."

I look over at my doppelganger, who is obviously confused.

"Look at this guy," I say, gesturing toward him. "He's exactly what you molded him into. What you molded me into. But I can't be that anymore. I'm already not that anymore. But that's okay, because it's not me you want anyway. It's him."

"You're the same."

"No, we're not. And that's a good thing. You can keep him forever."

I haven't quite been able to cut through Russ' stoic expression. I catch a hint of Bailly there, from when his fury boiled over and he ripped the world apart. I feel rather than see two versions of June as they come up behind me.

"Dad," she says, and the leading June rushes forward and clasps him in a hug.

When she pulls away all the knowingness and irony that usually defines June is nowhere to be found. She's simply Russ' daughter. The other version of June that was just pulled from the Carnival watches them, smiling.

"When I came here I was in a bad place," she says. "I don't know if I would've made it if it weren't for what you did."

"Everyone needs help sometimes," he says.

"It's true. When I first came here, I was scared to face the world, and all the shit I was going through. But I think I'm ready to go back. I need to face it. And guess what?"

Russ' eyebrows are raised as he watches both iterations of his daughter.

"That means you've done your job. It's time to allow all your hard work to take effect." She takes the other version of herself by the shoulder and nudges her forward. "Matthew's right. This is the version you should have." The doppelganger smiles. Russ rises from his chair. He studies her, as if trying to spot a difference between her and the real thing. Then he steps forward and wraps the alternate June in a deep hug.

I turn to my own doppelganger and, like looking in a mirror, he smiles back at me.

The Superstratum

"Russ, I have good news and bad news when it comes to getting them out of there," [REDACTED] says. She must be sipping tea because the volume of liquid in her cup decreases. "The good news is that yes, it can be done, and even better, I don't charge for that particular service. The bad news is that it's going to hurt quite a lot, and the vast majority of the pain is not physical. Is that understood?"

I nod.

"I would like to speak to each of them first, if that's okay."

"I guess—"

"I was only asking to be polite. Matthew?"

"Yes ma'am," says Matthew's voice from my mouth.

"Hi Matthew." Her tone is oddly motherly. "Are you ready to come out now?"

"Yes I am."

"Good. June?"

"Hi," says June, using vocal tones I never knew I had.

"This decision is final. Do you want to come out and return to the world?"

"More than anything."

"Good. Finish your tea. Russ, we'll start whenever you're ready."

I barely notice how hot it is as I gulp down the rest of the tea.

"Now, lie down and close your eyes."

I have this last opportunity to run out the door, to fight the powers inside me and keep things as they are. But aside from the potential consequences, I'm tired. A part of me always recognized that this was temporary. Whether by police investigation, or the obnoxious persistence of my own children, it couldn't last. But are those alternate versions of them enough?

"Russ?" [REDACTED] speaks firmly but not harshly.

"Yes. Okay."

I lean to the side, resting my head against the faded fabric of the couch's arm, and close my eyes.

Elsewhere

My body feels weird. In the Carnival, in the Hall of Echoes, in any of the places that constitute the not-here I've experienced for the past months, my existence was always slightly disembodied. Pain, hunger, fear, all of these existed, but they lacked any real biological urgency. They were more perfunctory nods to the appropriate feeling, rather than the feeling itself.

"How do you feel?"

I'm sitting on—maybe *in* is a better word—a plush green chair. An elderly woman leans over me. She has sharp features, which smile at me with something like grandmotherly concern.

"Hungry."

The woman puts a hand on my wrist and counts in her head. Satisfied, she straightens.

"To be expected, I suppose," she says. "We've never been introduced, not that Russ would be able to anyway. I'm Letti."

"Nice to meet you."

"I'm going to pull June out now. I would advise you look away."

Letti moves over to Russ, who is unconscious on the couch. He has a close-trimmed beard, graying hair, a slightly paunchy belly under a checked button-down. He's at least three or four inches shorter than me. More daintily built. There's nothing outwardly intimidating about him. I think about all the time we've spent together, the time spent building and executing the Plan. All with the goal of controlling my life, driving me toward college, and leaving the past behind. It worked, in its way.

I close my eyes. A sound comes from Russ that can only be classified as a *squelch*. When I open my eyes June sits next to me. She's still lanky, dressed in dark clothes, with an impressive array of bracelets on one arm, but her face is not exactly as I remember. Eyes slightly smaller, a few more acne scars on her cheek. She's more human. More full and real and alive.

Letti performs the same pulse-checking routine on June as she stirs. Her eyes pass the older woman and fall on me. She appears to go through the same recalibration I just did, adjusting to the more imperfect version of Matthew.

"Hey Matty," she says, voice hoarse.

"Hey J," I respond.

I reach out my hand through the short distance between our chairs. She takes it. Letti makes her way into the kitchen, and comes back carrying a plate of shortbread fingers, which she sets on the tea tray before taking a seat across from us.

"Please help yourselves. There's nothing like a stick of sweet, concentrated butter to remind you what it means to be alive. Have some tea too."

The first bite of shortbread is better than everything I tasted in the Carnival combined.

"You are adventurers," Letti says. "I'm almost envious of the journey you've been on."

"Mine wasn't anything exciting," I say. "Mainly labor disputes and hanging out on an island chain outside of time. The usual, really. June became the leader of an apocalyptic army. That's way cooler."

June is laughing to herself. We both give her quizzical looks.

"It's funny, isn't it?" she says through giggles. "All of it felt so important. Now when I think of those stupid Apocalyptians I can't help but laugh."

"You had a pretty badass cape, too. Don't forget that."

Letti watches us with the wrinkle of a smile.

"Can I ask you something?" I say. "You seem happy that we're out. Why would you be willing to put us inside in the first place?"

"He paid for my services and I did my job," she replies.

"You trapped us in there, knowing what it would do to us," June says.

"Human morality has never been something I've worried too much about. I am a conduit, not an actor."

"So you don't take responsibility?" I ask.

Letti crosses and re-crosses her hands, then sets them in her lap.

"Young man, I have been around a lot longer than you, and I will be around long after you are gone. If I took responsibility for every job I've done, I daresay my existence would become most untenable. I serve my purpose, nothing more." She points at Russ. "He is not the worst man to come to me. He is also not typical. There are many reasons for what I do, and ascribing goodness or badness to them is absolutely—and this is the last time I'll say this—not my job."

June rises shakily to her feet. She steadies herself on my shoulder, and walks over to Russ' still sleeping figure. She curls her finger and flicks him once, hard, on the nose. Then she reaches into his pockets and takes out his keys, phone, and wallet. She points the phone at Russ so it unlocks with facial recognition.

"Mattilda, let's go," June says.

We leave Letti alone with Russ. As we're leaving I notice a long coat hanging over the back of the door. It's thick and well made, but its edges have an odd flare that, if I didn't know better, I might think was made of feathers.

It takes us a while to find the car. The city feels different with the warmth of a summer night on our skin, and both of us were too involved with steering Russ to pay much attention to our route. When we do find it, June gets behind the wheel and I climb into the passenger seat. Russ' briefcase is already open. I toss it onto the sidewalk, watching pill bottle, glasses wipes, sunglass case, and an umbrella skitter across the pavement.

June nods her approval. "Good to see I've taught you something."

Traffic has died down somewhat, although the West Side Highway is never particularly pleasant. June guides us deftly. My eyes still feel sensitive to light. A couple times I catch June blinking as a car with bright headlights flashes by in the opposite direction.

"June, there's something I want to say before we get back," I say.

"Ugh this is going to be some real mushy shit, isn't it."

"Yes ma'am."

"You're sure it's something you have to say and isn't something you could, you know, not say?"

"Sadly no." I smile.

"Shit. Well go ahead. I hope you're prepared for me to vomit all over you and Russ' steering wheel."

"I just want to thank you. I don't know if I would've wandered the Wasteland forever without you, but I know I wouldn't have figured out how to enjoy the Carnival for a second. And I definitely wouldn't have figured out how to get out."

"It's really me who should be thanking you," June says.

She continues to watch the road, but she seems far away.

"I want you to promise me something," she says after a long moment. "If I ever give the slightest hint I want to go back, I need you to put a stop to it."

I hadn't considered the possibility that we could go back, much less that we would actually try.

"I need you to remind me," she continues. "Remind me what that place really is."

We continue to speed into the night, the traffic thinning as we get further out of the city. With each passing minute our anxiety grows. Neither of us remembers how to function in a world with so many rules. When you've lived without even gravity as a constraint, how can you return to such a constricted reality? Physical rules. Scientific ones. Cultural ones. Even the natural laws of money and capitalism. How do you live in a world you can't create yourself?

When we're within forty-five minutes of home, I text my mom from Russ' phone.

Received news about Matthew. Home in under an hour. Be sure Cass is there.

Then I add, like the righteous asshole June taught me to be: *Sorry I missed dinner. I'm the worst.*

I imagine it's the first apology anyone has typed on this phone. I can almost feel the virtual keys resisting me.

We pull into a quiet New Jersey neighborhood a little after 11pm on a Wednesday night. The lights are on in the two-story Dutch Colonial on the corner. Viburnum bloom in the front garden. My mom's maroon Hyundai is in the driveway, along with Cass' beat-up navy Honda Civic. The shades are open, and I can see two female figures inside. I can almost feel their expectant energy from here. Along with it is something more powerful. The bond they've formed in my absence, the one that Russ couldn't understand, lays like a gentle patina over the house.

I reflect that I've gone and stirred things up quite a bit, and not all of the resulting mixture has been bad.

June pulls up in front rather than in the driveway. She keeps the engine running.

"You're not coming in?" I ask.

"Last I heard, my mom was somewhere in North Carolina. I've got close to three-hundred dollars in cash and a stolen vehicle and cell phone. That should get me at least most of the way."

"Are you worried Russ will come after you?"

"He's a coward. He's always been a coward. Besides, once you've been inside a person's deepest thoughts, it's a lot harder to be scared of them."

I get out and lean into the car before closing the door. I sense more movement inside the house. They know something's up.

"Let me know when you find her. I'd like to meet her, if she's anything like you."

"Stop, I'm going to get emotional." She rolls her eyes.

"Okay, okay. But in all seriousness, come visit when you get a chance. I've really liked having a sister."

"Thanks bro," she says. I close the door. She makes a peace sign with one hand before cranking the car into gear and speeding off at an inappropriate speed down the quiet street. I watch her round the corner. The red glow of her taillights fades.

Scrubby grass encroaches on the stone walkway leading to the front door. Weed-whacking was my job, and I make a mental note to do that as soon as I get up tomorrow morning. I walk slowly, taking in the familiarity of the house, the front yard, the driveway.

For a moment my thoughts turn to Curi and her family in the While Isles. The citizens of the Carnival continue to go about their lives, building a rich society until it is inevitably torn down by the natural cycles of apocalyptic violence. I wonder if Curi will miss me, or if I've already become part of her story. A story where my chapter is finite.

When I hit the front step, the door is already opening.

347

Here concludes the story of *Carnival of the Mind*. I hope that the winds did not carry away my words, and that they have found fertile minds in which to grow their meaning

Acknowledgements

I would like to thank my family for their love and encouragement as I continue my writing journey. Perhaps most importantly, I would like to thank them for being nothing like Russ.

A big thank you to Sean Fletcher, who provided developmental edits on a late draft of this story. Your insights into the need for more clear stakes, and your flags about scenes that belonged in a different book, helped make this a much more enjoyable and cohesive read.

The beautiful cover of this book is by Casey Gerber, who was a delight to work with and created a perfect representation of the weird world readers are about to enter into.

And as always, thank you to Lauren, who has a front-row seat to how much joy writing brings me, and is always pushing me to seek that joy.

About the Author

Ethan Peterson-New (writing as E.M. Peterson) is originally from Western Massachusetts. He is a graduate of Middlebury College with a degree in English and Film, and lives in Brooklyn.

E.M.'s other books include *Of Earth and Sky*. It is the first book in the *Terraltum Saga*, a story of a magical floating world in the sky, a powerful force that threatens to take over both earth and sky, and the found family of teenagers who must stop it.

To find all this, head to em-peterson.com. Keep up with all his new releases and get insider news at newsletter.em-peterson.com.